No Sunshine When She's Gone

Read more Kate Angell

Sweet Spot (Richmond Rogues)

No Tan Lines (Barefoot William)

Unwrapped: "Snow Angel"

He's the One: "No Shirt, No Shoes, No Service"

No Strings Attached (Barefoot William)

The Sugar Cookie Sweetheart Swap:
"The Gingerbread Man"

No Sunshine When She's Gone

KATE ANGELL

KENSINGTON PUBLISHING CORP.
www.kensingtonbooks.com

KENSINGTON BOOKS are published by

Kensington Publishing Corp.
119 West 40th Street
New York, NY 10018

All Kensington titles, imprints, and distributed lines are available at special quantity discounts for bulk purchases for sales promotions, premiums, fund-raising, educational, or institutional use.

Special book excerpts or customized printings can also be created to fit specific needs. For details, write or phone the office of the Kensington special sales manager: Kensington Publishing Corp., 119 West 40th Street, New York, NY 10018, attn: Special Sales Department; phone: 1-800-221-2647.

KENSINGTON and the k logo are Reg. U.S. Pat. & TM Off.

ISBN-13: 978-0-7582-9128-8
ISBN-10: 0-7582-9128-0

First Kensington Trade Paperback Printing: May 2014

10 9 8 7 6 5 4 3 2 1

Printed in the United States of America

First Electronic Edition: May 2014

ISBN-13: 978-0-7582-9129-5
ISBN-10: 0-7582-9129-9

For Sarah: my white pointer.

*She's a canine rescue from Brooke's Legacy, Naples, Florida.
Who rescued who? can be debated. Sarah makes me a
better human.*

One

"This Psychic Fair is amazing," Lila Sims said to Aidan Cates as they strolled along the Barefoot William boardwalk. She rubbed her hands together. "I want to get a reading."

Aidan's gut clenched. He had his own sixth sense, and was pretty damn certain what Lila had on her mind. It involved him, unfortunately, and a walk down the aisle. She was one determined woman. He planned to dodge her bullet.

"What kind of reading?" he asked her, looking around at the numerous booths set up before the multicolored storefronts. Sufficient space separated the umbrella tables so no one felt crowded. He studied a few of the signs. "There's tarot cards, astrology, numerology, palmistry, crystal ball, channeling, clairvoyants, dream interpretation, and animal communication."

The psychic list went on and on, and the lines were long. He figured the wait would be an hour. Time he'd never get back.

He knew Lila well; she wouldn't stop with one reading. If the first psychic didn't tell her what she hoped to hear, she'd find someone who would. Her beauty couldn't mask her stubbornness. She wanted to know her future, and needed validation.

His sister, Shaye, had organized the event. There was no exam to be a reader at the fair. Their aunt was a renowned intuitive with an international following. Madam Aleta was presently in New York City filming a documentary on psychic detectives. She had solved many crimes in her lifetime.

Aleta had recommended several of her colleagues; people with credible and stellar reputations. Twenty psychics were presently in attendance. They'd arrived from the metaphysical heartlands of Sedona, Arizona, Lily Dale, New York, and Cassadaga, Florida. Each had a different talent. The metaphysical vibration was strong. The air was alive with excitement and expectation.

Aidan wanted only to escape. It was the first Sunday in March, and the Florida sun beat across his shoulders. He was feeling the heat. He'd turned his baseball cap backward to protect his neck from sunburn. He would've worn a T-shirt and athletic shorts instead of a long-sleeve white button-down and jeans had he known Lila planned to check out every gift table and booth.

The crystals and gemstones, the New Age books, and the silver, symbolic jewelry all fascinated her. She'd purchased a phoenix rising necklace. She was presently flipping through a pamphlet on being her own psychic. Perhaps she was seeking a career change, although she was well suited for her present position as a society columnist for *Sleek,* a glossy women's magazine.

She attended major events from the Kentucky Derby, yacht races, and designer fashion shows to pedigreed weddings. Her column reported on American royalty, who wore what and who was seen with whom.

But today was all about Lila, Aidan thought. She was on a mission for a reading. And what Lila wanted, Lila got. The woman knew no compromise.

"Sorry!" A lady bumped Aidan from behind and was

quick to apologize. A moment later a man elbowed him in the ribs. No apology there.

Enough was enough, Aidan decided. He moved beyond the crush of the crowd, finding a spot against the blue metallic railing that separated the boardwalk from the sugar sand. Wide wooden steps led down to the beach. Facing the Gulf, he breathed deeply. The scents of suntan lotion, cinnamon incense, and salt air surrounded him. A seagull squawked to get his attention.

He was so damn glad to be home. He'd been away too long. He could understand the tourists' fascination with his town. Here was a vacation spot where everyone exhaled. No one wore a watch. Laughter was plentiful and clothes were minimal.

The crystal-blue water rippled along the shore. Beachgoers sought space, then spread their towels. Those wanting to cool off floated on their air mattresses between the shoreline and the sandbar. The water sports shack was near the pier. Tourists could rent everything from surfboards to snorkel gear, air mattresses to paddleboats. Powerboats cruised offshore, and sailboats drifted with the wind.

William Cates founded Barefoot William in 1906, and generations of Cateses had lived and worked their inheritance. The northern cement boardwalk linked to a wooden pier. Amusement arcades and carnival rides drew a large crowd. The specialty shops sold everything from Florida T-shirts to ice cream and penny candy, sunglasses to sharks' teeth, and shells to hula hoops.

A century-old carousel spun within a weatherproof enclosure. Its walls of windows overlooked the Gulf. The whir of the Ferris wheel was soothing while the swing ride that whipped out and over the waves sent pulses racing.

Neon lights flashed at night and music poured from

many of the shops. People danced down the boardwalk, free and uninhibited. Many played blacklight volleyball on the beach. Glow-in-the-dark Frisbees were thrown along the shoreline. A few daring souls skinny-dipped near the pier after midnight. Kisses were stolen at high tide. Barefoot William was as honky-tonk as its sister city, Saunders Shores, was high profile.

Waterfront mansions welcomed the rich and retired to Saunders Shores. Yachts the size of cruise ships lined the waterways. Private airstrips replaced commercial travel. *Forbes* listed Saunders Shores as the wealthiest resort community in the country.

Despite the hundred-year-old feud between the Cates and Saunders families, Aidan's sister, Shaye, had married Trace Saunders. Aidan's older brother Dune had married Trace's younger sister, Sophie. The controversy had been resolved and peace restored between the families. Life was good. The southern paradise thrived.

Aidan caught a glimpse of platinum blond hair and a red tunic top from the corner of his eye and realized Lila was headed his way. "Hey, handsome, you hiding from me?" she asked, running her finger down the front of his shirt. Her nails were long and painted navy. There were times she wasn't as careful as he'd have liked when she touched him, especially when they were naked. Nails could scrape, score, and leave a man soft. She often scratched more than his ass.

"Not hiding, just needing some space," he told her.

"It's crowded," she agreed.

A successful psychic fair would keep the boardwalk in the black. That was his sister's goal. Shaye ran Barefoot William Enterprises while her husband, Trace, was CEO of Saunders Shores. The couple worked together on many building projects and land renovations. Both towns were flourishing.

Lila curved her hand about his neck and leaned closer, asking, "Do you want to have your aura cleansed?"

He shook his head. He'd taken a shower that morning, which was good enough for him.

"You could have your past lives unearthed."

"No thanks." He was happy with the present.

"Your runes cast?"

"I have no Viking blood."

"There's a psychic painter who can identify and draw you and your spirit guides," she suggested.

He didn't want to be pictured with metaphysical beings looking over his shoulder. It was too damn spooky. "I'll pass," he said.

She pressed a light kiss to his lips; her coral-cream lipstick was non-smear. "There are other choices. What would you like, Aidan?"

He eased back slightly and patted his stomach. "Lunch," he admitted. At least he was honest. The Blue Coconut was four blocks north. The peanut bar catered to a casual crowd. The beer was cold; the foam was as top-heavy as the waitresses. There were baskets of peanuts in the shell on each table. The shells were shucked and tossed on the floor. A jukebox played in one corner, and a life-size, neon Elvis statue leaned his elbow on one end of the bar. Dartboards and pool tables drew customers to the back room.

The bar's menu was limited; the owner served three kinds of sandwiches: pastrami, roast beef, and turkey. All came with potato chips and a jumbo dill pickle. A roast beef on rye sounded good to him now.

Lila sighed, pouting. "How can you think about food while world-renowned psychics are tapping into their powers on your boardwalk? Can't you feel their cosmic vibe? It's calling to me."

Better calling to her than to him, Aidan thought.

"We'll get your reading first and then I'll take you to lunch," he conceded. "Which psychic have you chosen?"

She looked over her shoulder and scanned the tables. "The lines are lengthy." She paused, went on to squeeze his arm. "There's a reader available two tables to our left. No one's around her."

No one? That didn't sound good. Perhaps she wasn't a competent psychic. Aidan hated to waste his money on a scam artist, even if his aunt had recommended the woman.

"Hurry, Aidan." Lila took off ahead of him.

He trailed slowly, focusing on the reader as he approached her. She sat in profile to him, a small woman with long chestnut-brown hair wrapped in a green-and-gold paisley bandana. She was casually dressed in a yellow crop top and khaki shorts. She looked like a Gypsy with her large hoop earrings and gold stacking bracelets on each arm. She was barefoot with toe rings.

Lila was quick to introduce herself to the psychic. She then motioned Aidan forward. He stepped up. He was a man who lived by first impressions. The reader touched him in a way that left him uneasy. He felt strangely drawn to her. His breathing deepened. He drew air from his gut, not his lungs. He found her sexy.

She was younger than he'd expected. He placed her in her early thirties, whereas the other readers were in their fifties and sixties. Her eyes were hazel. She had fine features and beautiful skin. Her mouth was full and her lips were parted, as if Lila had taken her by surprise.

Aidan read the printed sign on her table. Aries Martine was clairvoyant. She had the capability to see the past, present, and future. A ten-minute reading cost twenty dollars.

Such a short time wouldn't satisfy Lila, Aidan knew.

He'd bet she'd take a half hour. Maybe even an hour. The way he saw it, that was money tossed to the cosmos with no honest return.

Lila settled onto one of the two wooden folding chairs, facing the psychic. She patted the seat on the second chair, requesting Aidan join her. He sat down slowly, stiffly. He sensed his life was about to change, and not for the better.

Aries had yet to speak; had yet to fully close her mouth. He noticed the slight gap between her front teeth, which he found hot. A tiny crescent scar curved at the corner of one eye. He liked a woman who wasn't perfect; she seemed more natural, more real. More approachable.

Unfortunately for him, Aries appeared unsure of herself, which made Aidan uncertain of her. Not a good way to start a reading. Not good at all. Where was her confidence? Her positive energy? Her cosmic reception?

"This is Aidan." Lila was brief. "I'm the one seeking information. He's a skeptic."

"Ah, so you are not a believer," the psychic said to him.

"There's always room for doubt."

She shrugged a slender shoulder. "An open mind allows for new opportunities."

He was open to change, but on his terms.

Lila grew impatient; her future waited. "We're ready whenever you are," she told Aries.

"Very well," Aries agreed. "Allow me to center myself before we get started." She closed her eyes and drew in consecutive breaths, releasing them slowly.

Aidan stared, appreciating the rise and fall of her chest. Her breasts were full, firm, and held by a sports bra; the outline was visible beneath the cotton of her shirt. The depth of her breathing pulled the hem of her crop top high on her stomach. Her skin was pale. Sunshine had yet to kiss her belly. He liked her gold navel ring.

There was something about the Gypsy psychic that held his interest, for the moment anyway. Beside him, Lila anxiously tapped her fingertips on the tabletop. The noise was annoying. Distracting. Inconsiderate.

He glanced at his watch and wondered if Aries charged her clients for the time it took her to get focused. If so, she'd racked up a quick four bucks at two dollars a minute.

Blinking her eyes, Aries gazed at Lila. "How can I help you?" she asked. "Are you looking for an overall general reading or something more specific?"

Lila didn't hesitate. "Specific, please. Aidan and I have dated for six months now and I'd like to know where our relationship is headed."

Cosmic hell. He'd known this was coming, but had no way of stopping her, other than making a scene. He turned to Lila, keeping his voice low and even. "This is a personal matter, and not for the universe to decide. We've already discussed—"

Lila waved her hand dismissively. "Our conversations are one-sided. They satisfy you, but not me. I want to know our future."

He clamped his jaw. "You think Aries knows better than me?"

"She has powers."

Lila's persistence was not attractive. He was stuck at a table with a marriage-minded woman and a clairvoyant who could make his life miserable. Living for today worked for him, yet Lila wanted his tomorrows. They'd found no middle ground. He hoped that Aries wouldn't announce their engagement to the entire boardwalk. Perhaps if he left now—

"Sit down," Aries said in a calm but firm voice when he started to rise. "Skeptic or not, you may be interested in what I have to say."

He could leave, but something in her tone stopped him. Her voice hinted of a secret. He was suddenly curious.

He dropped back onto the folding chair and it creaked. The chair wasn't made for a big man. Aidan was six-four and weighed two-twenty. He was surprised the wood hadn't split.

"Fine, I'm listening." He forced himself to be polite.

"Your hand, please," Aries requested of Lila, extending her own. Lila was quick to grasp it. "Now yours." She wiggled her fingers at Aidan, encouraging him to take hold.

"Why do you need my hand?" he wanted to know.

"I want to feel the heat of your aura and see how it affects Lila. I can sense if you're her soul mate."

Heat of his aura? He didn't believe her for a second. He was a warm-blooded male. Her touching him would prove nothing. Lila wasn't the love of his life. His heart told him so.

Glancing down at her hand, he noticed she wore several hammered gold rings. She had a small half-heart tattoo on her wedding-band finger. Her nails were short and rounded with clear polish. The inside of her wrist had pale blue veins.

"Aidan"—Lila's whisper was sharp—"do as she says."

He felt very uncooperative at the moment. He wasn't willing to twine his fingers with the psychic's, so instead he laid his palm flat on the table. Aries covered the back of his hand with hers. Her touch was light and warm. Her skin was soft.

His attention was riveted on her; on the shimmer of sunlight at her back that gave her an ethereal glow. She appeared otherworldly. He hated the fact he was being drawn into a reading that would give Lila false hope for their future. He'd never led a woman on; he refused to do so now.

"Look," he stalled once again. "I value my privacy—"

"Yet you're getting a public reading," said Aries.

"Not by choice."

"Life is as you choose to make it."

She rode his last nerve. Several of his relatives passed by his table and slapped him on the back. His older brother, Dune, a retired professional beach volleyball player, stood off to the side and smirked. His sweet wife, Sophie, was wide-eyed beside him. This was not good. The Cates had a grapevine for news. Word would quickly spread that he'd gotten a reading. He felt silly taking part, even though the psychic fair was a major fund-raiser for his family.

Aidan glared at Dune until his brother and Sophie moved on. He didn't need them overhearing every word Aries said; especially if the psychic started humming the wedding march.

Aries dramatically cleared her throat. "Let me get a sense of each of you first," she said. "You mentioned dating for six months, but it does not appear that you know each other well. You spend more time apart than together. Is this a long-distance relationship?"

Lila's eyes rounded, and Aidan's narrowed. "You are correct," Lila said in awe. "We met at a black tie Paws and Claws Fundraiser last fall. The event benefited the humane society. I own a house in Tallahassee and Aidan sublets a condo. Sadly our work separates us often."

Aries nodded, looking sage and solemn. Serious. "Lila," she continued, "I see you attending parties and galas alongside a photographer. You mingle with the guests, taking mental notes." She paused, and her brow creased in concentration. "Are you by chance employed by a magazine or newspaper?"

Lila covered her heart with her free hand. "You are amazing! I'm a columnist for *Sleek.*"

Aries pursed her lips. "You have the opportunity to travel."

"My editor sends me to Europe several times a year," Lila confirmed.

"You've mingled with the rich and the royal, and"— Aries bowed her head, appearing deep in thought— "you've wished since you were a little girl that you could live in their world."

Heat crept into Lila's cheeks. "Spoiled is a nice lifestyle," she disclosed. "There's nothing wrong with having a lot of money."

Aidan stared at his date. Her aspirations were high. While he was well off, he didn't live in a castle or wear a crown. Everything about Lila was first-class. She wore designer clothing and platinum jewelry. She loved being seen with people who could advance her status. Why she dated him was beyond Aidan, although his family did own a town. But Barefoot William was all about sunshine, swimsuits, and going shoeless. There was no one to impress here.

He wasn't a man to stress, but tension rose in him now. He leaned back slightly and studied Aries. She'd pinned Lila down in a few short sentences. She was, however, reading the present, not the future.

Aries took a moment, then tilted her head left, then right, as if working a kink from her neck. Her hair swept over her shoulders, sleek and shiny. The ends tipped her breasts. She brushed her bangs out of her eyes.

Focusing once again, she gently touched the back of

his hand with her fingertips. The hairs on his forearm prickled. His thumb spasmed. "Feeling me?" he couldn't help but ask.

A hint of smile curved her lips, as if she were amused. "You, Aidan, are a force to reckon with." She looked more through him than at him. "You"—she hesitated — "build. Are you a carpenter or crafter?"

What the hell, how had she known? He grew more and more suspicious of her. His hands had known hard work; his body physical labor. He owned his own construction company. He worked the job sites along with his crew. He never minded the dust, dirt, and sweat that went into an honest day's work. He wasn't a pencil-pusher.

"Lucky guess," he muttered, more to himself than to her. She seemed to have the upper hand with her knowledge of him, when he knew so little about her. He didn't like anyone having that advantage over him, clairvoyant or not.

"You're involved in a big project, one that relates to . . ." She contemplated for several seconds before saying, "a sport."

Baseball, but that was common knowledge. It had been the talk of the boardwalk for many months now. Aries could have overhead any number of conversations. Cates Construction had been contracted to build the Richmond Rogues Spring Training Facility. Trace Saunders had fought to bring major league baseball to the Gulf Coast. Once the county commissioners unanimously voted to build the park, Trace had courted the team, as did the bigger cities of Tallahassee and Jacksonville. After several months of negotiation, Trace won over James Lawless and his executive board. The Rogues were coming to town.

It would be a huge economic boost for the adjoining

cities of Barefoot William and Saunders Shores to have a major-league club start their season in southwest Florida. The training park would be similar to James River Stadium in Richmond. Aidan had gone over the architectural plans so many times, he knew them by heart. The modern facility would accommodate ten thousand fans. His adrenalin pumped; he couldn't wait to break ground.

Lila tugged on Aries's hand. "We're aware of what's happening in the present," she stated. "I'm more interested in our future."

"It may not be what you wish or expect," Aries said. She released both their hands, sat still and meditative, and awaited their nod of acceptance.

Lila did not respond; instead she grew fidgety. She twisted one of the gold buttons on the front of her tunic until the thread came loose. This surprised Aidan, as she was not one to mess up her clothes. Ever. She then crossed her legs and flicked one foot. He could feel her nervous energy; it came off her in waves. She appeared almost frightened.

Resting his elbows on the tabletop, he steepled his fingers and said, "We're waiting."

Still Aries held back. "Be certain you are ready for what I have to say." Her words were meant for Lila.

Was she building anticipation? Or assembling a line of bullshit? He wondered. Time was ticking.

"I think so . . ." His date sounded reluctant.

Aries peered intently at Lila. Her voice was no more than a whisper when she spoke, as if she were sharing a secret. "I see two men in your life: Aidan and someone with dark blond hair."

Another man? Aidan didn't have to be a psychic to read Lila's expression. She flushed so quickly, so deeply, that he knew what Aries said was true. He exhaled sharply.

Lila jerked to her feet, her legs unsteady. "You're mistaken, there's no second man." She tugged on Aidan's arm. "We should leave. Who believes in psychics anyway?"

"*You* believe in them," he responded. "This was all your idea, remember? I wanted to have lunch." He nodded to Aries. "Things are just getting interesting. Let's see this through. You have our undivided attention."

Aries waited for Lila to return to her seat. She did so with reservation. Aries then rubbed her brow; palmed her eyes. "The man's name begins with the letter R, perhaps Robert or Roger. He's of medium height, wears black-rimmed glasses and business suits. Do you know such a person? He's here in Barefoot William as we speak."

All color drained from Lila's face. She slumped over and nearly slid off her chair. Aidan caught her. She was slow to pull herself together.

He had an idea who the man might be. "Could it be Roger Gardner?" he mulled over.

Aries shrugged. "Possibly, you would know better than me."

"The man owns *Sleek* magazine," he added. "Roger and Lila work closely together."

"Very closely, it seems," said Aries. "He may be her boss, but he's also her lover."

Shock dropped Aidan's jaw.

Lila looked horrified. He heard her moan, "Oh, no."

Aidan was taken aback. What the hell was going on?

Lila clutched the edge of the table so tightly, her fingernails scratched the paint. She hadn't expected Aries to be so precise. But then neither had he. He'd been afraid to lead Lila on, yet, according to the clairvoyant, Lila had slept around behind his back. He'd been duped, and that irritated the living hell out of him.

Lila recovered quickly. She turned on Aries, and her voice rose to that of a woman riled. "You're wrong!" she accused. "You're a fake. You can no more tell the future than you can fly."

Aries didn't take offense; she remained patient and calm. "You asked me a question, and I gave you an answer," she said evenly. "I'm sorry if my reading displeased you."

Lila was so upset she was close to hyperventilating.

"Deep breaths," Aidan told her. She was drawing a lot of attention to their table. He didn't want her passing out on the boardwalk.

"Water might help." Aries passed Lila an unopened bottle of FIJI.

Aidan twisted off the bottle cap and Lila took several slow sips. He glanced back at Aries, and couldn't help but ask, "Enlighten me further on Lila and Roger," he requested.

"There's nothing between us," Lila choked out. "Don't you believe me?"

Aidan was silent.

Lila's face contorted. "You'd take Aries's word over mine?" she hissed.

"She has powers," he said, repeating what Lila had said to him earlier.

"I refuse to pay for additional minutes," Lila stated. "I'm done here."

"My time, my dime," he told Aries. "I want details."

Aries gave it to him straight. "You are not Lila's first choice for a husband; she desires another," she stated. "She's using you to make another man jealous. That is all I can tell you at this time."

Aidan rocked back on his chair, crossed his arms over his chest, and took it all in. Relief replaced his anger.

He'd known Lila wasn't the woman he wanted to spend his life with, yet he hadn't taken her for a liar. He hated liars.

Silence settled around them, thick and oppressive. An invisible finger pointed at Lila. Aidan saw through her now, even as she tried to make amends. "This is my fault, and I take full responsibility," she rushed to say. "I should never have insisted we see a psychic. I love you, Aidan. Trust me, Aries can't be believed."

He tuned her out. Laughter from a nearby table drew him from the reading and back to the boardwalk. He scrubbed his knuckles along his jaw, debating his next move. His gut told him Aries was on the money. He owed her big time.

He mentally calculated her fee. They'd spent twenty eye-opening minutes at her table. He doubted Lila would pay her the forty dollars. His date still fumed. It was up to him now, and he would make it worth Aries's while. He slipped his wallet from his back pocket and withdrew two twenties and a ten. She deserved a tip. She was gifted. He slid the bills across the table with his fingers. "Thanks, it's been real," he said.

Aries refused his money. Instead she grabbed her shoulder bag and stood, seemingly done for the day. "Keep it," she said. "Have a drink on me later. Celebrate your freedom." She then eased around the table and slipped into the crowd, disappearing like an apparition.

Aidan felt her departure. She'd left, and so had the sunshine. It fled behind a cloud. He doubted he would ever see her again, there was no reason to. Psychic readings weren't his thing. Still, he felt an odd sense of loss.

Next to him, Lila stared entreatingly. "I'm so sorry," she said. "Forgive me?"

Her apology mattered little. He could forgive her, but he wouldn't forget what she'd done. Their relationship was over. He doubted they'd ever be friends. She'd kicked him in the nuts.

"How long have you been seeing Roger?" he asked her, wanting closure.

Lila sighed, came clean. "Roger's been in my life since the day he hired me. We're together as much as we're apart. Our arrangement is complicated and has never run smooth. He's a confirmed bachelor, whereas my biological clock is ticking. I thought if I dated someone equally as wealthy and handsome as Roger that I'd get his attention. I did to an extent. He came to Barefoot William when I told him that you were about to propose. I saw him last night, and"—she frowned—"he wished us good luck."

"He didn't fight for you then?" Aidan figured he knew the answer but he wanted to hear it from her.

She looked very sad. "Roger left me flat."

"But you still care for him?"

"Not as much as I love you."

His bark of laughter turned heads. "Get real, Lila, we're done."

"I'm planning to stay in town for a few days; maybe I can change your mind."

"You'd be wasting your time."

"What should I do, Aidan?" she asked, sounding lost.

"Book a flight home."

"I have no one waiting for me in Tallahassee."

He took pity on her. "Roger's a good guy," he said. He'd met the man on several social occasions. "Do your job, but don't be available to him. Maybe he'll come around."

"You think?" Her voice cracked.

How could he possibly know? She had played him, and he wasn't happy about it. Let Roger deal with her now. "I'm not psychic, I can't foresee the future."

"Aries Martine could see all." Lila shivered. "She scared the truth out of me."

Aidan hadn't been a believer going into the reading, but the clairvoyant had turned his way of thinking. He just might have to track her down. His sister, Shaye, would know where to find her. Most of the psychics were staying in town the entire weekend. The luxurious Sandcastle Hotel in Saunders Shores had offered free suites to those participating in the fair. An open bar and the beach buffet were also complimentary.

The scent of lavender preceded an older woman as she hustled toward them. "Were you waiting for me?" she asked, out of breath.

Aidan looked up. The lady was plump and wore a bright blue caftan. She sat down with a flourish and the wooden chair groaned. A pair of purple-framed eye-glasses rested on the top of her head. Her crystal prism earrings dangled nearly to her shoulders. She fanned her face with her hand and said, "I apologize for taking such a long break. I was in need of a cold drink. Are you here for a reading?"

"Thanks, but we just had one," said Aidan.

The woman smiled warmly. "I hope it was good for you."

"Aries is a wonder," Lila said halfheartedly.

The woman raised an eyebrow. "Aries, you say?"

"This is her table," said Lila. "We spent twenty minutes with her."

The woman shook her head. "That's impossible," she said, pushing up the sleeve on her caftan. She showed them the tattoo at her wrist: a ram depicted her astrological birth sign, and her name was scrolled between its horns. "I'm Aries Martine."

The tat didn't lie.

Then who the hell was the brunette? Aidan wondered.

He was about to find out.

He rose so fast he knocked into the table. His strides were long and purposeful as he took off after the psychic imposter. Being deceived twice in one day did not sit well with him. Not well at all.

Two

Jillian Mac walked with a purpose; she *sensed* she was being followed, no doubt by Aidan Cates. The sooner she left the boardwalk, the better. She had several blocks to go.

The thickening crowd slowed her pace. Plowing people down wasn't an option. She didn't want to draw attention to herself. She was already overexposed; she'd just given a reading based on fact, and not on psychic ability.

She was impulsive at times, and some would say she'd pulled a fast one. Others would call her a fraud. To her credit, she saw the reading as saving a man from a fickle woman. Although Aidan might not see it her way. He'd view her as interfering with his life.

She glanced over her shoulder and spotted a tall, dark-haired man in a white shirt bearing down on her. Her heart quickened. Was she being paranoid? Or was that Aidan?

There were too many tourists between them to be absolutely sure. She wasn't ready to face him. Hiding seemed a good idea. All the stores had adjoining walls and multicolored doors. She could enter a shop and wait him out. A bright tangerine door beckoned her. She ducked into Three Shirts to the Wind.

The store was packed; it was wall to wall people. She looked around and got the layout of the place. She decided on a disguise. The T-shirt shop had everything she would need.

She quickly selected a pair of sunglasses from the showcase on the front counter, then a red, wide-brimmed sun hat from a hook on the wall. A cotton shirt off a circular rack came next before she headed toward the dressing rooms. A man came out of one room, and Jill cut in line, drawing frowns from those waiting to try on clothes. She rushed out an apology that included the word *emergency*.

In her mind the situation *was* dire. A confrontation with Aidan would be a disaster. She'd seen his face when he'd discovered that Lila was a liar. A muscle had ticked along his jaw line, and creases had deepened at the corners of his eyes. Yet he'd remained cool; he was a man who could control his anger.

Pretending to be clairvoyant had come easy to Jill. Right time, right place. She'd told the truth, as she'd seen it. Aidan, however, might not see it her way. She would land on his short list of those not to trust. He appeared a strong, proud man, and would never admit he'd dodged a bullet. Not to her anyway.

She stood now in the small dressing room, barely big enough for one person. The lock was loose, with a screw missing. There was a full-length mirror on the wall and a row of pegs for hangers on the other. She breathed a little easier. Aidan would never find her here.

She hooked the strap on her shoulder bag on a short peg, then checked out the articles she'd grabbed as she'd torn down the aisle. All items were workable. She'd be unrecognizable. She exhaled, sighed, relieved.

She changed her top first. Pulling off her yellow crop, she slipped on her new blue tee. The gold logo read: *What Happens on the Boardwalk Stays on the Boardwalk*. She certainly hoped so. She didn't want her employer to catch wind of her antics. She was in town on business, and was expected to be professional at all times. Even a minor slipup could cause a domino effect down the road.

She next tucked her hair beneath the red hat. She curved the wide brim down low on her forehead. Her retro sunglasses had mirror lenses. Anyone looking at her would see his own reflection. She could have the price tags cut off at the cash register. Then wear her concealing outfit when she left the store. She'd mix with the townies and tourists. Easy enough, she thought, crossing her fingers.

However, nothing in Jill's life had ever been simple or trouble-free. Things got complicated in the best of times. A hard knock on the dressing room door made her jump. She nearly came out of her skin when Aidan Cates put his shoulder to the door and the lock broke. He walked in without an invitation. Heaven help her. He was a man on a mission.

She held up one hand, holding him off. "This changing room is taken." Her voice sounded unnaturally high. "You have no right to barge in."

"My cousin Jenna owns Three Shirts," he stated. "Being family opens doors."

The door closed behind him; the frame was slightly off-center. The space seemed to shrink. His presence pressed her back to the wall. She was trapped between the mirror and the man. He was a lot bigger up close than he'd appeared seated on the wooden chair. He stole all her air.

His gaze locked on her as he flattened his hands on either side of her head and leaned in. He was way too close for her comfort. "Aries Martine"—he got right to the point—"you and I need to talk."

So much for her disguise, she thought. The man was a

human bloodhound. He'd tracked her down. She lifted her chin and warned, "Get out or I'll scream."

"Be my guest, the louder the better," he dared her. "Jenna will come. Maybe you could give her a reading, too."

What an ass. Jill had heard the Cateses were numerous, and that they had each other's backs. That didn't bode well for her. She'd be seen as an outsider, when she needed to settle into the community. Quietly, and without drama.

A shift of his broad shoulders, and his body intimately touched hers. Everywhere. They stood so snuggly, he could've been her lover.

The hard bill on his baseball cap poked the soft brim of her sun hat.

His mouth was close enough to kiss her.

His lips were slightly parted; his breath was mint-scented.

His stubble was sexy and edgy.

Her breasts brushed his chest.

Her hipbones grazed his groin.

His stance was wide, and her legs fit between his.

His leather boots bumped her bare toes.

His cologne was sunshine and musk.

His intensity both shook and seduced her. She needed him to step back while she was still thinking straight. She could lose herself in this man, she realized. She couldn't let that happen.

She licked her lips, and he stared at her moist mouth. A harsh look meant to scare her. Instead of feeling fear, her stomach fluttered. "What do you want?" she finally managed.

"An explanation, woman."

She shook her head. "I have nothing to clarify."

"You're not psychic."

"I *sense* you're mad."

"I see guilty people."

"That's a gift."

His mouth tightened. He didn't find her funny. "I met the real Aries Martine shortly after you left," he told her. "She returned to her table."

Bad timing there. "How did you know she wasn't impersonating me?" she asked.

"She had her name tattooed on her wrist."

Busted. "You followed me here to tell me about her tat?" Doubtful, but she'd say anything to distract him.

"I came after you to press charges."

"Charges?" He had to be joking. The man was making a federal case out of nothing. Her mother had always said that if stretching the truth benefited someone or bettered a situation, then it wasn't a lie. It made life bearable. "Pretending to be psychic isn't a crime. As I see it, I did you a favor. You owe me."

His gaze narrowed. "Owe you? You're crazy, lady."

"I saved you from getting married."

His jaw worked. "There were no wedding plans."

"Lila thought differently."

"Our relationship was over."

"But you'd yet to walk away."

"I was about to take the first step."

"I gave you a push."

"I didn't need your help."

"I think you did."

"Don't do my thinking for me."

She couldn't make that promise.

He eyed her suspiciously. "How did you find out about Lila and Roger in the first place?" he asked.

She hated feeling cornered. She needed air. Flattening her palm on his abdomen, she pressed him back. He had stacked bricks for a six-pack, and didn't move a muscle. "Give me space and we'll talk," she bargained.

He eased back, gave her an inch. He then swiped the sun hat from her head and placed it on a hook. Her hair fell below her shoulders, mussed and unruly. He slipped off her mirrored sunglasses next, forcing her to look him in the eye. She crossed her arms protectively over her chest; her T-shirt stayed on.

"The truth," he said. "Start from the beginning."

"It's a long story."

"Give me the Cliff Notes. I don't have all day."

Neither did she. However, bossing her around would get him nowhere. She took her sweet time, silently counting to sixty before saying, "I arrived in Barefoot William yesterday afternoon." She'd been road weary. She and her administrative assistant, Carrie Waters, had driven separate cars straight through from Richmond. It had taken them eighteen hours.

They had reserved two adjoining rooms at the Barefoot Inn, a popular bed and breakfast. They would remain there until they could find the right apartment or house to rent. They'd be in town a year, maybe longer. The ball club had compensated their relocation. James Lawless wanted them comfortable. Jill hoped to find a place within walking distance of the beach; the ideal spot to spend her free time.

Carrie was the most organized person who Jill knew. She had walked into her bedroom and immediately unpacked. She'd then skipped dinner and gone to bed. Jill, on the other hand, had been exhausted, but too hyped to sleep. She felt as if she were still driving. She needed to keep moving. She'd taken a shower, and then rummaged through her antique suitcase for fresh clothes. The suitcase had once belonged to her grandmother. Made with fabric-covered wood, it was edged with leather and covered with travel stickers. Two brass buckles closed the case.

The remainder of her clothes hadn't been wrinkled, so she hadn't bothered to hang them up. She'd been known to live out of a suitcase for months on end. While she felt grounded with her career, she was still flighty in her personal life. A full satchel gave her a sense of freedom. She could pick up and leave at any time. She didn't do permanence well. She never had.

She enjoyed dining alone. She valued time to herself. She'd wanted to experience Barefoot William, and had chosen a restaurant within walking distance. It had felt good to stretch her muscles.

She blinked when Aidan snapped his fingers near her nose. "You're drifting on me," he said to move her along. "You arrived in town, then what?"

"I ate dinner at Steamers," she said, "the same restaurant as Lila and Roger. They were seated moments after me. Their booth backed mine."

The clam shack had a seafaring ambiance. Fishermen's netting stretched across the ceiling, and enormous boat anchors, oceanic photos, and street signs—LOBSTER CROSSING and BLUE CRAB WAY—decorated the walls. Hurricane lamps lighted the dining room. Scents of garlic and butter had whetted her appetite.

"I ordered seafood chowder and blackened sea bass," she told him. "The food was excellent."

Aidan wasn't interested in her menu choices. He tapped his watch, telling her to speed things up. She skipped the fact she'd had key lime pie for dessert.

"I hadn't planned on eavesdropping on Roger and Lila's conversation," she recalled, "but Lila doesn't know how to whisper. Her voice rose when she mentioned your name."

Jill had perked up when she'd heard Aidan Cates's name. He was one of her contacts in Barefoot William. His reputation preceded him, so she knew more about him than he knew about her. He wouldn't like that fact. She could tell he preferred the upper hand.

His construction company had been hired to build the Richmond Rogues Spring Training Facility. Her boss had indicated Aidan was the best commercial builder in the business. Aidan had traveled to Richmond, where he'd spoken with James Lawless, owner and CEO of the team.

Gossip among the women in the front office hinted that he was handsome and single with an engaging smile. Jill had only seen him snarl.

"What did Lila say about me?" he prodded.

"It's hurtful," she warned.

"I'm a big boy. I can handle it. I want the truth."

That was fine by her. "Lila said that she was dating you, but was in love with Roger."

His expression was unreadable. "Go on," he said.

She did so. "Roger very calmly told Lila that he cared about her, but he didn't love her. Lila lost it. She tossed a glass of ice water at him, and then threatened to marry you within a month. She stormed off. Roger started to follow her, but didn't take more than a few steps. He returned to his booth, wiped his face with a napkin, and ordered coffee and a piece of honey mango cake."

Jill had watched Lila leave in a swirl of black satin and clicking high heels. The spicy scent of her perfume had lingered. Roger had worn a tan suit. They'd both been overdressed for such a casual restaurant. The other customers sported T-shirts and jeans. Sandals and sneakers.

"That covers last night," said Aidan. "What about today?"

She picked up with, "I was on the boardwalk, checking out the shops and the psychic fair like everyone else."

The readings had looked like fun, but Jill wasn't one to stand in long lines. She was too impatient. Besides, she liked her future to unfold one day at a time. She wasn't in a rush. She didn't need anyone predicting her tomorrows.

"I was barefoot," she added. She'd left her beaded disc sandals in her car. "More than one person stepped on my toes, so I sat down to rest at the first free table."

Once seated, she'd wished that the wooden chair had been a hammock. She'd been in the mood for a nap. She'd left Richmond's blustery winds and cool fifty degree temperatures behind. The warmth of the sun had lulled her, leaving her drowsy. She'd started yawning.

But all relaxation had fled when Lila approached her for a reading. "I had no idea your date would mistake me for Aries Martine," she told him. "She obviously hadn't seen me at Steamers."

The couple's confrontation had rattled Jill. She didn't like arguments. She'd slumped down in her seat, not wanting to call attention to herself. Still, she'd heard their every word. Apparently Lila's focus had been on Roger and not on the other diners.

"Gathering what I had learned from last night, I decided to play along," she said. "I've been two-timed, and wished someone had told me what was going on behind my back."

Her stomach still twisted when she thought of Darrel Atkins. A man she had dated for seven months. She'd given him her heart and a key to her duplex. They'd lived together. She'd thought they were exclusive, until Sybil Bond, the neighborhood gossip, informed her otherwise.

Jill had learned that while Darrel spent his nights with her, he enjoyed the company of her landlady by day. The woman lived next door. Darrel delivered more than the rent check several times a week.

The news had devastated Jill. She'd never been with anyone who was good for her or good to her. She'd closed the door on Darrel. Recovery was a bitch, especially as she bumped into him daily, either in the landlady's driveway or at their sidewalk mailboxes. He'd had the nerve to smile and wave at her. She'd turned her back on him.

The job in Florida had come at a perfect time. She hadn't thought twice about leaving Richmond. She'd been ready for a change. Her landlady had released Jill from her lease. Darrel had stood in the doorway and watched her drive away.

Looking up at Aidan now, Jill said, "I used my powers for good. I got you out of a bad situation."

"I would never have married Lila."

"She seemed persuasive."

"I'm not a man to be pushed."

Jill believed him. Oddly enough, one look at Aidan and she'd felt an affinity for him. He had no idea who she was or why she was in town. Or that she was connected to the Richmond Rogues. She was their executive liaison for Community Affairs. She'd been sent to Barefoot William to connect with the locals and involve them in every aspect of the new spring-training facility.

James Lawless, along with the other executives, hoped to fill every stadium seat at the start of next season. Jill would make it happen. She planned to pack the ballpark to standing room only. James trusted her, and had given her full rein.

Her formal introduction to Aidan would come soon

enough. They'd eventually be working together. After the reading today, she now knew he hated liars. She could be honest. She'd do her best to be straight with the man.

A firm knock on the dressing room door turned both their heads. A woman with short blond hair and round glasses frames peeked inside. "What's going on, Aidan?" she said, her voice low and anxious. "My sales clerk saw you charge in the store and head for the dressing room. One that was already occupied. This is a family shop. You'd better not be fooling around."

He looked pained. "Trust me, we're not, Jenna."

Jenna's gaze narrowed. "Last summer—" she accused.

"Has come and gone," Aidan cut her off.

"I have a long memory."

"You never let me explain."

"I saw what I saw through the crack of the door," Jenna said. "Your date was *naked*."

"She was, but I wasn't."

"Your shirt was untucked—"

"Not by my hands—"

Jill listened, taking it all in, until they both stopped talking. This was family business, and they'd said too much in front of a stranger.

Transgressions on the boardwalk and sex in a changing room were all very interesting. If Aidan hadn't been caught, would he have dropped his pants or just unzipped? she wondered. The space was tight, even for a quickie.

Her imagination teased her. Then overtook her. She could picture his body getting hot and sweaty. His kisses would be deep as he drew out a woman's pleasure. He'd control the rock of his hips, the depth of his thrust. The mirror would reflect their orgasms.

Heat crept into her cheeks.

Her nipples were suddenly perky.

Perspiration dampened her cleavage.

Warmth settled in her belly.

Her panties grew damp.

She found it difficult to breathe. "I need air," she rasped.

Jenna pulled the door wide and allowed them to pass. Aidan let Jill go ahead of him. She stuffed her crop top into her shoulder bag and wore her new T-shirt. She kept the red hat, too, but left the sunglasses behind. She was no longer in need of a disguise.

The crowd had thinned, and there was no one in line at the cash register. She paid cash, and Jenna cut off the tags. The store owner eyed her curiously. Once she'd received her change and receipt, Jill bolted for the door.

Unfortunately for her, there was no quick exit. Aidan was again on her heels. The sound of his boots was heavy and closing in. He clasped his hand on her shoulder and turned her toward him. Her skin prickled where he touched her; prickled all the way down her spine to her bottom.

She rolled her shoulder, and he let his hand drop. She needed to get going. Her plans for the afternoon didn't include Aidan Cates. Releasing a long-suffering sigh, she asked, "What now?"

"You never gave me your name," he said.

"I never planned to." Their timing was off. He'd discover who she was eventually. She didn't want to rush their introduction.

"How long will you be in town?" came next.

"Long enough." She remained evasive.

"Stay out of trouble."

"I promise not to have sex in a dressing room."

One corner of his mouth curved, but he didn't fully smile. A hint of a dimple showed in his left cheek. He had a sense of humor.

Her heart gave a little squeeze. He could become a distraction, she realized. She needed to be cautious. "See
you around," she said.

"Yeah, around," he returned.

She took off at a fast pace. The farther she got from
him the better. Unfortunately, his image stuck with her.
The dog walkers, beachgoers, and an elderly couple
holding hands on the sidewalk nearby didn't erase him
from her mind. She shook herself.

Men would take note of his strength and physique;
women would want to trace his six-pack with their
tongue. His voice was deep and rough. His intensity
made her shiver. He was built for physical activity. And
sex.

Jill had always been a sucker for athletic men. Dark
hair and eyes did it for her, too. Aidan ranked right up
there with the hottest hunks she'd ever met, and she had
met many. Most were professional ballplayers who wore
strut and cockiness as easily as their uniforms. These were
men who knew their worth and exceeded fan expecta-
tions.

She admired those Rogues who had retired several
years ago, along with the new regime. Every male executive in the front office had played professional ball.
They knew the game inside and out. Respect for their
team ran high. They knew which traits were needed for
a ballplayer to succeed. They signed players with Gold
Glove potential and World Series drive. Dedication was
second nature to all of them.

Those just starting out were searching for their place
on the team. They made the occasional mistake and most
often recovered. Each man fought hard. Nothing was
handed to them. The team was young with growth potential. The average age was twenty-five.

That was one reason the front office had traded two of

their infielders to the St. Louis Colonels for center out-fielder Rylan Cates during their rebuilding year. Ry was a phenom with leadership qualities.

Born and bred in Barefoot William, he was the youngest of the four Cates brothers. He'd attended the University of Miami, and, at the end of his senior year, had been drafted in the third round. He'd played twelve years for the Colonels. He brought veteran experience and stability to the Rogues. The team hadn't won a World Series in six years. They were due. Let this be their year, Jill thought, crossing her fingers.

The cement was hot beneath her bare feet when she stepped from the boardwalk onto the parking lot. She jogged to a plot of grass close to where she'd parked her restored black 1955 Triumph TR2. The convertible sports car was her most prized possession. She stood beneath a Queen palm in the cooling shade. Caught her breath.

Jill was jarred from her musings by "Cheap Seats," the ringtone on her iPhone She scrunched her nose as Alabama sang about minor-league games where fans didn't know the players' names or how the team was doing, but crowded into the bleachers despite that fact.

Her crazy-ass brother had programmed the music; anytime she set down her shoulder bag and he was close by, he'd lift her iPhone and switch songs. Their taste in music differed greatly. He liked country western while she listened to the oldies. Her ringtone prior to "Cheap Seats" had been Bob Seger's "Old Time Rock and Roll."

She shook her bag and her iPhone surfaced. She checked the display. Carrie Waters's name and number now flashed. She touched her thumb to the screen to take the call.

"'Lo," Jill said.

"Jillie Mac, where are you?" asked Carrie, her voice

sounding rushed. "What are you doing? Why aren't you at the farmers' market? How long before you get here? I'm at the main gate waiting for you." She ran out of breath.

Jill couldn't help but smile. Carrie's questions rolled over each other when she was excited. "I got side-tracked," she confessed.

"That's the story of your life."

Carrie knew Jill well. They'd been best friends since they were both in diapers. Growing up, Carrie was always on the go, proficient and prompt. Jill was the opposite. She never wore a watch, and instead listened to her biorhythms. She often ran five to ten minutes late.

Jill so often jumped into life feet first and Carrie made sure she landed on solid ground. Carrie settled in easily wherever they lived; she was a nester. Jill, on the other hand, kept the back door cracked and a window open.

Carrie was one of the few who still called her by her childhood nickname, Jillie Mac. Jill didn't mind. The two women complemented each other, in an odd sort of way.

They'd both been raised in households by single parents on the poorest side of Philadelphia. Thugs and drugs and never leaving the house after dark had been commonplace. The girls had missed meals and outgrown their clothes. Jill had protected Carrie on more than one occasion. She'd learned from her brother that a baseball bat could be swung not only on the sandlot but to scare away bullies.

Jill had a lot of tomboy in her and lived in jeans, whereas Carrie was feminine and favored pastels. People were drawn to Carrie. She saw the good in everyone. She never doubted, and always trusted. She forgave.

Jill was pleasant, but cautious. She had a stubborn streak,

and made sure no one took advantage of Carrie. She'd been known to hold a grudge, when it was justified.

Jill's older brother had helped them escape their neighborhood. He was street smart, and his successful career allowed him to buy their mother and his five other siblings a new house in a safer district. Her friend Carrie was an only child; her mother had deserted her family when Carrie was six. Her dad spent more time at the corner bar than with his daughter. He'd called Carrie ugly and a burden and had cuffed her on the side of the head, often and hard.

Carrie had lost the hearing in her right ear. She would tilt her head when listening to people, so she could fully hear what they were saying. She often asked to have a sentence repeated and suffered occasional dizziness. Despite her hardships, Carrie never lost hope. She believed she deserved better. She stayed positive.

Jill had refused to leave Carrie behind when they'd moved. Her brother went to an attorney and had the paperwork drawn up, giving their mother custody of her best friend. Carrie's father had willingly signed the document. He'd never tried to contact his daughter.

Jill released the bad memories. She and Carrie were survivors. That's all that mattered. They were family.

"Jillie, are you still there?" Carrie sounded concerned. "Is everything okay?"

Her thoughts had drifted, as they so often did. "I'm twenty minutes from the market." She quickly calculated. She'd passed a promotional billboard on her way to the boardwalk. The farmers' market was rural. She was coming from the beach. "Where shall I meet you?"

"I'll be at the main gate. There's a coffee vendor close by, I'll grab a cup while I wait." She paused, then added, "You're on your way now, right? Not in an hour?"

"I'll be there shortly, promise."

She disconnected, then tipped her shoulder bag until her car keys appeared. She unlocked the Triumph and slipped onto the seat. The inside of the car felt like a sauna; the backs of her legs stuck to the leather seat. She rolled down the window by hand to let the hot air escape.

Her mechanic had serviced the vintage sports car before she'd left Richmond. The engine turned over easily and hummed. She drove to the outskirts of town.

She soon came upon the sign pointing to the turnoff for the farmers' market. The line of traffic seemed endless. The market stretched over five acres. Vendors from all over the state had set up stalls. Enormous sailcloth tents covered the produce and protected customers from the sun. Jill parked a half mile from the entrance. She grabbed her bag, slipped on her sandals, and power walked.

Carrie caught sight of her and waved. Her braces flashed when she smiled. She'd waited years to get her teeth straightened and, at thirty-two, finally had the funds to do so. Her hair was pulled into a high auburn ponytail; she wore an aqua sundress, and held two Styrofoam cups of coffee. Carrie sipped from one and handed Jill the other.

"Regular coffee with hazelnut creamer," she said. "How was the psychic fair? Did you get a reading?"

No, but I gave one. Jill hesitated. She'd never kept anything back from her friend; there were no secrets between them. However a part of her wasn't ready to discuss Aidan Cates. She wanted to keep him to herself a little longer. "The boardwalk was crowded," she said. "I'll stick with fortune cookies to tell my future."

"The last time we ate Chinese food, your fortune said

'Travel is imminent'," Carrie recalled. "And here we are in Barefoot William."

"Ancient words of wisdom," Jill agreed.

Carrie held up a flyer. "Let's get started. There's so much to see. We can produce shop 'til we drop."

Jill let Carrie lead the way. Her friend already knew the layout of the stalls. They strolled the grounds, unhurried and appreciative of the fruits and vegetables; the plants, flowers, and herbs; the baked goods and variety of nuts.

Carrie bought a red wicker basket to carry the items they purchased. Jill filled it with a container of raw Tropical Blossom honey and a small sack of sunflower seeds. Carrie chose an orchid plant and an enormous beefsteak tomato. She loved fried tomato sandwiches. She'd created the sandwich as a kid. Something easy to make. She would fry sliced tomatoes in a skillet, and once cooked, she'd put them on toast with a little mayonnaise.

Jill stubbed her toe on a crate of grapefruit as they exited a stall selling citrus. She'd been eyeing a bag of tangelos and not watching where she was going.

"You're leaving a trail of beads," Carrie said, looking down on Jill's sandals.

Jill lowered her gaze and saw that several tiny brown beads were missing on her favorite pair of disc sandals. She'd worn them for three summers now. "Better beads than bread crumbs," she said, grinning. "Whoever notices I've lost the beads is standing too close for my comfort."

Carrie scrunched her nose and said, "You can afford to buy a new pair."

Jill could, but she economized. She'd come from having nothing to having something. The nothing stayed with her, even after she had a regular paycheck and decent cash flow. She refused to spend unnecessarily. She'd wear the sandals until they fell apart, which would be any day now.

"By the way," Carrie said, "I contacted Trace Saunders this morning to let him know we were in town. During our conversation, his wife, Shaye, came on the line and invited us to supper. Does tonight work for you? I need to call her back."

Trace was Aidan Cates's brother-in-law and Shaye was his sister. It might prove interesting to meet his family, especially as Trace was so tightly connected to the Richmond Rogues. It seemed only polite.

"Works for me," Jill agreed. "Ask Shaye what we can bring. I don't want to show up empty-handed."

A semitrailer backed up close to one of the stalls, and a group of men began unloading produce. The noise level rose considerably.

"Be right back," Carrie said. "I need a quieter spot to make my call." She walked off.

Jill turned into a booth and considered a selection of cantaloupes, honeydews, and seedless watermelons. She picked up one cantaloupe, then a second. She was holding both before her when a young woman tapped her on the back. The redhead seemed to think Jill worked there.

"I'm in a hurry," the woman said. "How can you tell if a cantaloupe is ripe?"

Jill glanced over her shoulder, but couldn't locate the produce vendor. So she answered from experience. She'd worked at Cormet's Deli during high school; the deli had specialized in fresh fruit platters. She weighed both cantaloupes on her palms and said, "When it's ripe, the fruit should feel heavier than it looks. It should also smell musky and sweet. You should be able to press your thumb in slightly on the bottom side and there should be a lip around the stem."

"Thank you so much," the woman said. She quickly tested several cantaloupes for ripeness. Finding one that suited her, she sped off to a nearby checkout table where cash payments went into a metal box.

Jill moved out of the way of a teenager carting crates of bananas, only to step into another man's path. A man who cast a big shadow and now breathed down her neck. She knew before she turned around who stood behind her.

"So we meet again," Aidan Cates said.

Heat skimmed down her spine like a stroking finger. She felt a rush of nervous energy. He leaned in, so close his chest brushed her shoulder and his thighs bumped her bottom. "From psychic to produce vendor," he spoke low near her ear. "You do get around, don't you?"

Three

Jill's hand shook and she spilled her coffee. The splash barely missed her left foot. She refused to turn around. Let him talk to the back of her head. "This isn't my stall," she informed him, "but I was assisting a customer."

"You tend to be helpful." Aidan edged even closer.

"I know produce."

"So I heard." A sensual roughness deepened his voice. "I usually shake or squeeze for ripeness, although a thumb to the bottom sounds far more interesting."

Her blush was immediate. She'd never met anyone who made mature fruit sound sexual. She hated her reaction, hated worse that he'd embarrassed her. She drew a steadying breath and asked, "Are you following me?"

His chuckle was all male and dangerous. "Don't flatter yourself, babe. I've just returned to town, and have family and friends at the farmers' market. Coming here is the fastest way for me to catch up."

"Don't let me keep you." Her throat was tight.

"I'm going . . ." Still he stayed.

She decided to move if he wouldn't. She turned on him. Her gaze hit him square in the chest and she was forced to look up. "You have people to see," she prompted.

He stared down on her; his eyes were shielded by the

bill of his baseball cap. "I'll get to them. The market's open all afternoon."

What to do? Jill debated. There was no point standing there, checking out the width of his shoulders, the thickness of his chest. The flatness of his abdomen. The long length of his legs. She had the wild urge to touch him. To feel his muscles beneath her palms. She clenched her fingers instead; kept her hands to herself.

Where the heck was Carrie? she wondered. Her friend loved to chat on the phone. She would be Shaye's new best friend before their conversation ended. "I have someone to find," she said, rising on tiptoe and scanning the crowd.

"Male or female?" Aidan asked.

"Does it matter?" She took a sip of her coffee, playing it cool.

He shrugged. "I'm tall and can see over the crowd. If you describe—"

"I don't need your help." She hadn't meant to sound rude, but having him so near unnerved her. She'd locate Carrie on her own. "Excuse me," she said, easing around him.

"Wait," he said.

Now what?

He stooped down, picked something off the ground, and stood again. He held out his hand to her, and six brown beads rolled across his palm. "You might want these," he said.

She couldn't believe he'd returned her beads. She opened her bag and watched as he dropped them inside, one by one. "Thank you," she managed.

"There's a shoe repair on Gulfwing Drive," he told her. "Two streets off the main drag. I have my work boots repaired there. The soles wear out before the leather." His smile was slight. "No man discards broken-in boots."

She liked his way of thinking. He hadn't told her to toss her sandals and buy a new pair. Instead he'd given her directions to get them fixed. His suggestion set well with her. She'd locate the shoe repair shop tomorrow.

"'Bye, Aidan." She bumped his hip as she eased around him. His masculine heat branded her.

"I still don't know your name," he pressed.

"I'll tell you next time we meet."

"Our paths might not cross again."

"I'm betting they will," she said. "I've seen you twice in one day. The odds are good."

He appeared hesitant, but let her pass.

She went in the direction she'd last seen Carrie. Hurrying down the aisle, she cut around a corner stall piled with corn. She happened to glance back, hoping Aidan had moved on. He had not. He stood right where she'd left him. His gaze was on her, sharp and assessing. She'd never seen anyone look so serious. What was he thinking? Perhaps she was better off not knowing.

The man made her body tingle. Goose bumps rose over her breasts and skimmed her inner thighs. She hastened away from him, darting between booths of zucchini and cucumbers, quickening her pace.

She located Carrie near the edge of the tent. She stood beside a table stacked with red and green peppers. After disconnecting her call, she walked toward Jill. Her braces flashed as she smiled.

"We dine at seven p.m. at Shaye and Trace's beach house. I took down directions," Carrie said. "It's casual—Trace is going to grill. I asked Shaye what we could bring; she suggested mixed greens or coleslaw."

Jill proposed a layered salad. "We can mix fruits, veggies, and nuts."

Carrie agreed. "Sweet and crunchy. I like."

Jill followed Carrie up one aisle and down the other.

Selecting the salad ingredients was easy and fun. They paid each vendor as they went, splitting the price of their purchases. Salad dressing wouldn't be necessary. The juice from the fruit would suffice.

All the while they shopped, Jill kept one eye on the produce and one eye out for Aidan Cates. She never did see him again. She was as relieved as she was disappointed. Aidan added male dimension to her life. He made her stomach go soft and her heart flutter, purely feminine feelings.

The two women took a breather next to a stall with assorted herbs. Jill inhaled deeply; the scents of lemon balm, mint, and rosemary tickled her nose. Her mother had kept a small clay pot of mint on the windowsill above the kitchen sink. Her mom had never added mint to her cooking; she'd used it as an air freshener.

Their row house had been dark and in need of repairs. The building had smelled old, even when it was new. Growing up, Jill had stood at the sink and breathed in the mint. The clean fragrance erased the harshness of the outside world, where trash littered the streets and the smell of spilled liquor made her nauseous.

Carrie glanced at her watch. "It's almost three-thirty," she said. "Did you skip lunch?" When Jill nodded, she asked, "Do you want to grab a snack?"

"I can hold off until supper," Jill said.

"Let's go, then," said Carrie. "I feel dusty and in need of a shower."

Jill needed one, too. The air was humid and her skin felt gritty. They found the nearest exit, and then headed for the parking lot.

Traffic continued to file in. Those on their way out carried large grocery bags to their cars. Jill climbed into her Triumph and Carrie into her Nissan Cube. They'd each driven their own car from Richmond to Barefoot

William, as neither one wanted to depend on the other for transportation while they were in town. Carrie followed Jill back to the bed and breakfast.

One block off the beach, the Barefoot Inn was ideal for vacationers. Jill stood on the narrow stone sidewalk before walking up the steps. The relaxed atmosphere calmed her. Surrounded by tropical foliage and a wraparound porch, the sun-yellow, two-story inn offered ten guest rooms. A continental breakfast was served out by the pool. Jill had enjoyed a freshly baked orange muffin and a cup of coffee that morning before heading to the psychic fair.

Laugher now rang out poolside. She listened, smiling. Happy hour was underway. A chalkboard near the reception desk listed all daily activities. From four to six p.m., two drinks per guest would be blended at the chickee hut bar. The frozen cocktails included Paradise on Ice and a Barefoot Breeze; both were local rum-based favorites.

Carrie beat Jill to the front door. Her friend carried both bags of produce, by choice. "You coming?" she called.

Jill waved. "I'm right behind you."

However her steps slowed as her thoughts deepened. She was thirty-three years old, and had never had a real vacation, at least not one where time was exclusively her own. She had four days ahead of her to settle in and do exactly as she pleased. That included sunbathing at the beach, enjoying the rides and amusements on the pier, and shopping the boardwalk, all at a leisurely pace. She would welcome Carrie's company if her friend wanted to join her. Otherwise, Jill would go it alone. Carrie was confident and capable of entertaining herself. She was a homebody, whereas Jill had a restless streak.

By the time Jill entered the inn, Carrie had already consulted the owner, Sharon Cates, about storing their produce in the commercial refrigerator in the main kitchen. The food took up one shelf and the crisper drawer. Sharon was a gracious hostess.

"I'm tired," Carrie said, stifling a yawn as they left the kitchen and crossed the lobby toward the staircase.

Wide windows cast Florida sunshine over the entrance. Blond hardwood floors, pale aqua furniture, and brass accents completed the décor. A complimentary rack of tourism pamphlets directed guests to local and state attractions. Jill mentally added Disney World, Busch Gardens, Zoo Miami, and Key West to her bucket list.

"A nap would be nice," Carrie said as they climbed the stairs. "First impressions are important. I don't want to be tired when we meet Shaye and Trace."

Jill nodded. "Ditto that."

They showered in their separate rooms, then ended up sleeping longer than they'd planned. Ninety minutes later, they met again in the upstairs hallway. "I could use a cup of coffee," said Carrie. "Sharon has a Keurig in the kitchen."

They found their way downstairs. Carrie brewed two mugs of summer-sweet raspberry before they started on their salad. The flavored coffee tasted light and fruity. Carrie next removed their produce from the refrigerator and Jill washed the fruits and vegetables.

Sharon Cates had thoughtfully set out a glass serving bowl on the butcher block island, along with knives and a melon baller. The friends became creative. Hand-torn romaine soon lined the bottom of the bowl, followed by a layer of diced red apples. Jill halved the cantaloupe and scooped mini–melon balls. Carrie shaved a cucumber so thin, Jill could see through the slices.

Two diced bell peppers came next, one green and one yellow. Jill went on to peel an orange, then carefully chopped the sections into smaller bites. Fresh basil followed, cut into ribbons. Chopped pecans topped layers of blueberries and strawberries. The zest and juice of a lime was added last.

Jill popped a leftover blueberry in her mouth and admired their salad. "There's something for everyone," she said. "Cormet's Deli back home in Philly sold a ton of these salads. None of the other employees liked to layer, so I had job security as a kid."

Carrie leaned her hip against the island counter and grew thoughtful. "You were fourteen and gutsy," she said. "You snuck in the backdoor of the deli, picked up a knife, and started chopping carrots, without anyone noticing. Mr. Cormet finally saw you, and was amazed at how fast you worked."

"I begged for a job with my whole heart," Jill recalled. "I told Mr. Cormet I was sixteen. He stared me down, but never questioned my age. The deli was my lifeline back then. Mr. Cornet paid me cash. And his wife sent home leftovers, which my mom appreciated."

Jill crossed to the main counter near the sink and searched several drawers before she found a roll of clear Saran Wrap. Covering the salad, she placed it back in the refrigerator. She finished off her coffee, feeling relaxed and ready to face the evening ahead.

She was excited to meet their hosts. Trace had the connections and clout to bring the Rogues to Barefoot William. Shaye was also known for her strong business ethic. She kept Barefoot William in the black. They were a power couple.

Carrie tapped her watch, one with an oversize face and roman numerals on a red leather band. "It's almost six. We'd better get a move on. We need to change clothes, then locate their beach house. Neither of us is good with directions."

Somehow they managed to be punctual despite the

fact that Carrie changed clothes twice and Jill missed a turnoff. Carrie had had a tough time interpreting *Florida casual* and it took her thirty minutes before she tucked a blue-and-white nautical striped top into a pair of navy capris. Navy canvas wedges with bold white stars complemented her red toenail polish. Her feet looked very patriotic.

On the hour, Jill parked her Triumph in the Saunders's driveway. Carrie had held the salad bowl on her lap during their drive; she'd reminded Jill with every passing block not to hit a bump or pothole. She didn't want to jar the salad.

Jill had accidentally turned right instead of left on Pink Shell Lane, and was forced to make a U-turn. Several cars had honked when she'd blocked traffic. Still, they'd arrived safely with the salad layers intact. That was all that mattered.

Sliding from her sports car, she looked around. The sun was close to setting; the last of the daylight struggled to survive. The beach house was barely visible through the foliage. What she did see was amazing; two stories of glass and steel peeked between the palms.

A breeze off the Gulf flirted with the hem of her lavender sundress with a narrow, turquoise necklace strap. The dress was an extravagance for her, but Carrie had insisted she buy it. Feminine and flirty wasn't Jill's usual style, but the sundress updated her wardrobe. She accented with arm candy, the more bangles the better. She wore ten bracelets that glistened aqua, red, and champagne in the twilight.

"This place is incredible," said Carrie as she scooted from the car. She held the glass bowl to her chest; her eyes were wide. "Big bucks went into building this home."

Jill nodded her agreement. The back of the house

faced the street, the front stared at the ocean. They followed a blue pebbled path through the formal garden, taking time to appreciate their surroundings. An ancient banyan tree spread its branches across much of the grounds, providing shade. Topiaries populated the yard, shaped as seagulls, pelicans, and flamingos. Plants and flowers exploded with color from exotic birds of paradise and purple parrot tulips, to beach sunflowers and butterfly weed. The exotic floral scents mixed with the salt air.

Jill was so engrossed with the scenery that she stubbed her toe on the cement base of a decorative fountain where a dolphin spouted water. Additional beads broke from her right disc sandal. She scooped them up, slipped them in the side pocket on her skirt. She was glad she hadn't been carrying the salad. She'd have dumped it on the dolphin.

The path soon connected to a wide, wooden plank walkway that curved toward the main door. The windows reflected the coppery glow of the sunset. King Midas could live here, Jill mused, awed by the home and the coastal beauty. The scent of charcoal snuck around the corner of the house. Grilling would soon begin. She was hungry.

The door opened before she could ring the bell. A woman with curly blond hair and a warm smile welcomed them. She wore a yellow tank top and cutoff jeans. Her feet were bare. "Jill and Carrie, I presume," she said, shaking their hands, and then motioning them inside. "I'm Shaye. So glad you could join Trace and me for supper. James Lawless speaks so highly of you."

"We're excited to be here," said Carrie.

"We'll be calling Barefoot William home for the next year," added Jill.

Shaye took the salad bowl from Carrie. "You'll love our town," she said. "I travel with Trace on occasion, and whether we're away for a day or a week, I can't wait to get back to the beach. I will always have sand between my toes."

She led them into an enormous foyer. Two glass-enclosed staircases rose on either side of the entrance hall, connecting to the second story landing area with a wide balcony. The cream marble floor was richly polished.

"You have a beautiful home," Jill complimented as she and Carrie followed Shaye down a long hallway.

"The house was a wedding gift from my brother Aidan," she said easily. "His construction company started with residential homes before he turned to commercial buildings. We trusted Aidan with the architectural plans, and he added a lot of extras. Trace and I love it here."

This was a house that Aidan had built. Jill's jaw dropped. His company did amazing work. She was impressed. The living room looked out over the Gulf and seemed to stretch forever. The furniture was formal yet comfortable and blended soft buttery leathers with overstuffed chairs and ottomans.

A three-tiered bird cage sat in one corner of the room. A gray parrot perched on a swing. It bobbed its head, fluttered its wings, and set the swing in motion. *"Company's here,"* the parrot squawked as they passed.

Shaye stopped near the cage. "How's my favorite girl?" she asked.

"Hanging in," the parrot replied.

"Meet Olive, my very vocal Quaker," Shaye said. "She just turned five."

"Happy Birthday to me!"

"She's social, intelligent, and has a big vocabulary," Shaye added. "She can't keep a secret and mimics what she hears."

"I'm a smarty pants," said Olive.

"That she is," Shaye agreed. "Don't say anything around

her that you wouldn't want repeated. I swear she can hear through walls."

"Time for a quickie," came from Olive.

Shaye's cheeks pinkened. "Enough said."

Jill couldn't help but grin. If Olive could be believed, then Trace and Shaye had gotten busy before they'd arrived. The parrot liked to gossip.

Olive cocked her head and asked, *"Who you?"*

Jill stood before the cage. "I'm Jill," she said.

"Carrie." Her friend joined her.

"Olive is good with faces," Shaye said. "She'll remember your names. She recognizes every family member and most of our friends."

"Like Aidan best."

Shaye laughed. "My brother spoils her."

"He loves me."

Shaye nodded. "That he does. His work takes him out of town, but when he's home, he spends a lot of time with her."

"Gifts, gifts!"

"Aidan always brings her a special present," Shaye explained. "Olive gets all fluttery and excited. She screeches when she sees him."

Jill took it all in. She and Olive had something in common. Aidan made her heart beat faster, too. She looked forward to seeing him again. Under better circumstances.

The Quaker gave a long-suffering sigh. *"Olive hungry."* She sounded pitiful, as if she were starving.

Shaye tapped the tin food bowl hooked on one side of the cage. "You have sunflower seeds," she said.

Olive blew raspberries. *"Orange, please."*

"Nice manners," said Shaye.

"Thank you."

"Hope you don't mind," Shaye said to her guests as she rolled back one corner of the Saran Wrap on the glass bowl. Oranges made up a layer of the salad and she selected a small piece. She slid the fruit between the bars.

"Juicy." Olive took the orange in her beak and made a sucking sound.

Jill couldn't help but grin. "She sounds human."

Shaye smiled, too. "She can throw her voice, and often sounds like me. Trace has sworn I was in the house when I wasn't even home. Olive is that good."

To prove her talent, the parrot finished her bite of orange and said, *"Love you, babe,"* sounding just like Shaye.

"Love you, too," said Shaye before continuing down the hallway. Jill and Carrie followed her.

A wall of sliding-glass doors opened onto a wide gray slate patio. Shaye drew back one of the sliders and waved to the tall, dark-haired man attending an enormous outdoor kitchen. Jill had never seen anything like it. She stood and stared, awed by the sight.

Shaped in a horseshoe, a commercial stainless steel grill with access doors anchored the male cooking realm. A double burner and storage and warming drawers spread to the left, and a beverage area with an outdoor refrigerator, ice machine, and sink and faucet curved to the right. It was a man's grilling heaven.

"Trace," Shaye called to her husband, who wore a white chef's apron over his blue short-sleeve button-down and navy slacks. "Come and meet Jillian Mac and Carrie Waters."

Trace added more charcoal to the grill, then approached them. After shaking their hands, he put his arm around his wife and pulled her to him. He kissed the top of her head, then commented on the glass bowl she was holding. "Nice salad. It will go great with the chicken and ribs."

"Tonight is informal," Shaye said as she slipped from her husband's side and crossed to the refrigerator. She opened the door and set the salad on the top shelf. "Select something to drink," she encouraged. "There are pitchers of peach iced tea and pink lemonade, soft drinks, and beer. Glasses are in the cabinet above the sink. Help yourself."

Jill looked to Carrie. "Iced tea?" She knew her friend's preference. When Carrie nodded, Jill went to get their drinks.

She was bent over, her back to the group, when a deep male voice cut through the twilight, followed by heavy footsteps. "Sweet sister, I hope you have enough food for a couple of uninvited guests," the man said. "We don't come empty-handed. I have farmers' market corn and sweet potatoes. Mike picked up dessert from the bakery. Sadie came along for the ride."

Jill nearly toppled over. She clutched the refrigerator door for support. *No, it couldn't be. Not three times in one day!* However, a glance over her shoulder confirmed Aidan Cates's approach. She'd had no idea he'd be coming to dinner, but then neither had Shaye or Trace, given their surprised expressions.

Fate had played her, she realized. She'd wanted to put her best foot forward and favorably impress the Saunders family. She'd hoped to appear competent and capable and worthy of fitting into their community. Unfortunately, Aidan could blow her good intentions.

She stood and forced a calm she didn't feel.

She knew Aidan, but wondered who Mike might be.

And who was Sadie? His date?

"Aidan!" Shaye came to give him a hug. He handed over his contributions to their dinner. "I heard you were in town," she continued. "Dune sent a text that he'd seen you at the psychic fair with Lila, and that you were getting a reading. I figured you would show up eventually for a meal. Tonight is fine."

Aidan frowned. The psychic fair and the accompanying reading were best forgotten. He only wished he could get the brunette out of his head, yet she stuck with him. He might never see her again, and for some reason, that bothered him. They had unfinished business. In his thirty-five years, no woman had refused to give him her name. Not until today. He didn't like evasive women. He appreciated truthful and straightforward females.

"It's Thursday and traditionally Trace's night to barbecue," Aidan said to his sister. "His ribs are legendary."

His brother-in-law joined them. "Good to see you, man." The men bumped fists, thumped each other on the back. "We've got guests, but you're welcome, too."

"Guests?" Aidan felt bad he hadn't called ahead of time. "We can come back tomorrow."

"Not a chance," Shaye assured him. "You're here, you're staying."

"You're sure?" He didn't want to impose.

"Your timing is perfect, actually," Trace stated. "You can meet Jillian Mac and Carrie Waters. The ladies are with the Rogues Organization. They manage community affairs."

"Ladies, come and meet my brother Aidan." Shaye motioned to the two women. "He's the contractor for the spring training facility. You'll be working closely together."

Aidan had been so focused on Shaye and Trace that he hadn't noticed the twilight silhouettes near the refrigerator. A second later, the automatic timer for the pathway and landscape lights clicked on, illuminating the patio. That's when he saw *her,* the psychic imposter. He felt sucker punched.

This had to be a joke; that was the first thought that ran through his mind. He had hoped to see her again, but not under further pretense. Yet there she stood, staring at him, her expression closed, as if they'd never met. Once again she was pretending to be someone she was not. He was sure of it. There was no way she worked for the ball club. She was too damn flighty.

Shaye was not easily fooled, yet somehow this woman had pulled a fast one on his sister. The lady owed them an explanation. He would get answers.

The shorter of the two women approached him now. She was wholesome, pretty, and tentative. She tilted her head and gave him a shy smile. "I'm Carrie," she said, and he noted her braces.

"Nice to meet you," Aidan returned, keeping it friendly yet professional.

Jillian came next. Her steps were measured and her gaze was sharp. Her expression held the right amount of interest as if meeting someone for the first time. She gave nothing away. Carrie made the introductions. "This is my boss, Jillian Mac."

"Jillian," he acknowledged. He liked her name. He could almost taste the woman on his tongue.

"I prefer Jill," she returned easily. "It's a pleasure, Aidan. I had hoped to meet you when you were in Richmond this past October, but I was away from the stadium during your visit."

"We were involved with the local Chalk Walk," Carrie explained. "The event brings ballplayers together with the community. Fans pay big money to produce colorful chalk pictures alongside their favorite Rogue on the sidewalks downtown. Viewers donate a few dollars to vote for their favorite drawing. All proceeds go to cancer research."

"The team sponsors numerous events throughout the year," Jill went on to say. "My favorite is the St. James River Canoe Race in the summer. The Rogues paddle for Homes of Hope, houses built for single mothers."

"Jill and Carrie plan to raise fan awareness in Barefoot William," Shaye added. "The town is already psyched for spring training next year."

Carrie crossed her fingers, looking hopeful. "You build the stadium and we'll fill the seats."

"We're pushing toward the same goal," said Shaye as she carried the potatoes and corn to the butcher block counter near the sink. There, she washed the produce, then wrapped the vegetables in aluminum foil. She passed them to her husband, who placed them on the grill.

Aidan watched as Trace retrieved his tongs and turned the chicken and ribs. He then dipped a pastry brush in a container of sauce and spread it on thick. The sweet-tart scent of molasses, brown sugar, and a hint of vinegar drifted his way. Barbecue was a rite of summer. In his family, it was more than food; it was close to a religion.

He slowly returned his gaze to Jill. The woman knocked him off his game. Aidan wasn't sold on the idea of their working together. However he had little choice in the matter. He scratched his chin and said, "You look familiar, Jillian."

She dismissed him with a shrug. "I'm often mistaken for someone else. I have one of those faces, I guess."

Aidan disagreed. There was nothing common about her. She was stunning. She didn't look like anyone he'd ever met. Men would walk into walls, checking her out.

"I'm pretty sure I saw you on the boardwalk today," he insisted.

"You're mistaken."

He refused to let up. "You didn't attend the psychic fair? Didn't get a reading?" *Or give a reading?*

Her mouth tightened slightly. "Sorry, no."

"You're absolutely certain—"

"Aidan?" Shaye looked at him strangely. "Stop interrogating our guest."

He backed off for the moment, for his sister's sake. "My apology," he said, not meaning it for a second.

He stared at Jill, trying to figure her out. A light breeze off the Gulf pressed her sundress to her body. The lady was slender. He liked her bare shoulders. Her arms were sleek and toned. Her breasts were high and firm. She didn't need a bra.

A second gentle gust flattened her skirt against her belly, then snuck between her legs like the slide of a man's hand. There was no panty line. Her bracelets jangled. She wore the same sandals she'd had on earlier that day, the pair with the missing beads. Her toenails were painted a deep purple. He liked the color.

Jill was tricky; she turned the conversation on him. "Your sister mentioned you'd met with a psychic," she said.

"How did it go, Aidan?" Shaye asked as she started setting the round patio table that would easily seat six. She withdrew woven sea-grass placemats from a drawer, along with bright green plastic plates. Carrie assisted her, collecting matching glasses and silverware.

"People have e-mailed and phoned all afternoon," Shaye told him. "I've heard only good comments on the event. Who gave you the reading?"

Aidan set his jaw. He could tell Shaye the truth, point his finger at Jillian Mac and accuse her of pretending to be psychic. The woman in question stood before him now, her gaze unwavering. Only the rapid pulse at the base of her throat gave her away. She was nervous. She expected him to out her.

She was momentarily on a solid professional footing with Shaye and Trace. She'd put on her best face with them. His sister and brother-in-law would never hold Jill's prank against her. They would find it amusing. Shaye would praise her ingenuity for saving his ass. Trace wouldn't give it a second thought. They were good sports.

Jill, however, didn't know that. She wouldn't want her antics to get back to James Lawless. Aidan smiled to himself. He had her where he wanted her, and liked that fact. He kept her secret.

"Long story short," he began, "I was with Lila Sims, and she wanted a reading. Aries Martine immediately saw through her. Apparently Lila only wanted to marry me to make her boss jealous. We're no longer together."

Carrie was sympathetic. "Not so happily ever after."

Shaye smiled broadly. "That's amazing! I'm so glad Aries set you straight," she said, placing two rolls of paper towels at the center of the table. They would be used as napkins. "Lila wasn't right for you."

"How would you know that?" he asked.

"A sister's intuition," Shaye said as she passed Trace a large serving platter for the cooked food. "She seemed a social climber."

Aidan had to agree. Lila had often planned their dates. They would inevitably attend high-profile parties and events. He preferred low-key nights, where pizza, beer, and ESPN kept him company. The television didn't expect small talk or count on a charitable donation.

Woof! Sadie had arrived. Behind her came Mike Burke, Aidan's construction supervisor. Mike was tall and lean with a hard face and major attitude. He wore a *Tough as Nails* T-shirt and ripped jeans. Incongruously, he carried a pink bakery box. "Your girl sniffed every bush and tree on the property," he informed Aidan. "Then she wandered down to the beach and chased a crab."

Chased was an exaggeration, Aidan mused. Sadie was a white pointer of indeterminate age, although his veterinarian figured she was at least twelve, possibly thirteen. Her eyes were cloudy and her ribs showed despite her three meals a day. He gave her lots of treats.

Sadie was a stray. She'd found him in Tallahassee. She'd somehow managed to sneak inside the fencing where his crew parked the heavy equipment for the night. She'd been dirty and hungry. He'd given her a bath and fed her. She'd never left. His men had adopted her. She favored Aidan and Mike, and spent the day in their office trailer on different construction sites. Mike had an active social life, so Aidan took Sadie home with him each evening. He'd become her human. They suited each other. Neither asked for much.

Sadie came toward him now; her steps were slow and her hips sagged, but her tail never stopped wagging. She was always happy. She sat down near his feet, then leaned against his leg. He scratched her ears.

"I brought cupcakes," Mike said to Shaye. He handed her the oblong box; in exchange she passed him a Guinness, his favorite beer.

Shaye snuck a peek at their dessert. "Nice assortment," she approved. She immediately carried the cupcakes inside the house, so the frosting wouldn't melt in the heat.

"My name is on one of the devil's food," Mike called after her.

Carrie Waters gave Mike a small smile. "I like devil's food, too," she said.

Mike stared at her. Stared and stared to the point of rudeness. Aidan saw a flicker of interest spark in his eyes, so fleeting it could've been a play of light. "You're plain vanilla, sweetheart," he finally said.

He had called Carrie bland.

Heat crept into her cheeks.

Aidan cleared his throat. Polite wasn't Mike's strong

suit. He spoke his mind. His sarcasm often jabbed. The man could draw blood. He hadn't always been that way, but life had thrown him a curveball. He coped the best he could.

Jill visibly bristled; she was not pleased by Mike's comment. She was on him in a heartbeat. "Vanilla? Come again, dude?"

Mike shrugged. "Vanilla with sprinkles," he amended. "Happy now?"

Jill narrowed her gaze on him. "Definitely sprinkles with a sparkler on top."

Carrie flashed a smile.

Mike noticed her braces. "You have a full grill."

Carrie clamped her mouth shut.

Mike ran his own tongue over his teeth, testing the smoothness. "Aren't you a little old to have your teeth straightened?" he asked.

"Age is irrelevant," came from Jill.

"Total fender bender when you kiss, I bet."

"Why would you care?" Carrie braved.

Mike shrugged. "I don't, actually." He then looked to Aidan, lifted an eyebrow. "Who are these women?" he asked. No names had been exchanged. "Friends of yours?"

"We've just met." Although he and Jill seemed old acquaintances. Aidan made the introductions. Mike's jaw significantly tightened when he learned the ladies worked for the Rogues Organization. Major league baseball was a touchy subject for him. It was a dream lost. Building the spring-training facility would be bittersweet. He'd be on the outside, looking in. Fate wasn't always fair.

Aidan had known Mike for twelve years. He'd met the other man through his younger brother, Rylan. The two athletes had attended the University of Miami together. They'd lived in the same dorm. Both had full baseball scholarships. Ry played center field and Mike was the starting pitcher. Both friends were sport savvy and built to play ball.

Mike had ranked number one in college pitchers up until the night a crooked poker game and bar fight stole his future. Aidan was aware of the unfortunate incident. It had been tragic. Life-altering. Crippling.

Rylan and Mike had gone out for a beer at Humphreys, a local sports bar. They had joined a card game with four other guys they'd seen around campus, but hadn't known well. They'd had no idea at the time, but later learned that the men ran a poker scam and shared in the winnings. The bartender got a cut, too.

The crowd had thinned around midnight. The lights had dimmed. Few remained. Beer bottles littered their table. Baskets of pretzels were empty. Rylan and Mike were down several hundred dollars when Ry caught one of the players cheating. He had called Hudd Daniels out.

Rylan's accusation started a fight. Mike backed Ry. The remaining three guys sided with Hudd. Rylan and Mike took their fair share of punches, but finally got the best of all the guys but Hudd. He'd been a dirty fighter. Hudd had grabbed a Hammer Break pool cue from the rack, the heavy slammer that broke balls like cannon fire. He'd swung the cue at the back of Rylan's head with intent and anger, a deadly combination.

Ry never saw the blow coming, but Mike had. He'd raised his arm to protect Rylan, and taken the hit himself. Square across his palm. Fifteen bones had broken. His surgery had been successful, but recovery failed him. He'd never been able to fully grip a baseball. That took him out of the major-league draft. A draft that would've taken him first round had he been healthy.

Rylan went on to play professional ball. He'd been drafted in the third round by the St. Louis Colonels.

Mike had been heavily scouted by the Rogues, and would've given his right testicle to play for the team. Sadly, it wasn't meant to be. His dream had disintegrated. Disappointment darkened his heart. Depression left him moody. Sarcasm shadowed his regrets.

Aidan would always be grateful to Mike. He credited him for saving his brother's life. A severe blow to the head could have caused a skull fracture or worse. He couldn't imagine life without Rylan.

He'd hired the man when Mike graduated from college. Aidan paid him a good salary that included profit sharing. He would someday make him a partner. He'd always have Mike's back, even when Mike put people off. Tonight was such a night.

Aidan listened now as Mike spoke to Trace. "When did you get the Triumph?" he asked. "Vintage fuckin' A."

Shaye touched her fingers to her lips, shushed him. "Lower your voice. I don't want Olive picking up profanity."

"She's inside," said Mike.

"She can hear a pin drop on the other side of town."

"Sorry," he whispered.

Trace looked up from the grill. "It's not my car," he said. "It must belong to Jill or Carrie."

Mike rubbed his chin. "It's Jill's," he assumed. "Carrie is more Cube, square and boxy."

"That is what I drive," she quietly confessed.

"No surprises there," Mike said. "Bet you keep both hands on the steering wheel, stick to the speed limit, and have never gotten a ticket, am I right?"

Carrie dipped her head; didn't respond.

Jill looked ready to flatten the man.

"Safety first," Aidan said, smoothing over Mike's comment. Mike was being a dick. Aidan had no idea why he'd singled out Carrie. His jabs were sharp; uncalled for.

Aidan eased the conversation with, "I test-drove a Cube last year." He stretched the truth, just a little. In actuality, he'd sat in one at the dealership, but found it didn't have the leg room he needed. Still, he complimented, "It's a solid vehicle with lots of cargo space."

Jill eyed him curiously. A smile tipped her lips. She knew he was fibbing. "The Cube is Carrie's second car," she informed them. "She also has a Corvette."

Carrie tilted her head, as if to hear Jill better. Her eyes rounded, and there was a heartbeat of uncertainty before she said, "My red Corvette."

Mike's jaw shifted. "You wrap your ass in fiberglass? No way in hell, babe."

Aidan had his own doubts, too. He had a gut feeling Jill was fabricating to get back at Mike for his rudeness. She was quite the storyteller. Her life was a work of fiction, a real page-turner.

"Mike, I'm warning you," Shaye called to him a second time. "Clean up your language."

"That's crap," Mike corrected.

"Not good enough," said Shaye.

"Dubious then."

"Better," Shaye said as she began setting out the food. A plate of deviled eggs joined a bowl of steaming baked beans. Dinner was being served.

"I'll help you." Carrie chose to duck under Mike's radar.

She took pleasure in simple tasks, Aidan observed. Carrie's smile was soft when she retrieved the layered salad from the small refrigerator, removed the saran wrap, and set it on the table. She hummed as she fussed with the condiments. She brought out pitchers of tea and lemonade, then iced a metal bucket for the cans of beer. She seemed content and capable; a gentle soul. Mike preferred lusty, uninhibited women, those who broke sexual rules.

Aidan noticed Jill hadn't moved; she'd remained with the group. She turned on Mike, kept her voice low. "What's with you?" she asked. "Do you work at being a jerk or does it come naturally?"

"What you see is what you get."

"I don't like what I see," she stated. "Stop messing with my friend."

"Or you'll what?" Mike pushed back.

Her eyes glinted in a way that told Mike she'd dealt with assholes much of her life, and could handle one more. "You've been warned."

Mike's mouth pinched. "That I have," he said once she'd walked off. He jammed his hands in the pockets of his jeans, and the tips of two fingers broke through the worn denim. He scuffed the heel of his boot on the slate patio. Then shifted his stance.

Aidan pursed his lips and asked, "What's with the attitude, man? Why Carrie?"

"She likes devil's food cupcakes."

"That's definitely a reason to be a shit."

"I've acted worse."

"You better play nice," Aidan said. "I think Jill could take you."

"Yeah, I think she could, too."

Four

Aidan kept a close eye on Mike the remainder of the evening. Mike separated himself from Carrie, staying on his own side of the patio. That didn't stop him from staring at her when he thought no one was looking. Aidan caught each of his glances, and found the situation amusing. Mike's reaction to the woman wasn't normal. He had charm in him, when he chose. Tonight was not the time.

Mike had accepted a cold Guinness from Shaye, but he had yet to pop the top. Beer usually called to him, but tonight a woman held his attention. He'd gone quiet; his brow was creased. He tensed when Carrie laughed at something Trace said. He was on edge. The night rode his last nerve.

Bored by the men's company, Sadie pushed herself up with effort and ambled toward the cooking center. Deserted by man's best friend, Aidan mused. The pointer seldom left his side. She couldn't be hungry; he'd fed her before they'd left home.

Sadie sniffed the air and he could almost hear her sigh. The aroma coming from the grill enticed her. She would get her fair share of tidbits. Trace would fix her a special chicken breast without barbecue sauce. Aidan would peel off the meat. He didn't want her choking on the bones.

He watched as Sadie ambled toward Jill. Trace had put her in charge of the potatoes and corn. She clicked a pair of tongs. Sadie curled back her lip and gave Jill her crooked smile. Aidan had no idea how Jill would react. Did the woman even like dogs?

He was secretly pleased when she bent and scratched Sadie's ear. Sadie pushed her head against Jill's palm, and looked adoringly at her new friend. They'd bonded.

The night air slowly swayed, and a light breeze seduced the hem of Jill's sundress, pushing it up her thigh. Another gust cupped the material to her bottom. Her curves were again visible. Aidan appreciated what he saw, a little too much.

"Nice ass," Mike admired.

Aidan's chest squeezed. He didn't appreciate Mike eyeing Jillian Mac. He had no claim on her. Still, he was glad when Carrie stopped to massage Sadie's shoulders. Her timing was perfect. She distracted Mike.

Mike scrubbed his jaw with his knuckles and grunted. "It's going to be a long year."

Aidan understood. Instead of standing on the pitcher's mound, throwing one-hundred-mile-per-hour fastballs, Mike would be the construction superintendent of the Rogues' training facility. It didn't seem fair. Aidan felt bad for the man.

He valued Mike, so much so, he gave him an option. "The construction company has two big projects running simultaneously," he stated. "There's the expansion on the cardiac unit at Tampa Memorial Hospital as well as the sports center here in town. I've split our crew. Guy Clarion is supervising the Tampa project, but I can switch the two of you. There'd be less distraction, less pressure, if you took over the hospital. Your call."

Mike called it quickly. "Leave, and miss out on Trace's Thursday night barbecues? Not on your life," he said.

"You'll find a way to deal with the Rogues then . . . and Carrie?"

"She owns a Corvette, what's not to like?"

"Chances are good she doesn't."

"Yeah, I figured as much." Mike actually smiled. "Jill was misleading. She made up the second vehicle to make Carrie look good."

Jill had defended her friend. The lady was fierce. "The women are close," Aidan agreed.

Mike stared across the patio. "Carrie's stronger than she looks," he said.

"You know this how?"

He shrugged. "A gut feeling."

"Don't test that feeling," Aidan said.

"Jill would come after me."

"She'd take a nail gun to your testicles."

Mike winced. "That's a painful image." He then popped the cap on his beer and sipped deeply.

"Ten minutes and we eat," Trace called to the men.

Shaye glanced their way. "Aidan, you'd better go see Olive soon or she'll be breaking out of her cage to find you."

"I'll see her now." He patted his back pocket. "I brought her a packet of pistachio nuts, dried cranberries, and a mirror."

His sister nodded. "She loves you *almost* as much as me."

He lowered his voice, spoke to Mike. "Stand in cement." It was their man code to stay in one place until the other person returned.

"I'm not moving."

Aidan headed into the house. The sliding-glass doors silently opened, but the weight of his step on the marble floor clued Olive to his arrival.

"Aidan!" she gave a girly shriek when she saw him.

Her wings swept wide as she swayed on her perch. She danced for him.

He fitted the tip of his finger through the bars and smoothed the feathers on her head. "How's my best girl?" he asked.

"Better now." She pecked his finger; her way of giving him a kiss. *"Gift, please."*

"You only love me for my presents," he teased her.

"Diamonds are a girl's best friend."

Aidan chuckled. Shaye left the television on for Olive whenever she left the house. The sitcoms, movies, and commercials kept the parrot company. The Quaker picked up all sorts of slapstick and drama. She surprised everyone with her attention to detail. She loved Maxwell, the pink Geico pig. She imitated his *"wee wee wee"* all the way home.

"Sorry, no diamonds," Aidan told her.

"Pftt," Olive blew him off.

"But," he drew out, "I have nuts, berries, and a surprise."

"Mine, mine! Eat first."

He produced the unshelled pistachios and passed her one. Olive crunched through the nut in record time. She made a moaning sound, which sounded sensual. Aidan figured she'd overheard Shaye and Tracy having sex.

A cranberry came next, which Olive dramatically savored. She ate another berry before she screeched, *"Where's Sad?"*

Aidan rubbed his brow. No matter how hard he'd tried to coax the name Sadie from Olive, she referred to his dog as *Sad*. He went with it. "Sad's outside," he said.

"No," the parrot corrected him. *"Here."*

He turned slightly and saw that Olive was right. Sadie now rounded the corner of the living room with Jill close behind. What was it about this woman that made his stomach tighten and his dick twitch? He didn't wear underwear. The zipper on his jeans would leave track marks if he wasn't careful. He shifted, and made every attempt to breathe evenly.

"Have you met Olive?" he asked Jill. "She's quite the conversationalist."

"Earlier this evening," she told him. "She's amazing."

"Yes, I am," the Quaker agreed.

"I wanted to catch your exchange," Jill said. "Shaye said you spoil her."

"There's nothing wrong with taking care of your own." He paused, met her gaze. "Same as you do with Carrie."

"Carrie is like a sister to me."

"So I've noticed."

"Who is Mike to you," she asked, curious, "beyond your superintendent?"

"I'd take a bullet for him," he said honestly.

"I'll give a warning shout before I shoot."

"Good to know."

"More gifts?" Olive interrupted them.

He reached into his shirt pocket and removed a small, flat box. *"For me?"* Olive's voice rose.

"For you," said Aidan.

Jill leaned forward as he removed the top. Her hair brushed his arm; her hip rubbed his thigh. He sucked air. Set his back teeth. He was damn glad his shirt was untucked, hiding his erection.

Her effect on him was puzzling. He valued honesty, yet Jill danced around the truth. But then so had Lila Sims. He refused to be duped a second time.

Olive gave Aidan her full attention when he held up a rounded hanging mirror in a pink frame with a bell attached to the bottom. He slid it through the bars and clipped it safely to the cage.

"Mirror." Aidan sounded out the word for Olive.

She studied her reflection for several seconds. *"Who's the pretty girl?"*

"You are," he said.

The parrot preened and fell in love with herself. She then poked the bell with her short talon. *Ting-ting.* She arched her neck, nudged it again, listening for the tingle. The sound fascinated her.

"She likes your present," Jill said, smiling.

"Olive is easy to please." He lowered his voice, shared a secret. "Her next gift will be a ladder; after that, a toy car to push around."

"Maybe a matchbox Cube?" she said, tongue in cheek.

"Busted," he mused.

"White lies are forgiven," she assured him. "You were being kind to Carrie."

"What about her Corvette?" he asked.

"I pushed Mike's buttons."

"You did, too," he said, only to wonder, "Do you ever have a conversation when you tell the truth?"

"Guess you'll have to talk to me further to find out."

He could do that. He looked forward to getting to know her. He glanced at his watch, said, "Dinner is about to be served." He tapped the cage gently. "'Bye, Olive. Be a good girl?"

"Fuckin' A."

Jill's eyes rounded. "Oh . . . no."

Mike's profanity had reached Olive's sensitive ears.

His sister would not be pleased. "Bad word," he quickly corrected the parrot.

"So you say."

He grimaced. What would come next? Fortunately Olive's reflection caught her attention once again, and she went back to admiring herself.

"Can she get any cuter?" she asked her image.

Aidan took Jill by the arm, escorting her from the room. "Let's leave while she's into herself."

They crossed the living room. Sadie trailed behind them. Aidan slowed his steps to match Sadie's pace. Jill moved ahead of them. He took a moment to admire her backside. The bounce of her hair. The casual set of her bare shoulders. The nip of her waist. The sway of her hips. Nice, very nice, he thought. His dick agreed.

She stopped short of the sliding door, and he nearly walked into her. He caught himself just in time. He reached around her and pushed the slider aside. She passed through, returning to the patio.

"How was Olive?" Shaye called to him.

"She liked her mirror," he said.

"Did she thank you?"

"She had a few departing words for us," he informed her. "New words, I might add."

His sister frowned. "She overheard Mike, didn't she?"

"Her hearing is sharp."

Shaye shook her fist at Mike. "You're a dead man."

Mike finished off his beer. "I may be sentenced, but I deserve a last meal."

"Let's eat, then," Trace announced. He carried a platter piled with chicken and ribs to the table. Jill brought the corn and sweet potatoes. Carrie filled a squeeze bottle with extra barbecue sauce, then grabbed the butter and sour cream.

The group gathered around the patio table. His sister sat next to her husband and Aidan found himself between Jill and Carrie. Mike was on Jill's right. Everyone could see and talk to everyone else. Sadie nudged him with her nose and Aidan scooted his chair over, which put him closer to Jill. Their elbows bumped and their legs brushed. His groin tightened. His jeans tented. He had no physical control around this woman. He scooted his chair closer to the table.

Platters and bowls of food were passed around, and plates were filled. Shaye smiled at Jill and Carrie as she buttered her corn on the cob. "How was your trip?" she asked.

"We drove straight through from Richmond," Jill told her. "The weather was good and we made great time."

"We only stopped for gas and food," said Carrie. "Jillie Mac loves bagels and freshly baked bread. She could live on them. MapQuest located every bakery along the interstate."

"The Bakehouse on the boardwalk makes delicious bagels and cheese bread," Shaye said. "Get there early, when they're hot out of the oven."

"I'll make a point of doing that," Jill said, sipping her iced tea.

Aidan listened closely, taking it all in. He now knew that Jill liked baked goods. She must have a high metabolism to remain so slim. Either that or stretching the truth burned a lot of calories.

"How can I help you settle in?" Shaye wanted to know. "Tell me what you need."

Jill thought for a moment, and then said, "Rental space for our Rogues store. James Lawless wants team memorabilia available to the public. We'll sell everything from jerseys, T-shirts, baseball cards, and autographed photos of the players to bobble heads."

Shaye had a solution, which didn't surprise Aidan in the least. His sister was a mastermind. "The boardwalk would provide the best visibility," she said. "I will soon have a shop available. The Dairy Godmother has outgrown its spot and is changing locations. You could set up there, once my uncle clears out the display cases, dipping cabinets, and tables and chairs. Give him a few days to move."

Carrie smiled, big and bright. "Sounds perfect."

"Thank you," said Jill. "We can check that off our list."

"Where are you staying in town?" Shaye asked next.

Carrie answered, "We're temporarily renting rooms at the Barefoot Inn. We're quite comfortable."

"We'll stay there until we find something permanent," added Jill.

Aidan had a suggestion for them, but so apparently did his sister. Shaye jumped ahead of him. "How would you feel about living on a land-docked houseboat?" she asked as she scooped a generous portion of the layered salad onto her plate. "My grandfather gave me his vintage Horizon when it was no longer seaworthy. All repairs are in place, the boat is solid. It has two decks with all the amenities of home. I lived there for several years before I married Trace." She sighed. "The houseboat holds wonderful memories. I can't bear to part with it."

"A docked houseboat," Jill mulled over Shaye's offer. She exchanged a look with Carrie before saying, "We'd like to see it."

"My schedule is full for the next few days," Shaye said on a sigh. "Perhaps Aidan could give you the tour."

"I can do that." He then followed up with his own option. "I own an apartment complex two blocks from the beach. There's presently a vacancy." Beach Walk was eight months old. Aidan had told his manager to take his time filling the vacancies. Those filing an application went through two interviews and a background check. He offered furnished apartments, and preferred to rent to year-round professionals rather than seasonal tourists.

"The apartment has two bedrooms." He paused to give Sadie a bite of chicken breast without the skin or sauce. "I'd give you a good deal. Rent is negotiable."

"My houseboat is rent-free," Shaye was quick to say, as she topped off her glass of pink lemonade.

Trace turned to Mike and asked him, "Where will you be staying?"

Mike finished off his sweet potato, wiped his mouth with a paper towel, and said, "The construction trailer."

Shaye started to object, but Aidan held up his hand, stopping her. "It's his choice," he told his sister. "Mike likes being on site, he always has. It's him and the heavy equipment."

"Doesn't sound very homey," Carrie murmured, as she worked her way around a cob of corn. Aidan was amazed she did so well wearing braces.

Mike rolled his shoulders and said, "I don't need much."

"Neither does Rylan Cates," Carrie revealed as she passed the bowl of baked beans to Shaye. "Ry's very pragmatic; he likes the basics. He has five pieces of furniture at his condo, nothing more."

"How would you know that?" Mike's tone was harsh. "Have you been to his place?"

Aidan wondered why Mike would care. Why he'd raise such a question. Why he sounded so angry. Mike's pained expression gave new meaning to "turn back time," at least by thirty seconds. He reached for a second beer, grunted his annoyance. "Don't pay any attention to me," Mike stated.

"You're hard to ignore," Carrie said softly. She didn't have to explain how she knew Rylan, but she chose to anyway. "I met Ry when he arrived at James River Stadium. I showed him around town, lined him up with a real estate agent. I took him shopping and gave him a list of the best coffee shops, restaurants, and nightclubs."

"You frequent clubs?" Mike was at it again.

"Carrie knows her way around a dance floor," Jill answered for her friend.

"I took her for someone who waltzed."

"You look like someone with two left feet."

"He does," Shaye said. "I danced with Mike at my brother Dune and Sophie's wedding reception. He's a toe-crusher."

Mike grunted. "That's because the ballroom was crowded. We had a foot of space."

"Rylan couldn't make the ceremony," Shaye said. "He'd been chosen to play in the all-star game. It's hard to get all the Cateses together at one time in one place. We are numerous." She smiled then. "We do love family. Ry's a year older than me, but he remains the baby boy of four brothers."

"We picked on him as a kid, but that's what older brothers do," said Aidan. "He wanted to play baseball from the moment he could walk. He used to drag around a Louisville Slugger; the bat was bigger than he was."

"You'll see Rylan soon," Carrie reminded them. "He'll be in Barefoot William for the Rogues/community slow-pitch softball game in two weeks. He's a great guy, and always has time for his fans. He's a good person to know."

Aidan was aware of the upcoming event. It was scheduled for the weekend between spring training and the season opener. Several retired Rogues from the front office would be in attendance, along with two starting roster players. Rylan would be one of the starters. He'd volunteered to come home. Aidan looked forward to seeing his kid brother again.

Carrie had yet to mention Ry and Mike's college history, Aidan realized. Perhaps she wasn't aware of their strained relationship. Rylan had made several attempts to contact Mike, but Mike had never responded. Ry was living Mike's dream. Rylan's presence only reminded Mike of everything he'd lost.

"Jillie Mac and I need to form a local team," Carrie

said, hope in her voice. "Will you join us for slow pitch?" she asked the table at large.

Shaye was first to hop on board. His sister loved sports. "I'll play, and so will Trace," she volunteered them both. She'd caught Trace with his mouth full, so he couldn't decline. He nodded halfheartedly.

"Aidan, Mike?" Jill asked nicely. "Can we sign you up, too?"

Aidan rubbed the back of his neck. Slow-pitch softball wasn't his game. He'd once played in a coed charity event in Tallahassee; it hadn't been his greatest moment. Bricker's Backhoes had taken the field against Cherri's Hair Salon. The stylists weren't afraid to break a nail. The girls had kicked Bricker butt, wearing tank tops, short shorts, and high-top sneakers. They'd been distracting as hell.

Aidan had blamed his poor showing on not having the proper glove. He'd gone with a ten-inch baseball mitt instead of the larger fifteen-inch glove used in slow pitch. Which was his own fault; he hadn't had time to break in a new one. The pocket on his baseball mitt was meant to catch a nine-inch baseball, not the twelve-inch softball. He'd dropped two fly balls that day. His team had lost to the women who colored and cut, permed, and straightened hair. The defeat had not set well with the burly backhoe operators.

He should decline the upcoming game. It was in his best interests to do so. However the challenge in Jill's eyes had him relenting. "Sure, why not?" he said. He knew of a dozen reasons he shouldn't play, but kept them to himself. He would plan ahead this time. He'd purchase the proper glove and make a decent showing.

"Aidan's got long legs and he's a good runner," said Shaye. "Put him in the outfield."

"Mike?" Carrie nudged.

Mike pretended not to hear her.

Jill poked the bear. "Slow pitch isn't for everyone. It's all about timing and precision. You'd need to be an all-around athlete to participate. We understand if you don't want to play, Mike."

No response from the man.

Silence hung heavy over the table.

"You could always coach." Carrie gave him an easy out.

Mike looked at her. "Would you be on my team?" he asked.

She nodded, and Mike made a rude noise.

Jill leaned her elbows on the table and eyed Mike with fire in her eyes. "Carrie can hold her own in slow pitch."

Carrie didn't look very athletic, Aidan thought. He wondered if that was another of Jill's fabrications. "What about you?" he asked her. "Will you be playing for the home team?"

She shook her head. "I'll be with the Rogues," she said. "Carrie and I decided to split sides."

Mike's lip curled. "No surprise you chose the winning team."

"Slow pitch is a stretch for all players," Jill said. "The day isn't about winning; it's about fun and community involvement."

"That's what you say now," said Mike. "Wait until the score is tied going into the ninth inning. You'll be calling for a home run."

"Barefoot William will bring home the trophy," said Shaye, showing her competitive spirit.

"Psycho McMillan will be out for blood," Carrie said, grinning. "The man is a warrior. He gets hyped tossing horseshoes."

"His reputation precedes him," said Shaye. "I look forward to meeting the wild man."

"Psycho remains a fan favorite even after his retirement," said Carrie. "He still gets more mail than any other player. Requests for him to make public appearances are never-ending."

"He's passed his hell-raising days," said Jill, her face softening. "He's become a family man. His daughter is adorable, and his wife, Keely, is pregnant with their second child."

Aidan heard the fondness in her voice for the famous right fielder who was now the senior vice-president/general manager of the Rogues. Envy slammed him, an unreasonable emotion. Jill worked in community affairs and associated with all the players, veterans and rookies alike. She shared in many aspects of their lives. Baseball was a close-knit community.

"Make a decision," Jill prodded Mike. "Are you in or out of the game?"

"Chances are good I'll be working," he said.

"On the weekend?" again from Jill, her one eyebrow raised.

Mike glared at her. She glared back. Aidan wasn't sure whose stare was more intense. It became a contest of wills. Aidan couldn't determine the winner, they were both so stubborn.

Shaye pointed a rib bone at Mike. "A compromise," she said to diffuse the situation. "We'll pencil you in as coach."

"You're erasable," said Jill.

Mike tipped his chair back on two legs, caught the edge of the table with his knees, and kept his balance. "I'll play if you can answer one question," he said to Jill and Carrie. "How many stitches on a regulation major league baseball?" A shrewd question.

Aidan knew the answer, but did the women?

Jill didn't even blink. "There are one hundred eight single stitches or two hundred sixteen double. It's however you look at the ball."

"She's right." Aidan fought back his smile, but lost. Mike scowled at him, too.

"That settles it," said Carrie. "You've made a commitment, Mike, and I'm holding you to it." She raised her glass of iced tea, made a toast: "To Team Barefoot William."

"Here, here," said Trace, lightly touching his can of beer to Shaye's glass of lemonade.

Carrie held her own glass toward Mike. He ignored her, but she waited him out. Shaye cleared her throat and Mike took the hint, in his own time. He would never offend his hostess.

Aidan was relieved when he finally tapped his Guinness against Carrie's beverage, a little harder than was necessary. Tea sloshed over the rim. Mike surprised everyone by tearing off sheets of paper towels and blotting up the mess. He tossed the wet towels over his shoulder and into the trash can. He had perfect aim.

The men went on to have second helpings. Afterward, the women cleared the table. Shaye brewed a pot of coffee. Cupcakes wrapped up the meal. Mike retrieved his bakery box. Aidan eyed dessert. He let everyone select their favorite flavor before deciding on Butterfinger fudge. He noticed Mike polished off his devil's food cupcake at the exact moment Carrie finished hers. There was one devil's food left. He expected Mike to grab it, but he didn't.

Instead, he and Carrie stared at each other across the table. She was the first to reach for the cupcake. She picked up a plastic knife and cut it in half. She slid Mike's portion to him on a paper towel.

"You got the bigger half," Mike accused.

"That's because I'm the bigger person," she returned. "You're lucky I shared."

Mike almost smiled. One corner of his mouth curved as he took a bite of devil's food. He then chewed and swallowed his friendliness.

Carrie had been generous, Aidan mused. She could've eaten the entire cupcake herself, and no one would've said a word. Had Mike reached for it, Shaye would've slapped his hand. Carrie was company; Mike was considered family, albeit the black sheep. Guests had first choice. Always.

They sat around the table shooting the breeze for the next hour—until Shaye yawned, which Aidan knew was their clue to leave. His sister was tired. She often called it an early night, only to start her work day before the sun's own alarm clock sounded.

Aidan pushed back his chair and stood. "Time to fly," he said. "Thanks for dinner."

"I appreciated the meal," said Mike, standing now, too. "I don't cook, but I know the best restaurants in town. The next night out is on me."

"Works for us," said Trace.

Shaye nodded her agreement. "I like to cook, but I also support our local businesses several times a week."

Trace curved his arm about his wife's shoulders, kissed her affectionately on the forehead. "Shaye has Zinotti's Pizza, Fryer Clucks Chicken, and China Palace on speed dial."

"Those deliveries make my life easier," his wife said.

Trace smiled. "I like you easy."

Carrie collected the salad bowl and Jill finished off her iced tea. The group then moved from the table and trekked back through the house with Sadie ambling behind. Aidan stopped to say good-bye to Olive. " 'Night, sweet girl."

"Sleep tight."

"Miss me?" he asked.

"Fuckin' A" was a far cry from her usual *"with all my heart."*

Shaye stopped dead. She glared at Mike. "Olive overheard you," she groaned.

He grimaced. "How can I fix it?"

Shaye sighed. "I'll have to come up with a word she likes just as well."

"Hell." The parrot mimicked Mike's voice.

"Make that two words," said Trace.

They walked to the front entry. "Thanks for everything," Jill said as Trace held the door for her. She turned to Shaye. "I look forward to seeing the houseboat."

"Get with Aidan," Shaye said as they departed.

The four of them followed the path back to the driveway. Sadie took her sweet time, sniffing every plant and flower. No one complained. They allowed her plenty of time in the yard.

"When would you like to see the Horizon and the apartment?" Aidan asked the women once they reached their vehicles.

Jill leaned against the hood of her Triumph; gave it some thought. "We have this week free, so you pick a time."

He rubbed his chin. "Nine tomorrow morning," he suggested. "I need to be at the construction site in the afternoon."

"The trailers and heavy equipment arrive then," said Mike. "Aidan's girls should be in town, too."

Aidan's girls? Jillian Mac waited for further explanation, but Mike wasn't forthcoming. He just looked smug. The man could tick off a saint, she thought.

"I wanted my ladies to fly down from Tallahassee,"

Aidan said, "but they insisted on driving. They like to exert their independence on occasion."

Jill admired self-sufficient women. Apparently he had several such ladies in his life. Her brow creased. Her curiosity felt more like jealousy, she realized. She'd just met the man. It was ridiculous to feel anything but appreciation toward him. He was helping them find a place to live.

She looked at Carrie, who nodded, agreeing to the designated hour. "We'll be waiting for you," Jill told Aidan.

He opened her car door then, and Mike did the same for Carrie, much to Carrie's surprise. Once seated, Jill started her sports car. The Triumph hummed. She snuck a peek at the men in the rearview mirror. Aidan looked as good from the back as he did from the front, she decided. She liked the width of his shoulders, his tight ass, and his long legs. He had strut and purpose, yet tonight he slowed his pace for Sadie. The pointer walked between Aidan and Mike.

Jill caught Carrie adjusting her passenger-side mirror; she also wanted to catch one last look at the men. "Oh . . . how sweet," Carrie said with a sigh.

Jill understood what softened her voice. Mike pulled open the front passenger door of the black Armada and, instead of climbing in, lifted Sadie onto the seat. Sadie nosed his cheek, giving him a kiss. Mike then slid into the back.

Carrie brushed back her hair to get a better look. "Any man who gives up his seat for a dog has a heart," she said.

"Mike is a man unto himself," Jill reflected. "First impressions stick." Mike reminded her of the guys from their old neighborhood. Tough and not giving a damn. "He was rude to you."

"He got in my face, all right," Carrie agreed, still staring after him. "He didn't like me at all."

"That's his problem, not yours." Jill felt protective of her friend. "Stay out of his way."

"He may coach our slow-pitch team."

"You were determined to involve him, weren't you?" Carrie shrugged. "I merely made a suggestion."

Jill shifted the Triumph into reverse the moment Aidan pulled his SUV onto the main road. "You see something in Mike that I don't?" she asked.

Carrie bit down on her bottom lip. "He's broken," she said.

"You're not going to try and fix him, are you?" Jill feared Carrie's answer.

Her friend was a fixer. And a people pleaser. She was kind and positive, and always saw the good in a bad situation. She did her best to make everyone happy and comfortable, even if she got hurt in the process. Mike Burke would walk over her and never know he'd stepped on her heart.

"He needs more than I could give him," Carrie admitted. "I'll keep my distance."

Thank goodness, Jill thought. She doubted Mike would come looking for her friend. Their paths would cross only during slow pitch. That was if Mike kept his word to coach.

They arrived at the Barefoot Inn a short time later. Both women yawned their way from the parking lot and up the stairs to their rooms. "It was a good night," Carrie said, hugging Jill at her bedroom door. "Trace and Shaye are an amazing couple. Aidan is handsome and personable. He had his eye on you much of the night."

He'd watched her all right. Jill had felt his gaze. He'd been waiting to catch her in another white lie. She'd stuck strictly to the truth. Except for her comment on Carrie's Corvette.

"We'll see more of him tomorrow," Jill said. "I can't wait to board the houseboat."

Five

Five minutes aboard the vintage Horizon and Jillian Mac fell in love with the dry-docked houseboat. The boat sat on Land's End, a cul-de-sac off Houseboat Row. All the other vessels were anchored along a small wooden dock. Several Cates family members preferred the Gulf over a yard; they had less to mow.

Aidan assisted Jill and Carrie as they climbed the boarding ladder. It was steep. "Careful," he said to Carrie when she missed a step. He was quick to grab her arm.

He took Jill's hand next. His callused palm was right in line with his hard, muscled body. He felt like a man. She brushed against him as they stood outside the weathered front door. Goose bumps skimmed her arm. Heat touched her everywhere.

Aidan looked amazing, she thought, in his dark green pullover and khaki walking shorts. His topsiders were as broken-in as his work boots had been the previous day. He didn't wear socks.

A turn of the key, and the women followed him inside. Aidan began the tour. The houseboat had wide windows and bamboo blinds. Finished in maple, the compact space was decorated in summer-sand tones. The vessel had all the amenities of home. The living room connected to the galley, which was small, but modern. The orange countertops reflected Shaye's quirky personality. The center hallway led past two bedrooms. Both were fully furnished.

Shaye had installed a hot tub on the upper deck. A basket swing hung between two tall poles. The lush foliage of potted plants provided greenery and privacy. "My sister stops by every week to water her plants," Aidan told them. "This was her sanctuary."

Here was a place to meditate, Jill thought, or to sunbathe nude. The thought of no tan lines made her smile. She looked at the sky, painted a pale blue, and let the sun's rays play over her face. The air was still. Warmth and happiness soothed her soul. She could breathe here. "So serene," she said, running her fingers over the canvas cover on the hot tub.

Aidan pointed aft. "The water slide is your emergency exit," he said. "The fish finder is wired for security."

Jill's heart swelled. The houseboat was perfect. It welcomed her home. The two decks combined the freedom of the ocean with the security of solid ground. She could be happy here. She hoped Carrie would agree. She turned to her friend, wanting her approval.

One look at Carrie and her hopes for living on the Horizon were swept out on the tide. She stood across the deck, clutching the blue railing as if her life depended on it. Her shoulders were slumped, and her face was ashen. Her breathing came in puffs. Carrie appeared on the verge of collapse.

Jill hurried toward her. Aidan was right behind. She gently touched Carrie on the shoulder. "What's wrong?" she asked, deeply concerned.

"I'm queasy." Carrie's voice shook. "We're land-docked, but I feel the houseboat sway."

Jill's stomach tightened with worry. She knew the cause. "It's your ear, isn't it?"

Carrie managed a nod.

Jill felt sick herself. The abuse of Carrie's alcoholic father had left her gripped by dizziness and nausea at inopportune times. Land seasickness was as bad, if not worse, as being on the water.

"Help me get her off the houseboat," Jill appealed to Aidan.

He was there for her. Taking Carrie by the hand, he carefully led her down the narrow staircase to the lower deck. It was slow going. Carrie grasped his shoulder from behind, steadying herself. Jill came last; empathy for her friend made her own knees wobbly.

Carrie stopped in the hallway to catch her breath. She pressed her hand to her heart, her eyes were misty. "I didn't mean for this to happen," she whispered to Jill. "I'm so sorry."

"There's nothing to be sorry about," Jill assured her. "We had no idea the houseboat would affect you this way."

The Horizon was no longer an option, she realized. She swallowed her disappointment. They'd find somewhere else to live. Carrie was far more important than the houseboat.

She was close behind Aidan as he assisted Carrie down the boarding ladder and back onto the sidewalk. Carrie leaned against his side until her head cleared and she regained her land legs. Aidan stroked her forehead, like a father would his child. He was a kind man.

"Better now?" he asked, looking down at her.

"Much," said Carrie, although her voice was still weak.

Aidan released her, and Jill hugged her friend so tightly she wrinkled the pin tucks on Carrie's white poet shirt. "You frightened me," she said.

"I scared myself," Carrie admitted. "I felt claustrophobic on the houseboat; the walls seemed to close in on me. And standing on the upper deck made me nauseous."

Jill released her, easing back. "The apartment will be better," she assured Carrie.

Carrie studied her now, giving Jill one of her best-friend stares that got into Jill's head and read her mind. "I saw the look on your face when we were on the upper deck," she said. "You were excited."

Jill shook her head, was quick to deny it. "The Horizon was an option, but it's not for us."

Carrie wouldn't let her off the hook. "You wanted to live here."

"No, I did not."

Carrie frowned. "Don't lie to me, Jillie Mac."

Jill fingered the hem of her Rogues T-shirt. "I'd never lie to you."

Carrie actually smiled. "Oh, yes you would, and you have many times," she stated. "You'd say anything to make me feel better."

"The houseboat is already forgotten."

"Then why do you keep glancing over your shoulder?"

"It's a novelty."

"It would be a cool place to call home," Carrie insisted. "Just because I can't move in doesn't mean you—"

Jill held up her hand. "Don't go there. We made a pact, agreeing to stick together. We'll find the right place."

"Beach Walk is two blocks north," Aidan put in. "Take a look at the apartment; see what you think. Then you can make your decision."

They proceeded along the sidewalk to where Aidan had parked his SUV. Jill couldn't help sneaking one final peek at the houseboat. Her gaze lingered too long. She hadn't meant to sigh.

Carrie heard her. "Caught you," she said.

White lies came easy to Jill. "I was watching a seagull," she made up.

"The gray gull on the wooden piling that just dove for a fish?" asked Carrie.

"That's the one."

"There was no seagull."

Jill saw Aidan smile. The man was amused. "What's so funny?" she wanted to know.

"Carrie holds you accountable," he said. "I like that."

"There are two sides to Jillie Mac," Carrie revealed. "She can be so honest she'll make you blink. Other times she's known to fabricate and sugarcoat to protect her friends."

"Sugarcoat, huh?" Aidan raised his brow.

"I can be sweet," Jill informed him. She then opened the passenger-side door, offering the front seat to Carrie. "Hop in." She would've liked to sit next to Aidan, but she didn't want to seem obvious. She slid into the back, buckled up, then stretched out her legs in her skinny black jeans. She noticed her disc sandals had lost several more beads. She needed to locate the shoe repair shop.

Six times Aidan glanced at her in the rearview mirror on their way to the residential complex. Jill kept count. She'd had her eye on him, too. His glimpses were quick, direct, and hot.

Their gazes again met when he parked the Armada at Beach Walk. This time his stare was so sexually intense, he set her heart racing. She wiggled on the leather seat, and her fingers became all thumbs. She fumbled with her seat belt. It took her three tries to release the clasp.

Jill eased from the SUV and admired their destination. *Built by Aidan,* the six stories of pink stucco rose amid a landscape of Queen Palms. White hibiscus bushes bordered each corner. Terraces trimmed each apartment.

Keeping an open mind, she gave the complex a chance, even though her heart remained on the houseboat. She'd felt an immediate attachment to the Horizon. She'd been embraced by the indefinable sense of coming home. She shook off the feeling and concentrated on the residential building. It was massive and impressive.

She trailed Aidan and Carrie to the front entrance. Automatic glass doors gave way to an expansive lobby. A security guard sat at a desk off to the right. The floor was laid out in rich burgundy, white, and cool blue tiles. A center coffee and pastry bar welcomed the residents.

Carrie pointed to the display case. She flashed her metal smile. "There are bagels, Jill, and my favorite cake donuts."

Jill nodded. This was a nice amenity.

"Kylie Cates runs the kiosk," Aidan told them. "Sandwiches and chips are added over the lunch hour for anyone in a hurry who needs to grab a bite."

Jill liked having snacks on the premises. The food bar would provide easy access when her stomach growled and there was nothing more than a packet of ketchup in the refrigerator.

An elevator bank stood off to the left. A set of mailboxes lined the wall just beyond. Designed for conversation, two burgundy leather couches faced each other. A single chair sat separately for anyone preferring privacy.

"Let me grab a key," Aidan said, crossing to the manager's office. He returned in seconds. "This way." He ushered them to the nearest elevator. "Do you have an objection to a corner penthouse?"

Carrie's eyes rounded. "Sounds expensive. Maybe we should come down a few floors."

"It's brand new, completely furnished, and the only apartment I have available at the moment," Aidan said as they rode up in the elevator. "The view is great."

Carrie was all nervous energy and fidgety hands when she exited the elevator. Jill felt her friend's anticipation. Carrie was as psyched over seeing the apartment as Jill had been stopping by the houseboat.

Aidan slipped the key into the lock and then stepped back to let them enter. Carrie drew in a deep breath and walked in first.

Jill was a bit more reserved. Aidan sensed her hesitation. He placed his hand on her shoulder, a gesture of comfort, yet it jarred them both. His hand was big and his fingers were so long, they stretched to cover the swell of her breast. His fingertips reached nearly to her nipple.

Sparks flew across her chest, hot and sexual. Aidan felt them, too. He shook out his hand as if it were burned. Heat collared his neck. Jill's own color was high. His startled expression mirrored hers.

"Jillie," Carrie called to her from the breakfast bar. She'd propped herself on a tall swivel stool, the heels of her loafers hooked onto the bottom rung. "All the appliances are new and shiny," she was pleased to note.

"They've never been used," said Aidan. "You'd be the first."

"The first . . ." Carrie said so softly, Jill barely heard her. "When were we ever first at anything?" she asked.

They had never been first. They'd been second or third on a good day, and last more often than not. Their clothes had been handed down when they were kids. They'd shared half a sandwich at lunch. Jill hadn't tasted steak until she was sixteen. There had been few toys and fewer dolls. They'd invented imaginary friends. The invisible had seen them through the worst of times.

Their adult lives had changed for the better when they'd joined the Rogues Organization. They'd been hired within a month of each other. They worked in the same office. Friendships came and went, but theirs endured.

Jill watched Carrie now as she hopped off the stool and strolled into the living room. Her gaze was wide and her lips were parted. Her feet sank into the plush gray carpet. She appeared in a happy trance. She dropped down on a charcoal-gray leather chair. Her body sank deep. She lifted her feet onto a matching ottoman. Leaning her head back, she closed her eyes. "Soft as butter." She sighed.

Jill could tell from Carrie's expression that she was sold on the apartment. She was ready to move in today. They had little to relocate, only their suitcases and a few boxes. They could sleep here tonight.

Aidan came to stand beside her, but this time he didn't touch her. "My decorator furnished the apartment," he told them. "Nothing is set in stone."

Carrie started and looked around further. "What's not to like?" she asked. "I wouldn't change a thing."

"The one-hundred-inch projection screen television is like sitting in a movie theater," Aidan pointed out. "The custom shelving was built for books, photos, but could also hold a fifty-gallon aquarium."

"I like the art," Jill admitted. "The colors are vibrant." She was attracted to the floor-to-ceiling painting of crashing waves on the seashore. The white froth whipped up the sand and seethed between the seashells.

Carrie rose from her chair, motioned to Jill. "Let's check out the bedrooms."

They did. Aidan held his place at the corner of the breakfast bar, allowing them to move about freely. The master bedroom had a king-size bed and a modern, black lacquered dresser and desk. The bathroom hosted a Jacuzzi tub, deep shell-styled sinks, a heated towel rack, and padded vinyl toilet seat.

Carrie grinned. "Cushy tushy."

The price one paid for comfort, Jill thought.

A double bed fit comfortably in the second bedroom, and a mirrored armoire made for additional closet space. A half-bath was at the end of the hall.

They returned to the living room and found Aidan seated on the corner of the couch, talking on his cell phone. He rubbed the back of his neck, and his expression was serious. He appeared all business.

Carrie motioned Jill onto the balcony. She unlocked and pushed aside a panel of sliding-glass doors tinted against the harsh rays of the sun. Thick wrought iron railings secured the terrace. Two red-cushioned loungers were stacked against the building. An umbrella table would allow meals to be taken alfresco. A cedar Adirondack chair sat amid a small private garden. The view from the two-sided balcony was spectacular.

Jill noticed a brochure for the complex on the table and went to pick it up. Someone had left it behind, she guessed. She soon understood why. The pamphlet listed the size of each apartment and the rental fee. Beach access and the view came with a high price. Even if she and Carrie combined their yearly earnings, it wouldn't cover six months in the penthouse.

Jill quickly folded the brochure and stuck it in her back pocket. There was no way they could live here, even if Aidan gave them a good deal. The place was too rich for their blood. Disappointment was fast approaching.

Carrie eased down on the Adirondack chair. Her brow creased when she asked, "What do you think?" Her voice was hesitant, as if she were afraid of Jill's answer.

Jill stared toward the beach. The sun glanced off the Gulf in ripples of gold. Motorboats and Sea-Doos rode the waves. She squinted north, wishing she'd brought her sunglasses. Her heart slowed when she located Land's

NO SUNSHINE WHEN SHE'S GONE   93

End. She hadn't realized it would be visible from Beach Walk. There sat the Horizon, awaiting someone to move in. It just wouldn't be her.

"The penthouse is gorgeous," Jill responded, putting a smile on Carrie's face. "However we need to be realistic. The rent may be more than we can afford. A furnished apartment with this view will be costly." Which she already knew to be true. She just hadn't broken the news to her friend.

Carrie shut down, sighing. "I was afraid that might be the case."

"Rent may be less expensive than you think." Aidan now joined them on the terrace. He'd apparently caught the end of their conversation. He turned his back on the sun and leaned his hip against the railing. His gaze rested on Jill when he said, "My sister was generous in offering her houseboat rent-free. She wanted someone to live there and make it a home again."

Jill would've embraced the Horizon as her residence had Carrie not fallen sick. Her friend came first. Always.

Aidan shifted his gaze to Carrie. "How set are you on moving in together?" he asked.

"We've lived separately for years," Carrie told him. "The Rogues Organization provided us with a relocation allowance to get settled. We'd planned to share a place only so we could save money. We were looking for a year's lease."

"My suggestion is that you split up," he went on to say. "It's workable, if you can live with it."

"Live with what?" asked Jill.

"I just got off the phone with my apartment manager. He has yet to rent the penthouse, and we both hate to see it sit empty."

Who could afford this place? Jill almost said, but held back. She let Aidan finish.

He crossed his arms over his chest, tucked his thumbs beneath his armpits. "I can match Shaye's offer," he slowly said. "Carrie can live here at no cost, if Jill will reconsider staying at the houseboat."

Free was not a word the women heard often, if ever. Aidan's words took a moment to sink in. Even then, Jill and Carrie were so overwhelmed they couldn't speak. The silence on the terrace swelled with emotion. Tears shone in Carrie's eyes, and her lower lip trembled. Jill's throat tightened; she could barely swallow. Aidan's proposition gave them the best of both worlds.

Where was the catch? Jill wondered. Was this too good to be true? "Why are you being so nice?" she asked him.

"I'm a nice guy," he said easily.

Carrie was always practical. "You'll be losing money on the apartment," she said, giving Aidan a chance to change his mind.

He shrugged. "You were considerate of Rylan when he arrived in Richmond," he reminded Carrie. "Let me reciprocate with a little Barefoot William hospitality."

"It's not a fair trade, Aidan," Carrie softly insisted.

"Kindness doesn't have a price."

Jill understood. Her family meant everything to her. Her mother's love had been strong and supportive. Her older brother had been her lifeline. Carrie was her sister, if not by blood, by friendship.

"My offer's on the table," Aidan said. "No strings attached."

Carrie looked at Jill, waiting for her approval. She wouldn't accept unless Jill was in complete agreement. The very thought of living on the houseboat made Jill's skin tingle. The urge to jump up and down was great. She contained herself.

"You're a generous man, Aidan Cates," Jill said. The penthouse apartment would give Carrie a luxury she'd never experienced. She'd survived the hardships of growing up, and deserved to know the softer side of life. "Carrie would love to stay here and I'd be happy on the houseboat."

Aidan took two keys from his pocket. He tossed one to Carrie. She was shaking from her excitement and used both hands to catch it. Still, it fell in her lap. She cradled the key on her palm, eyeing it as a prized possession.

Jill grabbed the second key out of the air with one hand when he threw it to her. She clutched it so tightly she was certain she bore the imprint.

"Welcome home, ladies," Aidan said. "Electricity is on at both places. You can settle in anytime. I'm busy this afternoon, but I can send over one of my crew if you need help moving."

"We can manage," said Carrie. "I have three boxes and a suitcase, and Jill travels light."

So light, in fact, she could pack and leave at a moment's notice. Jill had yet to put down roots. A year on the houseboat would be the longest she'd stayed in one place. She had a good feeling about the Horizon. It was meant to be. Aidan was responsible for her good fortune. She'd find a way to thank him. Words didn't seem enough.

He glanced at his watch now, and moved them along. "It's eleven-thirty. I'll take you back to the Barefoot Inn, and be on my way."

Aidan was gone within two minutes of dropping them off. Jill stood on the sidewalk and watched him drive away. She liked the man. He was interested in her, too, if she read him correctly. His continued glimpses in the rearview mirror were engaging. They'd played eye tag.

He'd winked, and she'd winked back. He made her feel warm inside.

The friends waited until they were upstairs in Carrie's bedroom before pumping their arms and hugging each other. "The penthouse," Carrie was breathless. "It's like a palace. I feel like a princess." She blushed. "Does that sound silly?"

"Not silly, unless you start wearing a tiara," Jill teased her.

Carrie settled on her bed, sitting cross-legged. "Could the day get any better?" she asked, grinning. "What should we do first?"

"Let's pack, find Sharon Cates and pay our bill, then have lunch," Jill suggested. "We'll need to take inventory of our perspective places, and see what we should purchase. I'm assuming we'll need towels, bedding, and the like."

"I want silk sheets for my king-size bed," said Carrie.

"You won't find them at Goodwill or a thrift shop." Places they sometimes shopped at for good deals.

Carrie grew thoughtful. She grabbed a pillow and hugged it to her chest. "I'm willing to spend a little money to maintain my dream," she confessed. "You've got a nautical theme at the houseboat. Now would be a good time to get *Little Mermaid* sheets and a matching comforter."

A thought she might entertain if she wasn't thirty-three. "I'm too old for Ariel," Jill said.

"Age doesn't matter," Carrie said persuasively. "You might as well buy something you've always wanted."

That was true. Who would see her Disney sheets anyway? She wasn't dating anyone. She had the hots for Aidan Cates, but had no intention of acting on her attraction. Her inner child smiled. It might be fun to feel ten again. Why not?

"I'm in," Jill said. She then crossed to her adjoining room. "It will take me five minutes to pack."

"I need thirty," Carrie called after her. "I took the time to hang up my clothes and put things in the dresser drawers."

Forty-five minutes passed by the time they packed and hauled their suitcases and boxes downstairs. Sharon Cates was sad to see them go, but still pleased they'd found housing. Once their vehicles were loaded, they drove to Molly Malone's. The Barefoot William diner was a local favorite with a reputation for home cooking and large portions. They enjoyed BLTs on thick sourdough toast and vanilla milkshakes.

Full and satisfied, they stepped outside and into the sunshine. They crossed Center Street and strolled south toward Saunders Shores. Here was a world unto itself, Jill thought. The Shores differed greatly from the Barefoot boardwalk. The walkway shifted from cracked cement to cocoa-brown brick. Here, there were no in-line skaters, unicyclists, street singers, portrait painters, or vendors hawking their wares. There were no rickshaw pedicabs. No one wore swimsuits or ran around without shoes.

Those shopping the main city blocks were dignified and well dressed. The women were coifed and tailored. The men wore suits. Clientele carried designer boxes and bags. Money scented the air.

"I feel underdressed," said Carrie. "I'm not sure I belong on this side of the street."

Jill looked down at her Rogues tee. "I love baseball more than I like browsing."

Carrie slowed her steps. "Everything's so polished and perfect. Even the sidewalk is pristine." She pointed toward the shoreline. "There's not a grain of sand out of place."

Jill couldn't help but smile. "That's because cabana boys are raking the beach. No one gets sand in his crack."

"Such is the life of the rich," Carrie said on a sigh. "We don't have a lot of money to spend. I doubt these shops have sales."

Carrie was right. There wasn't even a small markdown. The friends strolled into several stores, only to hurry out. The prices made them blink. Carrie shook her head when they left In Step with the Shores. "Who pays four thousand dollars for a pair of shoes?" she asked, completely at a loss.

A woman passed them wearing the same black leather heels with delicate gold chain ankle straps that Carrie had admired in the glass display case. "She does," said Jill, eyeing the lady's white satin blouse, pencil-thin skirt, and the nickel-size diamond on her wedding finger. She lowered her voice. "She's a million dollars walking."

They next entered Dreams, a fancy boutique catering to a luxurious night's sleep. "This isn't Bed in a Bag," Carrie whispered, referring to a wholesale outlet in Richmond that they frequented.

A sales associate approached. "Ladies?" Her hair and black suit were as severe as her tone. She took her time deciding if they were worthy of the store.

Her mental debate had Carrie turning toward the door. Jill grasped her arm and stopped her from leaving. "Your collection of sheets," she said to the woman. "Silk for a king-size bed and a *Little Mermaid* set for a double."

"Silk we have," the woman said, her tone cool, "but we don't handle Disney." She sighed, as if it pained her to wait on them. "This way." She turned and walked down a center aisle toward the back of the store. Her high heels clicked on the ebony tiles, an impatient sound.

Jill was stubborn enough to follow her. Carrie was more hesitant. "Don't let her get to you," Jill said, dragging her friend along with her. Life had beaten Carrie down on more than one occasion. Jill refused to let it happen over silk sheets.

All along the aisle, beautifully made beds beckoned a person to slide between the sheets and sleep tight. Jill gazed appreciatively at a brass bed with lavender sheets and a lavender-and-blue paisley comforter. Jeweled throw pillows banked the headboard. A bed for slow, sensuous sex, she thought. Her mind strayed to Aidan Cates. The man distracted her, and she walked into a display of pillowcase covers. Fortunately for her, Carrie managed to save the pile from toppling.

The sales associate frowned over Jill's clumsiness. "Do be careful," she criticized. She crossed to a side aisle and pointed to a bed with an ornate Victorian headboard. The pale blue sheets on the bed glistened in sensual slumber. A silver tray with two champagne flutes and a bottle of Dom Perignon sat on a nightstand. Overhead, a crystal chandelier scattered prisms on the wall. Here was a bed inviting romance.

"Pratesi," the woman said, her voice glorifying the designer. "The sheets are made of Italian and Chinese silk and are hand-embroidered."

Carrie tentatively touched one corner of the sheet.

The sales associate cleared her throat. Apparently this was a look-but-don't-touch display.

"How much are they?" asked Carrie.

"You can't afford them if you have to ask," was the woman's reply.

"But she is asking." Jill wanted an answer.

The associate's lips pinched. "Fifteen hundred dollars for the set."

Carrie's face drained of all color.

"Does the set include pillowcases?"

"Two," the woman told Jill.

Jill kept a straight face. "Does the bedding come with a lifetime guarantee?" Heaven forbid the sheet tore. "Do they have to be dry cleaned?" She assumed so.

"Pratesi is dream decadence," the woman enunciated slowly. "The sheets are heirloom quality European luxury."

Jill nodded, taking it all in. Her only familiarity with brand names came in discount cotton. "I'd like to see your Midas Collection with the solid gold threads before we make a decision," she said.

Carrie covered her mouth, but not before Jill saw a flash of her braces. A grin was good. Jill never wanted her friend to feel less a person, just because they couldn't afford designer sheets. Who slept on these sheets anyway?

She was about to find out. "Two sets, Pratesi black," came from behind her.

Jill inwardly cringed. The man's voice was recognizable. She did a slow turn and found Mike Burke, Aidan's construction superintendent, standing behind them now. He wore a gray T-shirt designed with a hammer and scripted with *I'd Hit That* in white lettering. His jeans had more holes than the pair he'd worn the previous night. His scruffy appearance was in sharp contrast to the pricey silk sheets.

Jill waited for the sales associate to show him the door. The woman did not. Instead she welcomed him with a slow smile. "Always the color black, Mr. Burke?" she asked. "Can't I interest you in something lighter?"

"I like midnight in my bed," he said. He made easy conversation with the woman, ignoring Jill and Carrie. "How's it going, Sabrina?"

"I had several nice sales earlier this morning, but it's quiet now," she said. "These ladies are browsing, so I have a minute to put your sets together. I'll be in the back room if you need me." She then disappeared behind a brocade tapestry majestically draped on a long pole, used to disguise the storeroom door from the front floor displays.

Mike dropped onto the corner of the bed that Sabrina had insinuated that Carrie must not touch. He leaned negligently back on his elbows, patted the top sheet. "Care to share my bed, Vanilla?" There was heated challenge in his eyes.

Carrie kept her cool. "I'd hate to wrinkle the sheets."

"That's why I buy two sets," Mike said. "One is for sex, the other for sleep."

Expensive sex, expensive sleep, Jill thought.

Mike cocked his head, singled out Carrie. "I didn't take you for silk sheets," he went on to say.

"I took you for a sleeping bag guy."

Score one for Carrie, Jill mused. Her friend wasn't allowing Mike to intimidate her today.

"I work hard, sixteen-hour days, six days a week," he said. "I want my sheets soft as a woman's inner thigh when I sleep."

He'd made Carrie blush, and he seemed pleased by her reaction. His smile curved in sinful success. "Bedding is as personal as a bed partner," he added. His gaze fixed on Carrie's chest. "I want my pillows plump like a woman's breast."

Carrie had full breasts. Impressive C-cups.

Mike pushed off the bed, a slow uncurling of masculinity. He stood before Carrie so close their knees bumped. "Bury me in cleavage," he said.

"Back off, you're crowding her." Jill gave Mike the evil eye. "Stop being an ass."

"An ass sleeping on silk, Jillie Mac."

He'd called her by her nickname, reserved for family

and close friends. Was he trying to get a rise out of her, too? What was his problem? She liked him less and less.

The sales associate returned then, and the tension lessened. She carried a long box wrapped with the silver signature store ribbon. "Perfectly folded without a crease," she said. "I've charged your account, Mr. Burke. Sleep well."

The man had an account at Dreams. Jill was floored. Wasn't he living in a construction trailer? Maybe he'd changed his mind, deciding heavy equipment wasn't the ideal nighttime companion.

Sabrina escorted Mike to the main door. No other customers were in the store, so she lingered with him. She leaned intimately close, whispering, and grazing his arm with her nails.

Carrie bit down on her bottom lip. "Do you think they're lovers?" she whispered to Jill.

Jill shook her head, kept her voice low. "She's trying too hard to get his attention," she said. "He'd be far more into her if they'd been intimate. She sells him Pratesi; that's it."

Carrie seemed relieved. She brushed back her bangs, sighed. "He's still out to get me."

"Rudeness rides with the man."

"I've done nothing to him."

"You exist, and that seems to bother him a lot."

"I can't disappear," said Carrie. "We're in town for a year."

Jill took one final look at the designer sheets. "No bedding is worth that amount of money. Are you ready to leave?"

Carrie nodded. "Someday my dreams will be spun with silk." She ran her fingers lightly over the sheets. "Until then, we'll buy cotton. Denim Dolphin is on the Barefoot William boardwalk. The children's store should have bedding. *Little Mermaid* for you and Dorothy from *The Wizard of Oz* for me."

"Flying monkeys for Mike Burke."

They walked toward the main aisle, only to be confronted on their way out by an older woman with classic features. Sophisticated and classy, Jill thought. And no doubt the store owner.

"I'm Mila Carlisle," she introduced herself. "I was in my office on the telephone, and saw you through the two-way glass."

So, the gilded mirror spied on customers, Jill mused.

"I noticed your Rogues T-shirt, and had to greet you," Mila continued. "My family is originally from Norfolk, Virginia. My three boys grew up on baseball. My husband used Risk Kincaid as a role model when my sons took a bad turn. They were huge fans."

Jill knew Risk well. He'd played center field his entire career. He'd been team captain and a solid player, responsible for the final home runs in two World Series. When the previous owner of the club buried himself in debt, James Lawless, second baseman and heir to a hotel chain, purchased the team. Risk had invested heavily as well. He'd become managing general partner/co-chairman.

"Carrie and I work for the Rogues," Jill told Mila. "Risk is a generous man. He'll be in Barefoot William for the community slow-pitch softball game. I can drop off free tickets for any of your family members who might want to attend."

"There would be four of us. One son is out of town," Mila said. "I'd be happy to write a check for the event."

Jill shook her head. She liked the fact that this elegant woman would come to the park and cheer for the Rogues. Fans came in all shapes and sizes and bank accounts. "I'll get the tickets to you later this week," she promised.

Mila beamed, pleased. She then glanced at her associate, now walking toward them. Mike Burke was long gone, Jill noted. "Has Sabrina been of assistance?" she asked.

Sabrina stiffened, her smile forced. "I've returned for Ms. Waters's color preference on the Pratesi sheets."

"How lovely," Mila said. "My favorite spring hue is Moonlight Radiance, a luxurious ivory." She left Jill and Carrie to Sabrina's care.

"Choose a color?" Carrie asked once Mila was beyond earshot. "There's been a mistake."

Had Sabrina lied to cover her butt with her boss? Jill wondered. It was a strong possibility. "My friend has decided to pass on the sheets," she said.

Sabrina looked curiously at Carrie. "Mr. Burke has purchased your linens," she said. "Not only the Pratesi sheets, but matching pillows and comforter, too."

Jill and Carrie stared at each other. Neither spoke, neither had words to express their surprise. What the heck was going on? Jill had no idea. The man pushed Carrie's buttons, then put her to bed on designer silk.

Carrie swallowed hard. "I don't understand."

Sabrina came to her own conclusion. "It's called foreplay," she said.

"The man doesn't like her," Jill insisted.

"Hate and like often hold hands," Sabrina said. "They've been known to hop into bed together."

Jill freaked a little. Maybe she should've moved into the penthouse apartment with Carrie. She could've kept the wolf from her best friend's door.

"What if I don't accept the sheets?" Carrie asked.

Sabrina straightened her shoulders. "We have a strict no-return policy," she said emphatically. "Mr. Burke has paid for your bedding."

"You've already debited his account?" Jill found that hard to believe. The man hadn't been gone five minutes.

"His request was sufficient," said Sabrina. "The sheets have been purchased."

Carrie's brow creased when she frowned. "How many women have received sheets from him?" she wondered aloud.

"You are the first, Ms. Waters."

Still, Carrie hesitated. "I just don't know," she said.

Jill knew she wanted the sheets; she just didn't want them as a gift from Mike Burke. But she certainly couldn't afford such fine linen. Not today, not tomorrow, possibly not ever.

Jill set aside her own apprehension and encouraged her friend. "Take them," she said. "They come in a box that you never have to open. You can store them in a closet."

"Or you could make your bed and get the best night's sleep of your life," suggested Sabrina. "Pratesi is pure bliss."

"Bliss sounds nice," Carrie agreed.

Sabrina nodded her approval. "Trust me; you will not regret your decision." The associate then said to Jill, "I have a message for you from Mr. Burke. 'Sleep tight under the sea.' "

Jill's stomach sank. The man had amazing hearing. She should've spoken more softly. How could he have heard their conversation with Sabrina at his ear? Yet somehow he had. He now knew she planned to sleep with Ariel and Flounder. He was one up on her. That bothered her most.

"His departing words to you both were: 'Flying Monkeys, my next of kin,' " Sabrina said with a straight face.

She then took Carrie by the arm and, treating her as a valued customer, guided her back toward the Pratesi display. "English Garden is an elegant shade of green. The embroidery is rose."

Jill followed them. Her mind lingered on Mike and Carrie, only to shift to Aidan Cates. How could a woman

not think about sex in a store with designer-made beds?
She wondered as to his preference in sheets. Did he
spread cool, crisp cotton or sink onto Pratesi decadence?
Did he share his bed with a special woman? Her heart
squeezed. She hoped not.

Six

Aidan was hoping to find Jillian Mac at the houseboat. He'd spent a long, stifling afternoon at the construction trailer. Only one of the two window air conditioners was working. A replacement would arrive tomorrow. He now needed to breathe. He wanted to share air with Jill.

He navigated his SUV through rush hour traffic. The streets were jammed. Tourists were packing up after a day at the beach. Many had sunburns. Tired kids dragged their feet. Babies were fussy.

His white pointer, Sadie, rode with him. She sat on the passenger seat, wearing her dog harness, which clipped to the seat belt. Her nose was pressed to the window. She'd slept the day away, and needed a little exercise. Movement loosened her aging joints. The dog park was the perfect place for her to stretch her legs.

Aidan planned one stop along the way. He wanted to invite Jill to join them. He had no idea if she would or not, but it was worth a try. He'd like her company.

He was aware of her *Little Mermaid* sheets. Mike had shared the information when he'd returned from running errands. Aidan had chuckled over her selection. He'd never slept on little girl sheets. Perhaps Ariel would scoot over and allow him in Jill's bed, too.

Mike had relayed at length how he'd seen the women at Dreams. He'd intentionally confused Carrie once again. Mike's attitude toward the woman went beyond Aidan's comprehension.

Men could be boys; he'd witnessed such actions over the years. Mike reminded Aidan of a school kid on the playground, pulling a little girl's ponytail, teasing and taunting, and trying to get her attention. All because he didn't have the balls to tell her straight out that he liked her.

A crazy notion, Aidan thought, but he couldn't shake it. Mike didn't date nice girls. He preferred easy relationships. No caring, no sharing, no lingering. A single glance at Carrie and a man knew she wasn't a one-night stand. She seemed sweet and sensitive, and hopefully smart enough not to be fooled by expensive gifts.

Pricey sheets wouldn't win her over, if that was Mike's plan. Who knew? At the end of the day, what was meant to be would be. Fate had a way of dealing its own hand. Good or bad. Lady Luck didn't always kiss a man on the lips. Or slip him tongue.

Aidan turned down a side road that took him to Land's End. He assumed Jill had spent the afternoon settling in on the Horizon. He was damn glad she'd agreed to live on the houseboat. She had made his sister very happy. Shaye was attached to the land-docked vessel. Jill would now gather her own memories on the houseboat.

He parked his Armada next to her Triumph. Sadie perked up. She *woofed* when he unhooked her harness and lifted her out. They approached the craft together. Aidan gave her plenty of time. Despite her limited vision, she was a tracker at heart. She went into her arthritic pointer stance each time a butterfly brushed her nose or a lizard ran over her paw. Aidan praised her hunting skills.

He cupped his hands at the corners of his mouth and

called out once they arrived at the base of the ladder, "Request to come aboard." Shaye had asked all visitors to announce themselves. She didn't have a doorbell or a brass knocker. So shouting was a habit.

There was no response. He raised his voice a second time. Still nothing. Anyone within half a block could've heard him. Sadie whimpered, and concern crept over him. He hoped nothing had happened to Jill. He hefted Sadie onto the deck platform and then climbed the ladder himself. He found the door unlocked. He entered. Sadie followed. Silence greeted them.

Worry had him walking across the living room and into the galley. He leaned his hip against the orange kitchen counter. "Jill?" he raised his voice once more.

Maybe she was in the shower or relaxing on the upper deck. He hated to turn around and leave without knowing that she was all right. Sadie made his mind up for him. She ambled down the hallway. Aidan went after his dog.

The pointer led him to the master bedroom. The door stood ajar, and Sadie nosed it open. The afternoon sun filtered through the blinds. A vintage suitcase sat on the floor, the lid cracked. Clothes were folded inside, but Jill hadn't unpacked. He noticed her sandals had been fixed. She must have found the shoe repair shop. Full sets of brown beads now surrounded the gold discs.

Her bed was made, and Jill presently lay napping with the cast of *The Little Mermaid*. Sadie settled on the floor at the foot of the bed. Aidan drew a breath, hating to be intrusive. However this was a chance he couldn't pass up. He rested his shoulder against the doorframe and watched Jill sleep.

She looked soft and vulnerable, he thought. She lay on her side; her brown hair swept her cheek. Her shoulder was bare. One arm hugged her pillow. The sheet fluttered with the rise and fall of her chest. One nipple poked the cotton. The curve at her waist was evident; the outline of her hip and legs was visible.

The lady slept naked.

She slowly rolled over, just as he'd decided to leave. Flat on her back, the Disney sheet slipped, exposing one entire breast. The cotton settled between her legs in a ripple of characters. Sebastian the Jamaican crab wrapped his cartoon pinchers about her ankle. The seagull Scuttle perched on her knee. Flounder swam near the V of her thighs. Lucky fish, Aidan mused. His dick twitched in agreement.

He shifted his stance, adjusted himself. He then patted his thigh; the gesture told Sadie they'd be hitting the road. Her bones creaked as she got to her feet. She padded from the room.

Aidan stole one final glance at Jill and was surprised to see she'd wakened. She'd pulled the sheet up to her neck and plumped a second pillow behind her head. Her hair was sexy wild. Her gaze was questioning. Her lips were parted, but she didn't scream. He took that as a good sign.

"I wasn't expecting you," she said.

"I hadn't expected to find you in bed."

"Did you get an eyeful?"

"I saw more than you'd want me to see, but my focus was on Ariel."

"My boob says otherwise."

He ran one hand down his face. "I came looking for you, and Sadie found you."

"Where's Sadie now?"

"She's already left."

"And you should, too."

He deserved that. "I'm sorry."

"How sorry?" she asked.

"How sorry do you want me to be?"

She held his gaze, assessing the moment. Time was lost to them. He could no more move than she could roll out of bed. It should've been awkward, him standing in the doorway, fully dressed, and her naked beneath the Disney sheets. But it wasn't. She didn't blush or seem flustered. She was someone to challenge him. She did just that.

"Tit for tat, Aidan," she said. "Take off your shirt."

She wanted to even the score. He'd seen only one breast. She wanted to check out his entire chest.

Her smile teased him. "You could go one up on me and step out of your jeans."

The shirt would go, but not his Wranglers. He didn't wear underwear, and he wasn't ready to stand naked before Jillian Mac while she hid under the sea. He couldn't trust his penis not to point at her.

"I'm good with the shirt," he said, "unless you're willing to lower your sheet."

"All of me for all of you?" She shook her head. "I don't think so. You intruded; you need to make the bigger apology."

"I have a way to make it up to you," he told her. "Sadie and I wanted to invite you to Paws Park." The single mention of his dog got to Jill. Her face softened, as he'd hoped it would. "We'd planned to take a short walk and watch the other dogs play."

"Sadie doesn't play?" That seemed to bother Jill.

"She's social on the sidelines," he said. "Younger dogs can be rough."

"I'm in," Jill announced. "But first—"

He knew what she wanted. "My shirt."

"Smart man."

He tugged it over his head in one smooth move. Once his shirt was off, he clutched it to his thigh. She openly stared at him. Her expression was unreadable.

His body had never drawn a complaint from the women he dated. He'd never seen the inside of a gym. His muscle was built from hard work. He'd never minded sweat-soaked clothes or an ache in his bones. He worked to exhaustion most days. He liked it that way.

He waited for her to say something, to say anything, but seconds seized a minute and she still hadn't said a word. Maybe she wasn't impressed. Maybe she'd seen better. That bothered him a little.

"You're fit," she finally managed.

"You're firm." She had great breasts, although he'd seen only the one. He figured they were a matched pair.

"Your abdomen is cut."

"You've serious cleavage."

"Nice navel."

"Nice nipple."

"Mutual admiration?" she asked.

"We complement each other just fine." He drew his shirt back on. "Are we good? I've seen yours and you've seen mine."

She nodded. "Even Steven."

He turned toward the door. "Get dressed and we'll go." He found Sadie in the living room, asleep by the front door. She was resting up for their trip to the park.

Jill was ready in record time. She approached him in a white tank top and jeans. She was fresh-faced with a hint of lip gloss. She'd braided her hair. He liked her natural look. Bracelets adorned her wrists. She'd chosen tennis shoes over her sandals, a smart move for the dog park.

Sadie took that moment to waken. She rolled over, hoping Jill would rub her belly. Jill knelt down and gave Sadie a gentle massage.

Sweet mercy, Aidan thought, breathing deeply. He could imagine the play of her fingers on his own body, light and stroking. Teasing. Arousing. His stomach tightened, and his dick showed interest in her, too. He wished his T-shirt was a size larger and dipped lower. There was no hiding his erection. The longer Jill rubbed Sadie's tummy, the more difficult it became to stand still.

Jill surprised him by helping Sadie up. His dog was so relaxed she had noodle legs. It took her a moment to get all four paws under her. Jill supported her until she was steady.

"Lock up and set your security alarm," Aidan suggested as he walked onto the deck platform. "Barefoot William is a tourist town; we have little crime, but it's best to be safe."

Jill took his advice. Aidan showed her the security code. His uncle was the chief of police, and the station monitored the system. Anyone triggering the alarm would be on the receiving end of flashing lights and an ear-splitting siren. Squad cars would immediately be dispatched. Family protected family.

"How far is the dog park?" Jill asked him.

"Six blocks," he said. "We'll drive; the walk would wear out Sadie."

Jill reached for the handle on the back door when they arrived at his SUV. Aidan stopped her. "You can ride in front," he indicated.

"What about Sadie?"

"Her harness hooks easily to the seat belt and she can stretch out on the bench seat."

"Aidan, I don't mind—"

"I know you don't." He appreciated the fact she put Sadie first. "Sadie means a lot to me. She's lasted longer than most girlfriends," he ruefully admitted.

It was a short drive to Paws Park. Once there, Aidan lifted Sadie from the seat, then grabbed a red rubber ball off the floor mat. They left the Armada in the parking lot and wandered onto the acreage.

His family owned the land; until a year ago it had been overgrown and dense with vegetation. His brother Dune had initiated the off-leash dog park. The city council had agreed. The play area now offered trails for long runs, wide open spaces to chase a tennis ball or Frisbee, and social time with other animals. A pond allowed dogs to swim and cool down. Trees provided shade over wooden benches, placed throughout so the pet owners could sit and relax.

They passed through the gated entry. A four-foot fence surrounded the thirty acres. Sadie was the old lady at the park. A few familiar dogs came over and sniffed her. She sniffed back. They barked, encouraging her to play. She wagged her tail and sat in the grass.

Jill eyed the ball in Aidan's hand. "Will she fetch?" she asked.

"The ball's more for show."

"Pretend play?"

"We mostly come for the fresh air."

"A good reason to come to the park," she agreed.

A streak of gray came out of the blue. A charging Weimaraner rounded a corner on the dog trail. He was headed straight for Sadie. They were on a collision course. Jill reacted without thought—she jumped in front of the pointer, protecting Aidan's dog.

She waved her hands, attempting to slow the other dog. She didn't want him sliding into Sadie. The Weimaraner stopped on a dime. He was panting heavily, all wiggly and excited. He licked Sadie's face like an old friend.

"I gather they know each other." Jill's relief was evident as she stepped aside.

Her instinctive move to save his dog touched Aidan deeply. "Thanks for looking out for Sadie," he said. "This speeding bullet is Ghost. He belongs to my brother Dune. Ghost is young and playful and can get rowdy."

Dune showed up a moment later. He jogged toward them, tall and lanky in a tank top and running shorts. He bent over, slightly winded. "Ghost loves to race," he told them when his breathing eased. "I said 'get on your mark, get set—' and he took off. My dog beats me every time with a head start."

"He likes you to chase him," said Aidan.

Dune patted Ghost on the head. "That he does." He noticed Jill then, and his smile came slowly. "Have we met?" He seemed to recognize her.

She shook her head. "I'd remember you if we had."

His brother was six foot six and stood out in a crowd. He was hard to miss. Aidan introduced them. "Dune, meet Jillian Mac," he said. They shook hands.

Dune continued to stare at Jill, as if he should know her. He finally snapped his fingers, recognizing her. "The boardwalk, she was giving you a reading." He cut his gaze to Aidan. "Dude, are you dating your psychic?"

Jill grew very still. She looked at him, awaiting his answer, as did Dune. Uncertainty darkened her eyes.

Aidan wasn't ready to out her. He wanted to keep their first meeting a secret, for the time being. "She's not a psychic, she's employed by the Richmond Rogues," he said. "We met at Trace and Shaye's barbecue."

"I missed out on the eats." Dune sounded disappointed. "My wife Sophie worked late on Sunday. She runs the Barefoot William Museum, and was setting up a new exhibit," he added for Jill's benefit. "She loves our family's history. It's sometimes hard to separate her from the past."

"She knows the Cateses better than we know ourselves," admitted Aidan.

Ghost took that moment to nudge Aidan's hand with his nose. He'd located the rubber ball and wanted to play.

"I'll toss the ball," Jill offered.

Aidan passed it to her. She walked away from the men. Ghost bounced after her. Sadie seemed curious, and followed her, too.

The brothers stood off to the side and watched as Jill alternately threw the ball for Ghost to retrieve, then gently rolled it a few feet for Sadie to return. Sadie didn't tire as quickly as Aidan expected. His pointer loved Jill's praise and attention.

Aidan wasn't surprised when Dune pressed him again on Jill's identity. His brother should've been a detective. "Does she have a twin?" Dune tried a second time. "I'm good with faces; I could've sworn she was seated with you and Lila."

"Jill hasn't mentioned a sister," Aidan said, "but I haven't known her that long."

Dune reached into the side pocket on his athletic shorts, removed his cell phone. He flipped through a series of photos he'd recently snapped. "I took a picture of you getting a reading and sent it to Shaye," he said, pausing on a picture. "Not a great one— it shows the back of your head. I was hoping I'd gotten Lila and the psychic in the shot, too."

Thank goodness for bad photos, Aidan thought. "Shaye indicated the event was a success," he said, trying to change the subject.

"Shaye's all about building our economy," Dune said. "She's always thinking about ways to keep the boardwalk going. I stopped by to see her this morning. We discussed my summer volleyball clinic. I wanted her permission to renovate the abandoned warehouse east of town."

"Darren Cates's old feed store?"

Dune nodded. "It's sat empty for years, ever since he passed away. It's family property. I'd like to take it over."

"Sounds good to me," said Aidan. "Did Shaye agree?"

"Fuckin' A, she did," Dune said, trying not to smile.

"Olive." Aidan immediately knew Dune was imitating Shaye's parrot. "She overheard Mike the other night."

"Shaye's tried to coax the parrot into saying fussy, fuzzy, or fudge instead. It's not happening."

Aidan rubbed the back of his neck. "I'll make a point of visiting Olive tomorrow, see if I can help."

"Be sure to bring Sad along. Olive *loves her to death*," he quoted the Quaker.

Speaking of his dog, he noticed her energy had now waned. Sadie had chased her last ball. She wobbled over to him, her legs shaky from her exertions. Aidan hunkered down and hugged her. "You are a superdog," he whispered near her ear. Sadie gave him her crooked smile.

He pushed up and watched along with Dune as Jill continued to play with Ghost. The lady was slim, trim, and quite athletic, he noted. She stood her ground when the Weimaraner jumped up on her then bumped her hip in his excitement. Aidan appreciated the curve and stretch of her body with each throw of the ball. She was damn hot.

The shade from the trees held off the late afternoon sun. Dune glanced at his watch and called to his dog. It was time for them to leave. Ghost ignored him. The Weimaraner had a mind of his own. He took off in the opposite direction. He wasn't about to leave the park until he'd had his swim. The dog ran into the pond at breakneck speed, splashing those pet owners who stood on the bank.

"He minds well," Aidan mused.

"At least he doesn't swear."

Jill returned, just as Dune was about to retrieve Ghost. "Nice meeting you," she said to him. "Your dog is a handful."

"He tires me out," said Dune. He again stared at Jill, longer than Aidan would've liked. Obviously, his brother was still trying to place her.

Aidan would eventually reveal the truth to Dune. He hated the fact he'd lied to his own brother. Jillian Mac was a bad influence on him. He hadn't thought twice about telling the white lie. It had rolled off his tongue.

"Have a good evening," Dune said, breaking into a jog and heading toward the pond. "Ghost!" he called. The dog disobeyed him further, swimming deeper into the water. Aidan shook his head when Dune reached the bank and began wading into the pond. He grinned. "My brother is about to get wet."

He was right. Dune dove in without hesitation. He was a strong swimmer and overtook Ghost's slower dog paddle. There was no reprimand for Ghost. Dune simply turned him toward shore, and they swam back together. They both sent water flying when they shook off in the grass.

"I like your brother," Jill said as she watched the two pass through the park gate. Ghost continued to run circles around Dune. He still had energy to burn.

"But you like me more," Aidan hinted.

"Who said I like you at all?"

"You've seen my chest, what's not to like?"

She laughed at him. "The man has an ego."

"An ego that's being shot down."

It took her a moment to admit, "You're a good-looking guy, Aidan Cates."

"So, you're attracted to me?" Why not ask?

"There's a big difference between being attracted to someone and acting on the attraction," she slowly said. "We've just met. We're going to be working together. Relationships tend to complicate matters."

"I can separate business and bed." Could she?

"How do you feel about *Little Mermaid* sheets?" she asked.

"You looked good lying on them."

"I'd always wanted a set," she said with a sigh. "There were times I slept on a bare mattress as a kid. The sheets were a long-awaited gift to myself."

"I hear Carrie's sleeping on Pratesi."

"You've seen Mike, then."

"Seen and talked to him." He frowned slightly. "I'm not sure what he's after."

"It better not be Carrie."

"What if it is?" He wanted to be ready for any fallout.

A tiny smile flickered. "I think Ursula and her twin moray eels Flotsam and Jetsam from *The Little Mermaid* could take his flying monkeys."

Mike had mentioned Jill's comment at Dreams. "Let's hope it doesn't come to that. Mike won't have much free time once we start work on the spring-training facility."

"The ground-breaking ceremony is the same weekend as the slow-pitch softball game," said Jill. "James Lawless will be in town then. James, Trace, and you will dig the traditional first scoops of dirt. I've ordered Lucite shovels for keepsake gifts. There will be a lot of press."

He'd never been given a commemorative shovel. He liked the idea. The training complex was about to become his favorite project. He told himself it had nothing to do with the fact that Jillian Mac would be around for the next year. Who was he kidding?

"Do you have plans for the evening?" he asked, hoping to extend their time together. "You're new in town; you've seen the boardwalk shops, but what about the rides and amusements? I'll even toss in dinner."

Her eyes brightened. "Junk food?"

"Cheese nachos, chili dogs, cotton candy, candied apples, elephant ears, we've got it all."

There was a moment's hesitation before she asked, "I'm not taking you away from your girls, am I? Mike said they were arriving today. Shouldn't you be spending time with them? You don't have to entertain me."

His girls? He would've burst out laughing had Jill not looked so serious. Mike had mentioned the women, but not provided an explanation. Aidan rather liked the fact she appeared apprehensive, maybe even a little jealous.

"The ladies are fine," he assured her. "They'll be at the construction trailer tomorrow. Stop by and meet them." He purposely remained evasive. He wondered if she'd drive to the site out of curiosity. He'd have to wait and see.

She nodded then. "The pier sounds great." Glancing down, she showed concern for Sadie. "What about her?"

"Dogs aren't allowed near the beach," he said. "There are no exceptions. Shaye's gotten after me when I've tried to sneak Sadie onto the boardwalk."

He had an idea, if she'd agree. "Would you mind if Sadie camped at your houseboat? She's familiar with the Horizon. Shaye kept her overnight a few times when I was called out of town on emergency business."

"Food, blanket, toys?" Jill wanted Sadie to be comfortable.

Aidan liked Jill more and more. Lila Sims hadn't been fond of dogs. She'd never petted Sadie. She felt his dog smelled. Like cherry blossoms, Aidan thought. That was her canine shampoo. "I keep kibble in a ziplock in the glove compartment," he said. "All she needs is a bowl."

"And water," Jill added.

Aidan helped Sadie stand. They then took off for the main gate. His hand brushed Jill's along the way, and it seemed natural to twine his fingers with hers. It was a casual, friendly gesture with only a hint of sexual intent.

The half-heart tattoo on her wedding band finger had him asking, "Tell me about your tat?"

"It represents my open heart," she said. "I'll complete the heart when I meet my soul mate and marry."

The lady was romantic. "What about an actual ring?"

"The tattoo means more to me. It's permanent."

He understood. She planned to go the distance when she married. Some lucky guy would grow old with her.

They next drove to the houseboat and got Sadie settled. Jill pulled the cushions from the couch and padded the floor, making a comfy dog bed. Her compassion did it for him. Aidan could fall in love with this woman, given time. Bowls of kibble and water were placed by the coffee table. Sadie was set for the next couple of hours.

"You're sure she'll be okay?" Jill asked as they left the Horizon. She'd looked over her shoulder twice.

"She'll be fine, but will you?" Aidan teased her.

"I've never had a pet," she confessed. "I don't want her to feel left alone."

"She won't," he assured her. "You get the front seat," he said once they'd reached his SUV. He held the door for her.

When they arrived at the boardwalk, he parked in the reserved lot with spaces designated for the store owners. He pulled into the spot with a sign for Three Shirts to the Wind. "My cousin Jenna is gone for the day," he said.

Moments later they were on the boardwalk, headed for the pier. Pole lights came on at dusk. Musicians set the night to dancing. Every kind of music from contemporary to reggae was performed. People stopped to listen. Some clapped, some danced, and the majority of tourists tossed a few dollars into the instrument cases.

Aidan didn't have many carefree moments. Tonight he relaxed. He spontaneously pulled Jill to him and spun her around, moving to "Jamming" by Bob Marley. The lady had a little island in her. He was fascinated by the way she moved. Jill had rhythm and Jamaican spirit. She turned him on. He became hard. He gave her one last spin, then keeping hold of her hand, he led her toward the pier. There was bounce in her step, but not his. He was stiff-legged.

They passed a magician who turned a small sheet of white paper into a green origami swan. Jill was entranced, and Aidan gave the man a few dollars for the beautifully folded bird. He handed it to Jill; she slipped it in her jeans pocket for safekeeping. She squeezed his hand affectionately.

A few steps farther and she admired a caricaturist. The artist sketched in charcoal. They moved out of the way when two pedicabs approached. The drivers of the three-wheeled rickshaws gave beachside tours, relaying historical and fun facts as they pedaled.

Jill was so busy taking in the action, she bumped into a pirate. She stared, about to apologize, only to realize the man stood still as stone. He was a living statue.

"Human art," Aidan told her.

"Is he breathing?" she asked, concerned.

Aidan guaranteed that he was. "Theater freeze-frame is a new feature on the boardwalk."

"The man's got talent." She stared in awe. "I'd be shifting and fidgety."

Polka music from the vintage carousel wafted toward them on the night air. Twinkling white lights reflected across the hand-carved purple and white horses with the amber eyes and gold saddles. Children reached for the brass ring.

The lines were short for the rides. The arcade was nearly empty. The supper hour had passed, and the board-walk waited patiently for the nighttime crowd. Whether it was a weekday or the weekend didn't matter. The shops stayed open until midnight. Vacationers were drawn to the neon lights and the entertainments.

Aidan saw his hometown through Jill's eyes. She was mesmerized. "I feel like a kid," she said.

So did he. "What would you like to do first?" he asked.

"Let's go on a few rides before we eat."

Smart move. It wasn't wise to ride the scrambler or the swing ride that whipped out over the Gulf on a full stomach. "We can do the miniature scrambler," he allowed. "I'm too big for the swing ride." He didn't fit in the bucket-harnessed chairs. He also weighed too much. The limit was two hundred pounds.

Jill clutched the bar, then his arm on the scrambler. He couldn't keep his body from sliding into hers. They banged into each with every turn of the car. He feared she'd be bruised. Her grin at the end of the ride expressed only her happiness. She took his hand this time as they walked toward the swing ride. He could feel her excitement vibrating through her body and into him.

He paid for her ticket, then stood by the booth and watched as she took a seat on Wave Swingers. The chairs were suspended from the rotating top of a red-scooped carousel; they tilted for additional variations of motion.

Riders hung on tight as the chairs lifted and began to turn. The spinning accelerated, but Aidan didn't lose sight of Jill. He met her at the exit when the ride ended. He predicted she'd be light-headed, and she was. She walked toward him, unsteady and wide eyed. He tucked her into his body until she regained her balance.

He liked holding her, he realized. Loose strands had escaped her braid. Her face was flushed. Her breathing was rapid. The rise and fall of her breasts grazed his chest. He felt her nipples pucker. Her belly pressed his groin. His dick was unpredictable. He poked her.

Jill leaned back slightly, looked up, and met his gaze. She grinned. "That was fun," she said, "and arousing, too, I see."

He couldn't hide that fact. There was no saving grace, so he'd just have to live with it. "What's next?" he asked, letting her decide.

She checked out Whac-A-Mole, the basketball toss, penny pitch, and duck shoot. "How good are you at pinball?" she finally asked.

He'd been a pinball wizard in his teens. His initials were posted as the top scorer on nearly every one of the arcade machines. "I do okay," was all he gave her.

"Let's play then," she challenged.

He was all for it. They walked the short distance to the entertainment center. Aidan nodded to the arcade manager as they entered. The man kept the vintage machines and classic games in perfect running order. Aidan casually chose the 1962 Rack-A-Ball as their first pinball competition. The billiard-themed game was his favorite.

"Ladies first," he allowed. He'd never competed with a girl. He didn't want to run up the score right off the bat and beat her too badly. He'd save his bragging rights for later.

"The object of the game is to keep the balls in play as long as possible," he went on to explain. "You don't want them going down the drain. Do you have any questions?"

"I think I'm good."

He dropped a coin in the antique gold slot of the single player machine, and Jill got into position. She braced her feet, rolled her shoulders forward, and put her entire body into her play. She snapped the slingshot and the five small balls were set in motion.

She worked the flippers like a pro, aiming the balls at

targets then back up toward the top. Lights flashed as she racked up points. Obviously, she knew the inner workings of the game, and had a few tricks up her sleeve, too.

Only a proficient player could bump the table at the right moment to influence the movement of the ball. The trick was legal. She knew exactly how hard to hit the machine without triggering the tilt mechanism, which would then stop the game.

Jill's hips became a major distraction. She used her body like no player Aidan had ever seen. She was skilled and sexy. Shame on him for thinking he could beat the pants off her.

He stepped to the side and put some space between them. A small crowd had gathered. A group of young boys now surrounded her. They eyed her technique along with her bottom. They were old enough to appreciate a great ass. Jill had the best female butt Aidan had ever seen.

He glared at the kids, and they took the hint, focusing solely on her game. An hour passed, and he couldn't believe the depth of her concentration and endurance. She was in the zone. All five balls remained in play; a record for most gamers.

"Wish I was that good," Aidan heard a redheaded boy say. The kid appeared eight or nine, but was tall for his age. His T-shirt had a hole at the shoulder. His jeans were dirty and could stand on their own. The boy hadn't bathed recently either. A ring of dirt circled his neck.

Jill's motions slowed, Aidan noticed, as she took an interest in the red-haired kid. Aidan watched her watch the boy in the reflective back glass. Her expression softened.

She surprised them all by asking, "Who wants to take over my game?"

Excitement rippled the air. There was minor pushing

and shoving as those boys standing near Jill tried to get even closer. Aidan held out his arm, not wanting them to bump her. "Easy does it," he said. They backed off.

Her gaze never left the pinball machine as she called over her shoulder, "I'm thinking of a number between one and thirty. Whoever guesses it correctly stands in for me."

Numbers were shouted from all sides. The moment the group quieted, awaiting the winner, Jill announced, "Number sixteen, front and center."

The redheaded boy was stunned. His friends cheered and nudged him forward. He was so excited his hands were shaking. Their transition came next.

"Stand on my left," Jill instructed the boy. "On the count of three, I'm going to ease right. You'll need to slip your hands under mine and grab the flippers. Make it fast. Got it?"

The kid had started to sweat. Perspiration beaded on his brow and his upper lip. "I'm ready," he said.

The exchange went smoothly. The boy stepped into Jill's shoes and racked up his own points atop hers. His friends shouted encouragement.

Jill circled the group and came to stand by Aidan.

He leaned toward her, kept his voice low. "Lucky boy, guessing sixteen," he said.

"He needed an opportunity to shine."

"You knew this how?"

"I must be psychic."

Not necessarily psychic, but compassionate, Aidan thought. He glanced at the gamers. Jill's protégé was the center of attention. He was the man of the moment, and would remain a pinball star long after the game ended.

"What time is it?" she asked.

"You don't wear a watch?"

"Never have," she said. "I live by my inner clock."

"Does that clock have a morning alarm?"

"I wake up between seven and eight, always have."

He checked his Luminox. The watch was sturdy, but scratched. It had been a gift from his family when he'd completed his first commercial project. The black leather band had been replaced twice. The watch was as much a part of him as his worn work boots. "It's almost nine o'clock," he told her.

She blew out a breath and apologized. "Time got away from me. You didn't have a chance to play."

"Not a problem." He grinned then. "You've got skills, babe."

"Thanks to my older brother," she told him, smiling. "He taught me hand-eye coordination. I learned from the best."

That she had, Aidan had to admit. He wondered about her family, especially her brother, but saved his questions for another day. Tonight was all about fun. He didn't want to get serious.

Hunger snuck up on him. "Let's grab a bite to eat."

Jill was all for it. "I could go for cheese nachos."

They sat on a bench and shared hot dogs and two baskets of nachos. Jill chose blue cotton candy for dessert, which left her mouth and tongue blue. Aidan bet her lips tasted sweet and sugary.

"What else would you like to do?" he asked her when they'd finished eating.

She looked down the pier, then back toward the boardwalk. She grew thoughtful. "I don't have to do everything in one night," she confessed. "I'm taking a few days for myself. There's so much to do and see. I want to ease into the community."

Aidan understood. Barefoot William was fun in the sun. Life had its own pace at the beach; no one was in a rush. Time slowed to capture memories. The boardwalk and pier were as inviting today as they would be tomorrow. Jill had a year to explore and embrace his town.

He stood then, held out his hand, and she took it. He pulled her to her feet. They walked back to the parking lot. They were comfortable with each other, and there was no need for conversation.

He liked the way she squeezed his fingers to get his attention. She did so often, pointing out a unicyclist, a juggler, and a man walking on stilts. All familiar sights to Aidan, but he liked seeing them through her eyes.

They drove to the houseboat. She climbed the boarding ladder ahead of him, and he followed her up. They found Sadie with her nose pressed to the door, awaiting their return. She was glad to see them.

Aidan gave the dog his undivided attention for several minutes before saying good-bye to Jill. He faced her next, wanting to touch her, but keeping his hands to himself.

"Thanks for a fun night," she said appreciatively.

"We'll have to do it again sometime." But he didn't say when. He leaned toward her, kissed her lightly on the cheek. Had she moved the slightest bit, his kiss would've met her mouth. Her lips parted. Desire and indecision darkened her eyes.

A man knew when a woman was ready for him. His time with Jillian Mac was yet to come. He made her decision for her. He didn't want to rush with this woman. Seeing her arousal was foreplay enough. He'd wait her out. He'd let their anticipation build.

Somehow he would manage. Cold showers, long runs, and working late were in his future. He hoped Jill would be there, too. Eventually.

He touched her arm as he turned to leave. "Don't forget to stop by the trailer tomorrow," he encouraged her. "I want you to meet my ladies."

"I'll think about it," was all she would give him.

He hoped her curiosity would get the best of her. "See you soon."

She nodded, and he and Sadie took their leave. He thought about his bed and his own navy cotton sheets on his drive home. Under the sea was far more appealing.

Seven

Sleeping at the administrative construction trailer was not appealing. Not tonight, possibly not tomorrow night either. Beach Walk was always an alternative. Mike Burke had an open-door policy with Aidan Cates. He could request a key from the manager or security guard whenever he wanted a change in scenery.

It was after midnight, and the guard just coming on duty indicated the penthouse was available. Mike now rode the elevator to the sixth floor. He stepped out into the hallway and let the silence settle his nerves. It had been one hell of a day. He'd walked the perimeter of the site as the chain-link fencing was being installed. The heavy equipment along with five double-wide trailers for the subcontractors had arrived. He'd directed traffic. He felt dusty, grimy, and in need of a shower.

He was also hungry. Starving, actually. He'd had a cheeseburger at lunch; that hadn't tided him over. He could call and order a pizza. There were a few places in town that delivered until two a.m.

He stuck the key in the penthouse lock, but it didn't immediately open. He jiggled and twisted the key six times before he heard the release click. He walked in and reached for the light switch. His fingers never connected with the lever.

Whack! He was hit on the head by something solid. Tired and taken off guard, he staggered in the dark. His shoulder banged against the wall. His hip bumped the breakfast island.

"What the hell?" he growled with the second strike. A third hit, and he'd had enough. He dove low and tackled his attacker.

They both went down. Mike pinned him to the floor. Sprawled across the body, he quickly realized the person beneath him wasn't a man; it was a woman. Her softness and delicate almond scent stunned him. He'd never hit a female. He wasn't about to start now. She, however, was out for blood. She slapped, pulled his hair, and drew up her knee. He was nearly rendered impotent.

"This isn't a home invasion," he growled, right before she punched him in the nose. Cartilage crunched. "Damn it, I'm not going to hurt you."

She went instantly still, then exhaled sharply. Her voice shook when she asked, "Mike Burke, is that you?"

She had identified him, and he recognized her now, too. "Vanilla?"

"My name is Carrie." She pushed on his shoulders. "Get off me."

Darkness pressed them to the floor, and he lay atop her. She was no longer fighting him. He liked the way she felt. She had nice breasts, he noted. Her belly had softened against his abdomen. His cock settled at the V of her thighs. Settled, and wanted to stay.

She was the first to move. She rolled her hips, and he slid off her. He pushed up, and then ran his hand along the wall, searching for the light switch. He found it. Flipped it on.

He looked at her then, and his gut tightened. His surprise arrival had scared her. Her hair was as wild as her eyes. Her face was pale. Her granny nightgown had twisted, hanging off one shoulder and riding high on her thighs. He saw a lot of leg and the shadow of her sweet spot. He groaned inwardly.

He held out his hand and helped her up. That's when he noticed her weapon. She clutched a sterling-silver candle holder. It was tall and heavy and designed for a thick pillar candle. He rubbed the top of his head and felt a small bump. The candle holder had done its job. Touching his fingers to his nose, he noticed blood. "I knew you had fight in you," he said. "You're more than Jill's shy sidekick. You're stronger than you look."

She straightened her nightgown. "It was pure fear and adrenalin. Jillie's older brother once showed us how to throw a right hook."

Mike walked around the island breakfast counter and into the kitchen. He stood at the sink, turned on the water. He cupped his hand and cleaned off his nose. It stung a little. Vanilla packed a punch.

He glanced at her over his shoulder. "What are you doing here?" he asked her.

"I live here now."

"Since when?" She had to be joking.

"Since today. Aidan offered the penthouse as a place to live and I moved in this afternoon."

"How can you afford this place?" He was damn curious. Beach Walk was an exclusive rental property. The people leasing these apartments had money to burn.

Her face softened. "Aidan gave me a really good deal."

A hell of a deal, Mike thought. Aidan hadn't mentioned her taking over the penthouse. But then, Mike hadn't seen much of his boss during the day. They'd dealt with separate problems and issues, and Aidan had been long gone by the time Mike called it quits.

"Is Jill here, too?" he asked. Maybe she was sleeping.

"She's at the houseboat."

"The two of you parted ways?"

"Jill fell in love with the Horizon and I liked the pent-house view," she told him. "You'd be out cold had Jill been here. She keeps a baseball bat for protection."

"I wasn't aiming to hurt anyone," he said. "I was merely looking for a bed and a few hours sleep. This is a two-bedroom apartment, right?"

"Yes . . . it is." She sounded uneasy.

"I need somewhere to crash."

"What's wrong with the construction trailer?"

"It's uninhabitable," he said. "Boxes and file cabinets were hauled into the bedroom before we left Tallahassee. There's a lot of shifting and sorting to do. I didn't have time tonight. I'm too damn tired."

"So you showed up here?"

"There's usually an apartment open at Beach Walk. I'd hoped to have the penthouse to myself. It seems I'm stuck with you."

"This is my place," she said.

"Yours and mine for tonight," he corrected her.

"I haven't agreed to let you stay here."

"You haven't kicked me out either."

"I'm still debating."

"Make up your mind, sweetheart. I'm hot and sweaty and spreading dirt like Pig-Pen from the *Peanuts* cartoon."

His mention of Pig-Pen won her over. "Use the guest bathroom."

He was relieved. She'd given in, which he hadn't expected. He'd been ready to leave. He could be a hard ass, but he'd never have pushed her further. Crashing with Aidan and the Cateses wasn't an option either at this late hour. He did have a few manners.

He would never impose. Vanilla had saved him from driving the main strip, looking for a hotel with a vacancy sign.

He left the kitchen and headed down the hallway. "Towels?" he asked over his shoulder.

"They're hanging on the warming rack."

Warm towels—the penthouse had it all. Aidan had spared no expense. Mike would be considerate and shower in the guest bathroom, although his muscles would've appreciated the pulsing jets of the Jacuzzi tub off the master suite. He could make sacrifices.

He showered with a fresh bar of almond soap, but didn't shave. There was no suitable razor. The girly pink Schick wouldn't cut his stubble. He needed an electric razor with a dual-edge blade. His whiskers stayed with him.

He used one bath towel to dry off, then wrapped a second about his waist. The ends split over his hip, barely covering his man parts. He'd gone from home invader to flasher.

His clothes were filthy. Most of the apartments had a stacked washer/dryer combination, usually hidden behind louvered doors. He hoped Carrie had detergent.

She did, he soon discovered. Sixty-four ounces of Fresh Wash. A bargain brand. He removed his wallet and keys from his jeans pocket, set them on the shelf. He then dumped his clothes in the machine, poured in a capful of the off-brand, and set the short cycle. He returned to the kitchen while the tub started filling.

Carrie was still up. She'd put on a robe, fluffy and blue. She now sat on the edge of the couch; her expression showed concern and contemplation. Uncertainty.

"Are you waiting up for me?" he asked. "It's late."

"I'm wide awake, and it's all your fault," she accused,

sounding grumpy. "You woke me. I need eight hours of sleep to function."

"I have insomnia most nights," he admitted. "I'm lucky to get three hours. Tonight I'm really tired. I'll be down for six."

Her gaze flicked over his chest and white towel. "Where are your clothes?" she asked, staring at his groin.

He shifted, and hoped he stayed covered. "In the washing machine."

Her sigh was long-suffering. "You're using my washer and my detergent?" She wasn't happy about that fact. The lady needed to learn how to share.

"Half hour max," he assured her. "A ten-minute wash, and a twenty-minute dry."

"You'll sleep in your clothes then?"

"Yeah, right." Naked did it for him.

She wasn't convinced. She tucked her robe tighter around her, looking like a mummy.

He was too hungry to debate prude or nude. "Do you have anything to eat?" he asked.

"You expect me to feed you, too?"

"I'm your guest." He returned to the kitchen and opened the nearest cabinet. He was rewarded by a box of Fiber Flakes. He'd never heard of the cereal, but there weren't a lot of choices. The lady's cupboards were bare. "Hope you don't mind," he said, opening the top without her permission.

"That was my breakfast."

"I won't eat it all." He stuck his hand in the box. "I don't need milk." He sampled the contents. The damn flakes were dry. They tasted like cardboard. "Does the fiber keep you regular?" he asked.

She blushed. "I have no idea. I've never tried the cereal. It was on sale."

Bargain flakes. Great. He grabbed another handful, hoping the taste would improve. It didn't. The cereal sat heavy on his stomach. It would be hard to digest. One last scoop and he returned the box to the cupboard. He belched.

"Are you staying up?" he asked. She hadn't left the corner of the couch.

She yawned. "I've haven't decided yet."

"I'm going to wind down with ESPN," he said.

He walked to the opposite end of the sofa and dropped down. He adjusted his towel. Free-balling was no fun unless a woman snuck a peek. Carrie's gaze was on the ceiling.

"Which bedroom is mine?" he asked.

She rolled her eyes. "Which one do you think?"

"The master bedroom has a king-size bed." He'd checked it out when he'd returned from his shower. "I'm tall, you're small. I like to spread out. I imagine you sleep fetal."

"I don't curl in a ball." She was huffy.

He cleared his throat, said, "You made your bed with silk sheets."

"You have no business in my room."

"I saw it from the hall." One corner of his mouth curved slightly as he stared at her robe and granny gown. "You need to unwrap, Vanilla. Pratesi is best experienced naked. Silk feels good on your skin."

She worked her bottom lip.

"You'd feel uninhibited and sexy, and might even take a lover. You could use a good—"

She left the room then, without a good-night, sleep tight. What had he expected? He'd been rude to her. He was damn lucky to be sitting on the sofa in her penthouse. He could've landed at a hotel or, worst scenario, he might have been reduced to sleeping in his car. There wasn't a lot of room in his Porsche. He'd have been poked by the stick shift, and not in a good way.

He located the remote control on the coffee table and turned on the big-screen television. He felt as though he was sitting at the ESPN desk himself. He listened to the basketball scores, but changed the channel when it came to major league baseball. He hadn't watched a game in years.

The time had come for him to fight his demons. The Rogues were coming to Barefoot William. He would soon have to face his past and all he had lost. His stomach tightened at the thought.

He flipped the channel and caught the end of a sitcom. He bored easily. Turning off the TV, he took to pacing. His clothes were soon ready for the dryer, and he changed them out. Alone in the hallway, he stretched, scratched his belly, then his balls.

He had the sudden urge to look in on Carrie. Had she taken his advice and slept nude? He might never know. Her preference was her preference. He'd caused her enough grief for one night.

He entered the guest bedroom and was greeted by white cotton sheets. No surprises there, he thought. He dropped his towel, tucked back the comforter, and slid onto the bed. His last fleeting thought before he fell asleep was of Carrie. He punched his pillow. Of all the women in his life, why her?

Carrie Waters wakened slowly. Apprehension pushed her up on one elbow. She smelled coffee, which meant someone had made a pot. That person was Mike Burke. He was still at her penthouse; still making himself at home. That irritated her enough to roll out of bed. Nude.

There was no denying she'd slept well. The silk sheets were a nighttime caress. She was on vacation, and could take a nap later in the day if she so chose. She just might. The idea was appealing.

She pulled a face. There was no easing into her day, not with Mike rummaging around her kitchen. She needed to see what he was up to. All that noise didn't come from him finishing off her Fiber Flakes.

She crossed to her dresser, opened the top drawer, and selected a sports bra and high-cut bikini panties. She shook out a folded *Virginia is for Lovers* T-shirt, slipped it on. A pair of gray sweatpants came next. The carpet was so plush, she hated to put on shoes. She let her toes go naked.

She swiped a brush through her hair, then pulled it into a high ponytail. She walked into the master bath, wiped a wet washcloth over her face, and gargled with mouthwash. She wasn't primping for Mike. There was no point. The man didn't even like her.

She found him in the kitchen, wearing the same clothes from the night before, only cleaner. His T-shirt was actually gray; she'd initially thought it was brown. His jeans rode low and Emporio Armani was visible on the waistband of his black boxers. He liked his silk.

"I bought breakfast," he announced when he saw her. "The food kiosk in the lobby had an assortment of doughnuts, muffins, and bagels. I didn't know what you might like, so I—"

"Purchased one of each?" She was amazed at the variety. Bakery items filled a white square box.

He poured her coffee into a cobalt blue glass mug. "I went through the cupboards and drawers and found paper plates and napkins, but couldn't find any cream or sugar," he said.

"I drink my coffee black."

A corner of his mouth curved. "So do I." He seemed amused they had something in common.

He set out plastic knives, along with butter and cream cheese packets. He leaned his hip against a breakfast bar stool and faced her. She noticed the bruise on the side of his nose. Fortunately the bump on his head wasn't visible. "Help yourself," he said.

She preferred to sit. She hoisted herself up on a stool, eyed the selection, and chose a plain cake doughnut.

"No surprises there," Mike muttered, but she still heard him. He stood on her left, and her left ear was her good ear. She heard very little in her right.

"What's wrong with my choice?" she asked him.

"It's predictable," he said, reaching for an onion-rye bagel. He cut it in half and spread two packets of cream cheese in the middle. He took a big bite. He'd downed two bagels by the time she finished her doughnut.

"I like what I like," she defended herself.

He passed her a crème-filled, chocolate-frosted doughnut sprinkled with coconut. "Be daring, go crazy."

She gave it a try. It was delicious. "What time do you have to be at work?" she asked, hoping it would be soon.

He shrugged. "I don't punch a time clock. Yesterday I put in eighteen hours. I work until the job's done."

"You managed to squeeze in a little shopping, too."

He narrowed his gaze on her. "Dreams was on my way to the bank."

"How fortunate they were in the same vicinity."

He topped off his coffee, added a few drops to her mug also. "Are you giving me a hard time?"

"No worse than you've been giving me."

His jaw worked. "Feeling brave this morning, aren't you, Vanilla?"

"Courage comes from a good night's rest."

"Pratesi did it for you?" He was smug.

She didn't allow him the satisfaction of a response. "Did you sleep well?" she asked instead.

"Like a virgin on those white sheets."

She couldn't help herself; she smiled. "You're far from innocent."

He covered his eyes with the back of his hand. "Close your mouth. You're blinding me with your braces."

His words hurt her a little, but his tone wasn't mean. It was teasing. "Be glad you're leaving then," she said. "I'm living in a penthouse and I plan to smile all day."

He looked toward the living room. "It's nice here," he agreed.

"Don't get too attached."

They sipped their coffee. She had nothing further to say to him, and he seemed finished with her, too.

"I better get going," he finally said. "I have a shitload of stuff to do today."

"Does that include organizing the construction trailer?"

"I need to find my bed under a ton of boxes." He rubbed the back of his neck. "If worse comes to worst, maybe I'll—"

She didn't like the direction of his thoughts. "You'll *what?*" she asked.

"Spend another night with you."

"Go with Plan B."

"You wouldn't know I was even here," he said, warming to the idea. "I wouldn't get in until midnight; you'd already be asleep. I'd take a quiet shower. Sleep, and leave in the morning before you've got one eye open. It's doable."

"For you, but not me." She slid off the stool, started for the living room.

He blocked her path. "Think about it."

"I have other things to think about today."

He reached into the front pocket on his jeans, pulled out his wallet. He removed a fifty, and tossed it on the counter. "For last night," he said. "Put it toward your rent."

He had no idea she was living in the penthouse rent-free. She couldn't take his money. She picked up the bill, pushed it into his chest. His very hard chest. "I can pay my own way."

He curved his hand over hers, squeezed the fifty in her palm. "Buy some groceries then. You can't live on Fiber Flakes. They're disgusting."

"I'm fine with the flakes."

"I'll fill your refrigerator—"

"You won't be around to eat the food."

"Cut me some slack, Vanilla."

He frustrated her. "Stop pushing into my life."

"You wouldn't let me in otherwise."

That took her aback. Her stomach tightened. "You want in?" she asked, finding it hard to believe that he wanted to be around her.

He released her hand, and then fisted his own at his side. His expression hardened. His gray eyes cooled. He gave her an invisible push away from him. "This isn't about us; it's about a place to stay. Don't confuse the two."

At least he was honest. She wasn't looking for a relationship either. Particularly with a man who ran hot, then cold, then indifferent. He'd never allow her to get close.

However there was something about him that drew her. She could put a roof over his head. What was one more night? *Twice the fool,* her conscience warned.

Her best friend Jill would say she was out of her

mind. That she needed her head examined. "I don't want anyone to know you're staying here," Carrie went on to say.

"I can live with that."

She made one final request. "Please don't bring a woman home with you tonight. Save your sleepovers for your own place."

His brow creased. "You don't think much of me, do you?" he asked.

"You don't make a good first impression."

He shrugged as if he didn't give a shit. He stepped around her then, and walked toward the door. She looked after him. "I'll see you if I see you," he said, leaving abruptly.

"Thanks for breakfast," she said to the closed door. There was a lot of food left over, enough to enjoy several morning meals. She had no idea if Mike would be here, too.

She slipped the fifty dollar bill in the silverware drawer for safe-keeping, then washed his coffee mug and put it away. She was in the midst of storing the bakery goods in ziplock bags when someone knocked on her door. Her heart skipped a beat. Had Mike returned? She crossed to the entrance, hoping so. She answered with, "You have a key—"

Only to have Jillian Mac reply, "No, I don't."

Her best friend leaned against the doorjamb, wearing a pale blue tank top, jeans, and a smile. She carried a small brown bag. She gave Carrie a morning hug before asking, "Who were you expecting?"

"The locksmith," came immediately to mind. The sound of Mike fiddling with the lock had wakened her last night. Her own key had stuck earlier in the day. She'd planned to call the apartment manager and have it fixed.

She just hadn't gotten around to it yet. The white lie kept Mike a secret.

Carrie motioned Jill inside. "You're up early," she said. Jill followed her back to the kitchen.

Jill's eyes widened when she saw the leftover muffins and doughnuts, not yet put away. "Did you raid the kiosk downstairs?" she asked.

"My eyes were bigger than my stomach."

Jill set the small bag on the counter. "I stopped at The Bakehouse and picked up breakfast, although it looks like you've already eaten."

"I'm full, but I'll sit with you," Carrie offered. "There's coffee." She poured Jill a cup and topped off her own.

Jill slipped a glazed doughnut from the bag and divided it in thirds. She ate slowly. "How did it feel sleeping at the palace?" she teased.

"Amazing," Carrie said. It was all thanks to Mike Burke. "I slept on Pratesi."

"Are the sheets as comfortable as they look?"

"Even better," Carrie said on a sigh. "They're heaven on a bed."

"I was going to call you last night," Jill told her, "but Aidan and Sadie dropped by the houseboat. We went to the dog park, then took a walk on the boardwalk. I played pinball."

"Sounds like a nice evening."

"It got late," Jill added. "I didn't want to wake you if you'd turned in early."

"I was asleep by ten," was a half-truth. Stranger danger had rousted her at midnight. It had taken an hour for her heart to slow and her mind to calm after her confrontation with Mike.

Jill didn't comment further, which was unusual for her. Her friend was vibrant and usually embraced life. Not so this morning. She was quiet and distant, and seemingly in her own world. Something was off. Carrie guessed the obvious. "Tell me about Aidan," she said.

Jill ran her finger around the rim of her coffee cup, then played with the corner of her napkin. She was procrastinating. "He shared his town with me," she finally said. "The boardwalk is fun during the day, but it comes alive at night. It rocks."

Jill hesitated, and Carrie didn't push her. "Aidan invited me to stop by his construction trailer and meet his girls," she managed.

"Will you?" Carrie asked.

"I'm not sure," Jill evaded. "*His girls* sound like a harem."

"He's a good-looking guy," Carrie said. "I'm sure he has his share of female attention."

"These women followed him from Tallahassee."

"They must be special."

"I'm thinking so, too."

Carrie eyed Jill closely. "Jealous, Jillie Mac?"

"I'd have to like the man to be jealous."

"You're giving him a lot of thought."

"Too much thought, maybe. We've just met."

Carrie touched Jill's shoulder. "I'm curious about the girls, too," she admitted. "When do we leave for the site?"

"You'll come with me?" Jill looked relieved.

"What are best friends for? I want to check out your competition."

Jill laughed then. "I'm not planning to date him."

"So you say now."

"So I'll continue to say for the rest of the year."

Carrie didn't believe her for a second. There was something in Jill's expression that said she hoped for

more. "Another cup of coffee before we leave?" she offered.

"I've had enough caffeine to face the day."

Carrie persuaded Jill to let her drive to the construction site. The road had yet to be paved. Ruts and potholes wouldn't be kind to Jill's Triumph. They took
Carrie's Cube.

Carrie's heart quickened when she saw Mike Burke at
the security gate. He was talking to the guard. She slowed
her vehicle at the entrance booth. An enormous sign announced THE FUTURE HOME OF THE RICHMOND ROGUES
SPRING TRAINING FACILITY.

She rolled down her window, unsure of her welcome.
Mike stared a hole through her windshield. He wasn't
happy to see her. Not at all.

She wasn't here for him; she had come along for Jill.
Screw the man, she thought. He could be obstinate.

The guard held up his clipboard, asked, "Your name?"
He wanted to be sure they were allowed on the site.

"Carrie Waters and Jillian Mac to see Aidan Cates,"
she stated.

The guard shook his head. "Sorry, you're not on the
list."

"Perhaps you could call him?" Carrie suggested.

Mike was being no help at all. He stood off to the side,
crossed his arms over his chest, and watched as she was
denied access. What a bastard.

"Mr. Cates isn't on site," the guard told them.

"The man works banker's hours," mumbled Carrie.

Jill shifted on the passenger seat. "Let's go then."

Carrie was about to shift in reverse when Mike walked
toward her vehicle. He had athletic swagger and a badass
attitude. "I see you're driving the bread box." His tone
was snide. "Why are you here?"

"Aidan invited us."

"He's running late," Mike stated.

"We'll come back another time," said Jill.

"Or you can wait for him in the administration trailer," Mike suggested, giving ground. "You can hang with his girls."

Carrie glanced at Jill. Jill seemed uneasy. "We're here, we might as well stay," Carrie said.

Jill nodded. "Let's get this over with."

"Get what over with?" Mike asked, with more than a little interest.

"It's none of your concern," said Carrie.

His jaw worked. "You're on my construction site," he reminded her. "Everything that happens here is my business."

"We were hoping for a tour," was the first thing that came to Carrie's mind.

"You're into trailers and heavy equipment?"

"And guys in hard hats," Carrie said, when a truckload of men pulled up behind her vehicle. "Do they all wear tool belts?"

A muscle ticked in Mike's jaw. His gaze was as hard as his voice. "They're subcontractors, and have their own special tools for their trade," he said. He then slapped his palms against the side of her vehicle. "Follow me. I'll take you to the main trailer."

He waved them through the gate, and then climbed into a silver Porsche parked just inside the fence.

"Dickhead drives a hot car," said Jill.

Yes, he did, Carrie silently agreed.

"Did you see his shiner?" Jill asked. "I'm sure he deserved the punch."

"His nose looks sore."

"He gets no sympathy from me."

Carrie felt bad enough for both of them.

Mike gunned the engine then and took off. He left them in a cloud of dust.

"That was rude." Carrie quickly rolled up her window. She didn't want to breathe the grime.

Jill covered her mouth, coughed. "He's not my favorite person."

Carrie gave him the benefit of the doubt. She'd seen the considerate side of him when he'd brought her breakfast. Unfortunately, there was nothing nice about him now. The man could backslide.

Mike was already out of his Porsche by the time they reached the double-wide trailer. They joined him. He let them pass ahead of him. They made their way up the steps.

"No need to knock," he said to Jill, who was ahead of Carrie. "Go on in."

Carrie was about to follow Jill when Mike pushed the door closed. She was one step above him, and looked down on him now. "Why are you really here?" he questioned. He seemed to know there was more to their visit than they'd let on.

"We were in the area, and wanted to see the site," she hedged. "This will be the Rogues' second home."

"There's nothing to see," he said flatly. "It's a dust bowl. The road has yet to be paved. We won't officially break ground for another week."

"Aidan invited Jill to meet his girls, and"—she didn't want to give too much away—"this was as good a time as any."

A slow look of understanding crossed his face. "Jillie Mac is curious about the ladies. She's checking out the competition, isn't she?" He smirked.

Carrie would never give up Jill's purpose for the trip. "You're wrong."

"I'm right." He seemed pleased with himself. "Jill's not

busting my balls. She's quiet and nervous. She's imagining babes in their twenties, hot and single. All of them into Aidan."

"How involved is Aidan with the ladies?" Carrie hoped for inside information.

Mike gave her a strange look, then barked his laughter. "Do you really want to know?"

She bit down on her bottom lip, held her breath. "Tell me." She could take it. But could Jill?

"Come inside and see for yourself."

Eight

Jillian Mac was one step inside the construction trailer when she realized Carrie was not behind her. She'd hoped for her friend's support. Instead the door had abruptly closed. She worried about Carrie being stuck outside with Mike Burke. They had nothing in common, and even less to say to each other. The guy was an ass.

"How may I help you?" the receptionist asked Jill. The older woman was seated at a desk so large, it seemed to swallow her small body. She could barely be seen behind an enormous bouquet of yellow roses.

She had a fragile but friendly face, from what Jill could see. Her auburn hair had hints of gray, and was pinned in a loose bun. Wire-rimmed glasses sat low on her nose. She wore a peach blouse with a string of short pearls at her neck. Her scent was classic Chanel. *Agnes Spencer* was scripted on her nameplate.

"I'm Jillian Mac, and I'm here to see Aidan Cates," she said. "I've been told he's off-site at the moment."

Agnes glanced at the wall clock, which was big and round and easy to read. "He phoned a few minutes ago, and is on his way back now," she informed Jill. "Can I assist you in any way?"

Not unless you can introduce me to Aidan's girls, Jill wanted to say, but didn't. She hesitated. "It's personal."

Agnes didn't question her further. She nodded to a row of straight-back chairs, lined against the wall. "You're welcome to wait."

"Thank you." Jill chose a seat at the far end. This gave her a vantage point of the comings and goings and all that was happening in the office. She'd yet to see any young, hot women. Did Aidan prefer blondes or brunettes?

She looked around. The office was immaculate. This wasn't just any construction trailer; it appeared custom made. The overhead fluorescent lighting was modern. There wasn't a single scuff mark on the white vinyl tile floor. Framed pictures hung on the back wall. She squinted. They were family photos, parents with their children.

A second woman stuck her head around a partition. Her gaze was narrowed and her brow was creased. Her long gray braid draped over her shoulder. She wore a high-collared blue blouse. "Agnes," she called to the receptionist. "Did Weller Plumbing drop off their project invoices?"

"Not that I'm aware, Mary," Agnes replied.

"I'm printing checks for Aidan to sign," Mary went on to say. "I'd wanted to include Weller in this week's accounts payable."

"I can give them a call," a third woman said, coming from the back of the trailer. She walked with a cane. Tall and full-figured, she was the oldest of the three, if Jill was any judge of age. Jill figured her close to seventy. She wore her hair in a snow-white bob. Her black pantsuit was perfectly tailored. An antique cameo was pinned to her lapel. She appeared all business.

"Nora, I'll take care of Weller," Mary said to the statuesque woman. "You're in the middle of reviewing project contracts and bids. Johnny on the Spot has yet to deliver the porta potties. We're still waiting for several insurance binders."

Mary then ducked back behind the divider. Jill assumed she was the bookkeeper, since she had access to the checkbook.

The door opened, and Carrie and Mike entered. Carrie's eyes were wide and her color was high. She looked a little frantic while Mike wore his usual smug expression.

Carrie came to sit by Jill. She nudged her friend, whispered, "We need to talk privately."

"Difficult to do," Jill said.

"Trust me; it's a need-to-know."

That sounded important.

Nora interrupted whatever Carrie might have said, noting her own concerns. "Michael, we need you to refill the watercooler, please," she requested. "Mary wanted hot tea and the dispenser gurgled at her. We were able to lift off the empty bottle, but the full five gallons were too heavy for us to replace."

Michael, Jill mouthed to Carrie. The man didn't flinch. Jill forced back a smile. This was a side of him she'd yet to see. Michael sounded very professional. The man with his hands jammed in his pockets was hardcore Mike. Jill sat back and watched him deal with the older woman. He surprised her.

Mike looked pointedly at Nora. "You shouldn't attempt to replace the spring water," he said firmly. "The no-spill water guards can leak. I don't want you slipping and falling. Absolutely no lifting, do you hear? You could pull a muscle or crack a rib. Aidan would be all over my ass if anything happened to you."

His jaw shifted. "I'll deal with whatever you need, I've told you that. Just ask me."

"You're so busy, Michael, we hate to bother you," Nora said. "We like to do things ourselves, when we can."

"You're a little too independent at times," Mike muttered. "I'll change light bulbs and fix the leak in the kitchen sink later today. Wait and let me do it."

"You take such good care of us." Agnes beamed. She slid open the bottom drawer on her desk, removed a small cookie jar in the shape of a brown bear with a red bowtie. "Lemon sugar cookie?" she asked, lifting the lid.

Mike was at her desk in a heartbeat. He snagged two. He winked at Agnes. "Will work for cookies," he said.

"Leave the cookie jar out then, Mike has a full schedule," Aidan Cates said as he came through the door. He kicked it wide. He was carrying Sadie, who couldn't make it up the steps on her own. He set his dog down gently. Sadie surveyed the room, spotted Jill, and wagged herself over to her. The pointer was glad to see her.

Jill caught Aidan watching her as she scratched Sadie's ears. He had *handsome* written all over him. He filled out his white button-down and packed a pair of jeans. His work boots were dusty. His dark eyes were warm and his smile came slowly. "Welcome," he said easily.

Mike finished off his cookies. "I know why Jill's here." He was amused.

"I do, too," Aidan said. "She came to meet my girls." He moved from the door and went to stand before Jill. "Glad to see you."

"Shit," Mike said. He'd wanted to be the one to break the news to his boss.

Nora *tsk-tsked*. "Language, Michael," she said.

Mike's jaw shifted. "Shaye got on my case recently and now you."

"What you say on the job site with your men is one

thing, how you speak in the office with us is another."
Nora sounded like his mother.

Aidan eyed his superintendent. "I just came from the
beach house," he stated. "You've created a monster parrot. I spent an hour with Olive, coaxing her not to
swear."

"Were you successful?" asked Mike.

Aidan shook his head. He flashed a telling glance at the
ladies and then a warning look on Mike. He lowered his
voice, so as not to offend his office staff. "It's only gotten
worse. My sister is beside herself. She invited several city
council members to the house for lunch yesterday, and
Olive ended everyone's sentences with the F-bomb."

"Shaye should've covered Olive's cage," said Mike.
"The parrot would think it was night."

"Shaye did try the cover," Aidan informed him. "Olive
screeched 'I can see you' in a scary voice from a horror
movie."

Jill felt sympathy for Shaye. Olive was a sweetheart.
She'd come around eventually, hopefully sooner rather
than later.

Aidan touched Jill on the shoulder, and motioned her
to stand. He then pressed his hand low on her spine, and
gently rubbed her back, a possessive yet comforting gesture. Mike raised an eyebrow.

"Jill," Aidan began, "I'd like you to meet my girls.
Agnes is my receptionist, and she always has cookies.
Nora's my administrative assistant, she keeps my day running smoothly. Mary's my bookkeeper." Mary poked her
head out, waved. "Jillian Mac and Carrie Waters are with
the Rogues Organization. You'll be seeing a lot of them."

It took a moment for Aidan's words to soak in. Jill
blinked. His *girls* were old enough to be grandmothers.
She felt embarrassed and foolish. And very relieved. She'd

worried herself sick for nothing. She realized she liked this man more than she was ready to admit. They'd known each other less than a week, but feelings weren't based on time.

The girls were pleased to meet Jill and Carrie. Good wishes flowed for a successful joint venture. "I'd like a Rogues jersey on your next visit, if it's not too much trouble," requested Agnes. "Size small."

"Me, too," Mary called from behind the partition. "I'd need a large."

"Large for me as well," Nora said. "The jerseys would be perfect for our casual Fridays."

Jill loved their enthusiasm. "Jerseys all around," she said. "I'll deliver them next time I'm on-site."

Aidan's girls smiled at her.

"There are a few things we need to discuss," Aidan next said to Jill. "My office?"

"Carrie?" she asked, wanting to include her.

"Take care of business," Carrie said. "I'm happy here."

"I'll be around for a while, too," Mike informed Aidan. "I've a few odd jobs for the ladies; afterward I need to straighten my own office."

"Your office," Nora spoke up, frowning, "has become the storage room. I'm sorry, Michael, we don't have enough space. Your cot had to go."

Mike remained remarkably calm, Jill thought, for a man who'd been booted from his bedroom. She saw the look he shot Carrie, and that made her nervous. She hoped he had other alternatives that didn't include her friend. He could always tough it out; perhaps buy a sleeping bag and camp on the floor.

"I spend most of my day in the field," Mike managed on an even note. "Still, I'm going to need a desk and a computer."

Aidan stepped in. "Order a partition and whatever else

he needs," he said to Nora. "It might get a little tight, but let's find room for him."

"Tight works," Mike said, "as long as I can sit close to Agnes."

The receptionist giggled. "You're after my cookies."

Mike winked at her. "I also like older women." His words made Agnes blush.

"Let's get down to business," Aidan said. "This way." He directed Jill through Nora's office and into his.

A masculine domain, she thought, pausing in the door-way. His desk was massive, and his leather chair looked comfortable enough for a nap. Organized chaos, she admired. His administrative assistant no doubt kept him sane.

"Feel free to look around," he said. He stood at his desk and read through a stack of messages. "James Lawless called," he told her. "He's made travel arrangements for the ground-breaking ceremony next week."

The Rogues would be coming to town. Jill's heart warmed. Every person in the organization was like family. "I wonder if he's picked his roster for slow pitch?"

"He has strong athletes to choose from," said Aidan. "What position will you play?"

"Second base or shortstop," she said.

"The infield move fasts."

"I want to be part of the action."

"You sound as competitive as my sister, Shaye."

"As my brother used to say, 'Winning isn't everything, but the alternative sucks.' "

Aidan grinned. "I understand where he's coming from." He continued with, "Where's your brother now? What does he do?"

Jill had her own reasons for distancing herself from her brother. She didn't know Aidan well enough to discuss family. Not yet anyway. Avoiding an awkward silence, she gave him a half-truth. "My brother's a Philadelphia boy. He handles sporting equipment."

"Does he work for a large chain?" Aidan asked, showing interest.

"Large enough, I guess." She'd circled his office and admired his plaques for achievement and appreciation. There were framed newspaper articles and photos of finished projects. She especially liked the no-kill animal shelter in Miami and the senior citizen village in Boca Raton. Honor and respect came with each one.

"Tell me about your girls," she said, taking the focus off her brother. "They seem very nice."

Aidan took a seat and she sat on a chair facing him. His desk separated them, but he felt a lot closer. He rested his elbows on the desktop, steepled his fingers. Smiled at her with his eyes.

"My girls may be older, but they are productive and efficient. They're smart and pleasant. They can handle Mike, and he respects them, too. I hired the ladies six years ago when my company was in Panama City building a resort hotel. My previous staff was much younger. They partied during spring break, were always late for work. Two quit without any notice.

"I ran an ad in the newspaper for temporary help. The three ladies showed up together. They were friends. Agnes and Mary lost their jobs when their bank merged with another financial institution. Nora was given a pink slip on her sixty-fifth birthday. She's seventy-one now, and works harder than two thirty-year-olds.

"The women are widowed. They wanted more in life than a rocking chair and knitting needles. They weren't ready to retire. They told me at their interview, it was all for one and one for all. They wouldn't be split up. I was impressed and hired the threesome. They like traveling and don't mind relocating with each new job."

"Lucky you, lucky them," said Jill. "You give them a reason to get up in the morning."

"I'm glad their reason is here with me," he said honestly. "Mike calls them my girls. It's an office joke."

Jill now saw the humor. "I have to admit I was curious," she admitted.

"I'm glad," he said. "It shows you're interested in me."

"Don't be so sure of yourself."

"To be honest, I had concerns you wouldn't come."

"If I hadn't?" she asked.

"I know where you live."

He would've turned up at her houseboat. Jill appreciated a persistent man. "You'd like to see me again?" She was hopeful.

"Tonight, actually," he said. "How would you feel about miniature golf? I built the course. It has a seaside theme. The fourteenth hole is designed around a mermaid."

"Sounds great," Jill said. She hadn't played mini-golf for a long time. Barefoot William brought out the kid in her.

"I'll pick you up at seven," he said. "We'll drop Sadie off at Shaye's. Olive requested Sad pay her a visit. I agreed. My sister plans to let Olive out of her cage tonight so she can stretch her wings. Olive flies around the house and Sadie follows at her own pace."

An interesting friendship, Jill thought, the dog and parrot bonding. She rose then and said, "You've got a lot to do, and I'm headed to the beach. We'll talk later."

"Enjoy your vacation day," Aidan said as he stood, too, and showed her out. "The area near the pier is least crowded. There's shade should you want to cool off."

She would take his advice. "The day after tomorrow Carrie and I can move into our boardwalk store," she told him. She felt a rush of excitement. "We have a lot to do before the slow pitch softball game and the ground-breaking ceremony."

"You'll be busy."

She'd make time for him, if he wanted to see her. She didn't tell him that. She'd let him do the chasing. She liked being pursued. She might even let him catch her.

Jill returned to Carrie in the outer office. She found her friend chatting with Agnes. They shared a love for romance novels, and were comparing authors. Mike had disappeared. He had likely departed when their conversation turned to larger-than-life heroes and half-naked cover models.

"Ready to go?" Carrie asked Jill when she approached her.

Jill nodded. "Let's head out," she said.

They took their leave. Carrie headed slowly down the dirt road, not wanting to cast a lot of dust on the work crew. Mike was back at the guard gate. Carrie waved at him as they passed through. Mike gave her a short nod. His communication skills were improving.

"Your plans for the rest of the day?" Carrie asked Jill as they drove back to town.

"I'm off to the beach, then have a date with Aidan. How about you?"

"I have a few errands to run. I need groceries and want to set up a local bank account. I may even buy a new swimsuit."

Jill's two-piece was four years old. She'd spent time at Virginia Beach, but not enough to warrant new beachwear. Her navy suit was slightly faded, but who cared? She was going to the beach for a tan; she wasn't looking for a man.

An hour later, Jill found the perfect spot near the pier. She'd debated long and hard, then broken down and purchased a new beach lounger. Extravagance was not her style. She saw the lounger as an investment, living so near the Gulf.

She set up her lounger, laid a beach towel over the yellow-and-white vinyl. She slipped off her tank top and untied the string on her gray athletic shorts. She was already barefoot. She reached into her beach bag for her red wide-brimmed straw hat. She next retrieved her sunglasses. She uncapped her bottle of sunscreen and rubbed it on thickly. She wished she had someone to put it on her back. She didn't feel comfortable asking a stranger.

She'd brought two women's magazines to read. She'd found them under the coffee table at the houseboat. They were a year old. The fashions might be outdated, but the articles looked good. She sat down carefully, not wanting to tip the lounger and land in the sand, since she was covered in sunscreen. She flipped open a Christmas issue of *Cosmopolitan,* and began to scan the pages.

She'd read both magazines by the time her stomach growled. Her biorhythms were telling her it was close to noon. She looked down the beach, saw both a hot dog and Popsicle stand. There was her main meal and dessert, she decided. She rummaged in her beach bag for her wallet.

"Are you Jillian Mac?" A young woman now blocked her sun. She had curly blond hair and a curious smile. She carried a picnic basket.

"I'm Jill," she said.

"I thought it was you." She seemed pleased with herself. "My cousin Aidan described you perfectly."

Why would he be describing her to someone? Jill wondered. What had he said about her? She was about to find out.

"You're brunette and beautiful," the blonde said. "Aidan figured you'd be wearing a red sun hat."

He thought she was beautiful. Jill's heart fluttered. Compliments were new to her. She liked hearing them.

"I'm Violet Cates-Davis," she introduced herself. "My husband, Brad, and I own Molly Malone's. We purchased the diner from my Aunt Molly last summer."

Jill had eaten lunch there with Carrie. "I love your milk shakes."

"They are good," Violet agreed. "Aidan called me a bit ago. He asked that I bring you lunch."

"He did?" This surprised her, in a good way.

"It's hard to judge what a person might like," Violet continued. "I didn't want chicken or egg salad to spoil in the heat. I went with our famous peanut butter and jelly sandwich."

Jill remembered seeing the sandwich on the menu. Made with one slice of rye and one slice of pumpernickel, it was then spread with crunchy peanut butter on both. Grape jelly and strawberry preserves were added. When she'd been there before, others in the diner had ordered the sandwich. It had looked thick and tasty.

Violet handed Jill the small basket. "There are two kinds of chips, a double-fudge brownie, and a bottle of iced tea. I hope that works for you."

"Totally," Jill said, excited over her picnic.

"Do you have a cell phone with you?" Violet asked.

Jill nodded.

"Give me a call if you need anything further." She turned to go.

"How much do I owe you?" Jill called after her.

"It's on Aidan."

"Thank you."

"Thank him." Violet gave her a final smile and walked away.

Jill definitely would. She ate her lunch as if she hadn't

seen food for a week. Every bite hit the spot. The Gulf
provided the perfect view. It was an iridescent blue.
Wave runners raced beyond the sandbar. Sailboats drifted
on the breeze. Swimming lessons were being offered by
a lifeguard in the shallows of the shore.

Jill pinched herself. She couldn't believe she was in
Barefoot William. Working for the Richmond Rogues
provided her job security. Meeting Aidan Cates was a
definite perk. Life was good.

She finished her lunch, feeling full. The sun was at its
zenith. She stretched out her legs, and that's when she
noticed her feet looked red. Lobster red. She'd applied
sunscreen on her legs, but not to her ankles and feet. She
was in trouble now.

She decided it was time to leave the beach. She packed
up, and walked to the wooden steps that led to the
boardwalk. Hot and gritty, the sand chafed her feet. They
itched like crazy. She was hot-stepping by the time she
reached the stairs. She tried walking on her heels on the
boardwalk, which was a bit better, but still not great.

She quickly returned the picnic basket to Molly Malone's, then headed for the visitor's parking lot. Her steps
were slow and painful. She winced more than once.

Driving a clutch nearly killed her. She kept the Triumph in first gear on the way home. The vintage sports
car grumbled, growled, and lurched, but didn't stall out.
She arrived safely at the houseboat, then hobbled onboard.

Jill discarded her swimsuit and showered. Once dry,
she searched her medicine cabinet for body lotion. She
found a bottle of Vaseline Intensive Care.

She went into her bedroom, pulled an old pair of
lounging pajamas from her suitcase. She had yet to unpack. She sat on the edge of her bed and massaged the
lotion on one foot, then the other. She left a thick pro-

tective layer. Soft socks came next. Her feet felt squishy, but at least she could walk. A short distance anyway.

She returned to the living room, and lay down on the sofa. She planned to watch some afternoon television. Maybe catch up on her favorite soap operas. Instead she fell asleep.

She woke to the evening news. She'd slept for several hours. She felt revived. She sat up on the couch and wiggled her feet. Her skin felt raw. A blister had formed on her big toe. This was not good. She had a date with Aidan Cates in two hours. They were to play miniature golf. She would not let sunburn stop her.

Their date would be casual. Jill dressed in a gray top and her favorite black jeans. Her feet presented a minor problem. She lathered on more lotion, wore the same pair of socks. She then slipped on her Isotoner PillowStep slide slippers. They'd been a gift from Carrie. The slippers were meant for the bedroom, but could be worn outside in an emergency. She had no other choice. It was the slippers or stay home.

She brushed her hair, left it loose. She added six gemtoned bracelets to her right arm. She was ready to go. This was as good as she was going to get.

Aidan arrived at seven. He wore a rugby pullover, tan with a wide burgundy stripe across the chest, khakis, and loafers. He defined masculine.

"Where's Sadie?" she asked, looking over his shoulder.

"She's stretched out in my SUV. I lowered the backseat, so she has lots of room. The windows are cracked. I figured you'd be ready, so she wouldn't be left alone for long."

Jill wasn't always prompt. She tended to run late, but her date with Aidan had inspired her to be on time. She'd been counting down the minutes. "Let's go then."

He stopped her at the door. "There's lotion oozing from the top of your socks."

Yes, there was. She sighed, confessed, "My feet are sunburned. They hurt. I squeezed half a bottle of lotion in my socks."

"You must really want to play miniature golf."

"It's my sport of choice." She wanted to spend time with him, whatever the cost.

"You killed at pinball the other night."

"I have golf skills, too."

Still he hesitated. "Sunburn is no fun." He appeared concerned. "We can make this another night."

"Do my slippers embarrass you?"

He shook his head. "Blue and fuzzy do it for me."

Aidan Cates did it for her. She set the security system and they were off. She walked slowly, and he stayed by her side. He didn't rush her.

Sadie welcomed her with a wagging tail. Jill reached over the passenger seat and petted her. They buckled up and hit the road. "We'll drop Sadie off at my sister's," Aidan said. "Then play By the Sea, Barefoot William's beach-themed course."

There was only one car in the Saunders's driveway when they arrived at the beach house. Shaye met them at the front door. A bandana wrapped her hair and dirt smudged her cheek. "Trace is working late and I'm cleaning," she told them. "Can I get you to pull out the refrigerator, Aidan? I tried, but it won't budge."

Aidan frowned at his sister. "The Northland's heavy. You don't want to hurt your back. You should've waited for Trace."

"I hate waiting when I want to do something now," she stated. "I've got the cleaning bug."

"You should hire a housekeeper," said Aidan.

"It's been a long, chaotic day, and cleaning clears my head," Shaye said. "I like putting things in order."

"Aidan, is that you?" Olive squawked from the living room. She had heard them arrive. *"Sad, too?"*

"And Jill," Aidan said as he crossed to her cage.

The parrot tilted her head. *"Jill."* Olive recognized her. *"White lies are forgiven."*

Jill was speechless. The Quaker had the memory of an elephant. Aidan and she had stood near the cage the night of the barbecue and discussed honesty and stretching the truth. Olive remembered Jill's exact words.

"Did someone lie?" Shaye overheard Olive.

"No one," said Aidan.

"Tell the truth," Olive said.

Aidan stuck his finger through the cage, gently stroking the parrot on the head. "It was a private conversation, and you're spilling our secrets, aren't you?"

"Fuckin' A."

"I see her language hasn't improved," said Aidan. "She has such fun saying it."

"Too much fun," Shaye said with a sigh. "I'm working on replacement words. I just haven't hit on the right ones yet."

"Chat with Olive while I move the fridge," Aidan said to Jill. He and his sister took off down the hallway.

"What's on your mind?" asked Olive. She sounded so human, it was hard to remember she was a parrot.

"My feet are sunburned," was what concerned Jill most at the moment.

"Ouch." Olive's sympathy sounded genuine.

Sadie arrived a moment later. She looked up at Olive and her tongue lolled out of her mouth. *"She loves me,"* said the Quaker.

"Lucky you," said Jill.

"I like Aidan."

"Me, too."

Olive screeched her approval. *"Jill likes Aidan."*

Jill's heart stopped. Heaven help her! There was no saving grace, she realized. She'd spoken the words and Olive would repeat them to her dying day. She wished the parrot would start swearing again.

"What's this I hear?" Aidan came around the corner. Amusement darkened his eyes. One corner of his mouth curved and his dimple flashed.

"Jill likes Aidan."

"That's what I thought I heard."

"Olive misunderstood," Jill was quick to say.

"Olive doesn't make mistakes." Aidan grinned. "How much does Jill like me?" he prodded the parrot.

The Quaker fluttered her wings and danced on her perch. *"For me to know and for you to find out."*

"She has one heck of a vocabulary," Aidan praised.

"Heck?" Olive mimicked him, as if trying the word on for size. *"Heck, heck, heck."*

"She may not know what the word means, but it's far better than her previous one," Shaye said from the hall-way.

"Let's hope it sticks," said Aidan.

"Heck sticks," Olive said.

"I hear you like my brother," Shaye teased Jill.

Jill cringed. "I think all of Barefoot William now knows. Olive's squawk carries."

Shaye didn't press further. "Enjoy your evening." She walked them to the door. "Olive and I will take good care of Sadie."

"Heck, yes," Olive agreed.

Aidan opened Jill's passenger door once they reached his SUV. He blocked her when she would've climbed in. "So," he asked with a gleam in his eye, "is what Olive said true?"

"I like you enough to want to know you better." She was honest.

"There's no better way to get to know a man than to play him in miniature golf."

Jill soon found that to be true. By the Sea was a challenging mini-putt. They selected colored putters and matching balls at the entrance booth. Jill played with red and Aidan chose black. The eighteen-hole course was created with lots of mounding and varying elevations. Rippling streams and waterfalls accented the landscape. Various robotic creatures and characters, lifelike and mobile, were activated at each hole.

Aidan was competitive. He played hard for a big man on a miniature golf course. He got frustrated when he missed a shot. He had a few choice words for his putter. She laughed at him often. He was down by three by the time they reached the tenth hole. Jill was even par.

"I built this course, you'd think I'd play better," he said at the twelfth hole.

"You'd think so." She grinned at him.

"Smart mouth," he said, just before he leaned in and kissed her, a soft, light kiss that surprised her. She lost her concentration. His kiss had thrown off her game. It took eight strokes to sink the next putt on the thirteenth hole. Aidan managed to land the ball in the cup in three. He was quite pleased with himself.

They faced a robotic mermaid sitting on an enormous boulder on fourteen. Her long silver tail swung like a pendulum, making it difficult for the ball to pass through a hole in the rock. Jill successfully beat Aidan by one stroke.

"Ariel let you win the hole," he said.

"Us girls need to stick together," said Jill.

Jill liked the sixteenth hole best. It offered a long pier that resembled the one at the beach. Navigating around tourists and fishermen was a difficult task. Jill jerked and ducked when a robot fisherman cast his line. Her ball went over the side of the pier and landed in a water hazard. Aidan retrieved it with a small fishing net. She was penalized a stroke.

The eighteenth was the toughest. They faced a stand of flamingos, hot pink and long-legged. The first stroke set the birds in motion, and their webbed feet began to shift.

"A flamingo shuffle," Jill said, amazed by the intricate mechanisms. It took her forever to shoot between their feet. She lost count of her strokes. "Five or six?" she asked Aidan.

"Nine."

She finally closed her eyes and putted blind. She squinted to see if the ball had rolled back to her. To her surprise, it shot between the shuffling flamingos and landed in the cup.

Aidan fared better. His brow creased with concentration. His focus got him a hole in one. He won the round.

Jill had been so absorbed in mini-golf, she'd been distracted from her sunburned feet. Now, at the end of the course, she realized how much they hurt her. They felt on fire. She needed to return to the houseboat.

Aidan sensed her pain. "Let's grab a soda from the vending machine and head back to the Horizon," he suggested. "Miniature golf tired me."

He didn't appear tired, Jill noted. He looked big, and strong, and ready to go another eighteen holes. Easily. "Are you sure?" she asked.

"Nora and I have an early morning conference call with James Lawless and Risk Kincaid," he told her. "We're still ironing out a few kinks in the stadium design."

Jill believed he had a call coming in, but she wondered what he considered early. She knew James seldom got to the office before ten a.m. The team owner spent mornings with his grandfather. Heir to a hotel chain, James did his best to keep his finger on the pulse of his inheritance as well as the team. She suspected that Aidan had fibbed to make her feel better.

Jill was limping by the time they returned their equipment to the entrance booth. Aidan offered his arm and she leaned on him heavily. Each step was excruciatingly painful.

She sighed with relief when they reached the houseboat. Once inside, she removed her slippers and socks. No lotion remained. Her feet were beet-red and swollen. She looked around for her bottle of Vaseline Intensive Care. Aidan stopped her before she could reapply it.

"My grandmother had a remedy for sunburn," he told her. "Let's give it a try. Do you have a washcloth?"

"There's one in the bathroom cabinet."

He retrieved two, and dampened them both. "Tap water, so the cloths aren't cold," he told her. He knelt before her then, settled both her feet on his thigh, and laid the washcloths across them.

Relief was immediate. "Bless your grandmother," she said.

Aidan set her feet off his leg; went to wet the cloths once again. He repeated the process a dozen times, until the swelling lessened.

"How is that?" he asked.

She was so taken by his kindness she could barely speak. "I'm feeling much better, thanks," she managed around the tightness in her throat.

"I'd do anything for someone who liked me."

She liked him more the longer she knew him.

"You need to rest," he said. "Apply the cloths a few more times before you go to bed. You should be fine in the morning, although it's going to take a few days for the sunburn to fade."

"I can't believe I forgot to put sunscreen on my feet," she said with a sigh.

"Live and learn, babe."

He rose then, stood over her. "We've both got busy schedules the rest of this week and next," he said. "I'll attend slow-pitch practice; that will burn my free time."

She would miss seeing him, but she understood. "I won't be at practice, since I'm playing for the Rogues. Carrie wants to keep the team's tactics a secret."

Aidan smiled and said, "We'll take our turn at bat, we'll play the field, that's the extent of our performance."

"It will be a fun day."

He stared down at her, indecision in his gaze. "I'll be in touch," he finally said. "Take care of yourself."

He gave her a good-night kiss.

One that was far too short.

Corner to corner, he brushed his lips across hers.

His kiss was gentle, yet unsettling.

Arousing, yet soothing.

He left her wanting more, a whole lot more.

She had a restless night, not from her sore feet, but from wanting Aidan Cates. In her bed and under the sea.

Nine

Carrie Waters was headed to bed. It was only ten p.m., but her silk sheets called to her. She turned off the television and left the couch. She blew out the pillar candle she'd purchased that afternoon. The summer breeze fragrance filled the living room. She couldn't look at the candleholder without thinking of Mike Burke. He had invaded her life.

She stretched and smiled to herself. She loved living at the penthouse. Her life couldn't get any better.

But it could get worse, she realized, when someone pounded on the front door. Her heart quickened. Her gut told her it was Mike. At least he had the courtesy not to barge in on her as he'd done the previous night.

Her feet sank into the carpet as she moved to the entryway. Her toes got lost in the deep pile. She looked through the peephole. There stood Mike, looking tough and tired and in need of her, she thought. She cautiously opened the door.

"You knocked," she said.

"I wanted you to invite me in."

"If I didn't?" she asked.

"There's always the hall."

She stepped back, let him pass.

He carried an athletic bag and a designer box from

Dreams. The man had brought his own sheets. Somehow that didn't surprise her at all. He liked his silk.

He walked through to the living room. She followed him. He set the bag and box on one end of the sofa. Dead on his feet, he dropped down, ran his hands through his hair. It spiked. He palmed his eyes, as if trying to focus. "One more night?" His voice was hoarse.

She figured he'd inhaled a lot of dust on the job site as he'd shouted to be heard over the roar of heavy equipment. "Will that lead to a week or a month?" she asked, wanting him to be honest.

"However long you'll have me," he said.

"I'm here for a year."

"Not sure we'll make it twelve months."

She doubted it, too. They were too different.

"Let's get through tonight," he suggested. "We can discuss this further in the morning."

That she could do.

"I hate to cut this conversation short, but I could use a shower," came next.

She wrinkled her nose. "You smell." Dark and musky, but not really offensive.

He slowly rose, and stood within a foot of her. "Man sweat, babe, from physical labor."

"I thought you were the superintendent."

"I do whatever needs to be done."

"Feel free to shower."

"I was thinking Jacuzzi tonight."

She shook her head. "Think again. My bath connects to the master bedroom, and I'm about to tuck in."

"I could be quiet."

"Don't push me."

"I'd tiptoe—"

"I would still hear you." She'd sense his presence, even if he were as quiet as prayer in church.

"Difficult woman."

"Irritating man."

He blew out a breath. "Fine, have it your way." He hefted his athletic bag onto his shoulder, then picked up the box. "Are you sleeping skin to silk?" he asked as he stepped around her.

Her cheeks heated. "That's none of your business."

"Your blush says yes." His grin was wicked.

He walked off, and she stared after him. Mike Burke was built. He had the swagger of ten men. He was difficult and moody with sinfully good looks. His sarcasm put her off, but not as much now as when she'd first met him. She'd have her hands full with him living here. She sensed he was here to stay. That didn't bother her as much as it should.

Tomorrow they would make a list of rules. Abide by them. Or so she hoped. She would sleep on it.

Morning came too soon. Dawn peeked through the blinds. Carrie slid her body across the silk sheets, feeling cool and comfortable. She'd fallen in love with Pratesi.

She jerked when Mike banged on her bedroom door. The man had no respect for her space. Or the fact she might still be sleeping. It was six a.m.

"What do you want?" She sounded grumpy.

He cracked the door, but didn't look in. "Can I have one of your bagels?" he asked.

"You bought them yesterday," she reminded him. "They're as much yours as they are mine."

"I didn't want to take any food without asking."

That was a first. Boundaries were good. "Help yourself," she said.

"Can I bring you breakfast in bed?"

"No."

"Come join me then."

The man wanted company? That surprised her. "Let me get dressed."

"I have an hour before I have to be on-site." He closed the door.

She purposely took thirty minutes. Ten, and she'd slipped on a floral-print blouse and white jeans. She sat the remaining twenty on the end of her bed. She didn't want to appear anxious to see him.

She strolled into the kitchen and found him standing by the kitchen counter, buttering a blueberry muffin. He narrowed his gaze, gave her the once-over, and then looked away. Pouring himself a second cup of coffee seemed more important than her appearance. Maybe she should've combed her hair. Put on mascara. It was too late for that now. She settled on a swivel stool.

He passed her several ziplock bags. The man had eaten two muffins and a bagel, she noted. He'd left her the plain cake doughnut. He filled her coffee mug. The brew was dark and strong. She was wide awake after her second sip.

She glanced toward the door. No athletic bag. No designer box with sheets. Apparently he wasn't leaving. She cleared her throat. "We need to set some house rules if you stay," she dared to say.

His gaze sharpened. "Are you laying down the law, Vanilla?"

"There's always flexibility," she said, trying to be fair. She sensed he'd break whatever rules she set anyway. But she had to start somewhere. She needed to be firm.

"I'm listening, let's hear them," he said.

"I'd rather write them down."

"Why do that?"

"You won't remember, and I want them listed."

He pulled a face and made a rude noise. "You haven't lived with a man before, have you?" he asked.

"No, why?"

"It's evident. Roommates are give and take."

"I won't let you take advantage of me."

"I've no plans to do so."

She snagged a sheet of paper off the notepad near the portable phone. A pen was at arm's reach. She tapped it on the counter, contemplating. "The penthouse is beautifully furnished," she said. "There should be no new items brought in unless we both approve."

"Guess I'd better cancel my pool table and beer keg."

He was pushing her buttons. "You need to respect my space." She jotted down. "No poking your head in my bedroom unannounced."

"You're welcome in my room any time."

She rolled her eyes. "Thank you, but no."

"Can I schedule time in your Jacuzzi?"

"Absolutely not."

"Not even when you're not home?"

"Not a chance."

"Damn, you don't share well."

"I have seniority, Mike," she said, reminding him that she'd been there first. This was officially her place. "The master bedroom and bath are off-limits."

"Not set in stone," he grumbled.

"I'm chiseling it in now."

"You could make me feel more welcome."

"You were never *invited*. You showed up and stayed."

"You'd rather I leave?"

"I'm not saying anything."

"Your silence says everything."

"I'm nervous and worried," she admitted. "I have no idea how this will work out."

"We won't know until we give it a try, will we?"

"I guess we won't."

"What's next?" he asked.

"We buy our own groceries and paper products."

"I can live with that," he agreed. "I'll leave an IOU if I borrow a roll of toilet paper."

"No borrowing."

"I'd repay you. Charmin two-ply."

She moved forward. "Cleaning the apartment," came next.

"Define *clean*."

"Spotless. You vacuum on Monday, and I'll dust on Tuesday. You wipe down the appliances on Wednesday. I'll—"

He held up his hand. "Slow down, Vanilla, you're a neat freak and I drop-kick my clothes. Let's consider a cleaning service."

"It's not within my budget."

"I'll pay the bill," he said.

"You don't take pride in mopping and polishing?"

"Not after putting in an eighteen-hour day."

She shrugged. "Do what you want then."

"That I will."

She cleared her throat. "No parties."

"Here I'd planned to bring my crew home tonight to play poker and pop a few cold ones."

She ignored him.

He pursed his lips, serious. "My life is all about building the spring-training facility. Aidan will throw a blowout party once the stadium is finished. I can wait."

"Remain fully clothed in shared areas." She added to her list. "No walking around naked."

"You can if you want."

"Dating?" she broached, holding her breath.

"I won't bring a woman here. I'll have sex at her place."

He was a red-blooded male. A fact she couldn't deny. Celibacy wasn't in his vocabulary. The thought of him with another female left her chest unexpectedly tight.

"Our arrangement remains secret," she added.

"We agreed to that yesterday."

Still, she wrote it down. She hopped off her breakfast stool and located a pineapple magnet in the silverware drawer. She posted their rules on the front of the refrigerator. A short, but satisfying list, she thought as she read them over.

She hoped Mike would keep his word and abide by a few. She knew in her heart he wouldn't follow them all. She expected him to sneak into her Jacuzzi and possibly parade around naked. It was who he was: arrogant, a law unto himself. He took what he wanted. Did as he pleased. He would step on her toes. Hard.

"You done here?" he asked, washing his coffee mug in the sink. He then tossed his paper plate in the trash. "See, I cleaned up after myself." He seemed proud of it.

"Be safe and have a good day," she called after him.

He paused at the door, glanced at her over his shoulder. He appeared surprised by her comment. Had no one ever wished him well? "Yeah, you, too." And he was gone.

Carrie was a list person. She decided to map out her day. She returned to the counter and ran her finger along the border of the notepad. She needed to contact Shaye Cates. The slow-pitch softball game was rapidly approaching. Team Barefoot William had four players. They needed eleven total. Nine on the field and two alternates. Just in case someone got hurt. She hoped Shaye could suggest additional people.

She also wanted to catch up with Jill; see how her date with Aidan had gone. She just might drop by the houseboat. They could set beach chairs on the dock, so she wouldn't have to board the Horizon.

Tomorrow they would take over their boardwalk shop. Today was all hers. She'd make the most of it.

★   ★   ★

Carrie had a productive day, better than she'd expected. Shaye had offered to meet her at Molly Malone's so they could discuss the team. Shaye had given her a list of names. At the top were the local athletes; the bottom consisted of those who could stand on a baseball field and not fall down.

Shaye had then taken her around town and introduced her to possible players. Their team had been formed by noon. They'd added Violet and Brad Davis, owners of the diner. Also Dune Cates and Mac James; both had played professional volleyball. Kai Cates, the resident boardwalk handyman, elected to play. An additional Cates cousin signed on. There was one spot left to fill. Preparation was key. The team agreed to three practice times before the big game.

Carrie had suffered right along with Jill when she saw her friend's sunburned feet. Jill wasn't moving very fast or very far. They talked business on the dock in the shade of a coconut palm. There were immediate concerns: setting up the Rogues' store, the ground-breaking ceremony, and the community softball game. They couldn't wait for the Rogues to arrive in Barefoot William.

Now, back at the penthouse, she exhaled, relaxed. It was seven p.m., and the apartment seemed inordinately quiet without Mike. She set her purse on the kitchen counter and walked into the living room. She could feel the man. He was everywhere. How had he taken up so much space in such a short time?

She glanced down the hallway and had the unexpected urge to look in his bedroom. He wouldn't be home for several hours. He would never know she'd checked him out. So why not? Her curiosity got the better of her. She cautiously walked down the hall.

She made it to his bedroom door; her heart was pounding so hard she could barely catch her breath. She was snooping. And she wasn't good at it. She glanced over her shoulder, making sure she was still alone. It would be just her luck to be standing by his bed should he arrive home early. She crossed her fingers. That wasn't going to happen.

Still, she called out his name before she entered his room. No answer. What had she expected? She turned the knob, stole inside. She could tell a lot about a person by his belongings, yet Mike had so few. She already knew he had silk sheets; his alarm clock was basic Big Ben.

She peeked into his top dresser drawer. There were several folded T-shirts in basic colors. His jeans were in the second drawer. Three button-down shirts and four pullovers hung in his closet, along with one pair of dark dress slacks. He had no shortage of tennis shoes or work boots.

She snuck into his bathroom; saw his toothbrush, paste, and dental floss on the counter by the sink.

Electric razor and deodorant. His medicine cabinet revealed a bottle of aspirin and a box of condoms. Ribbed and lubricated.

Returning to the bedroom, she had the uneasy feeling she was not alone. She wasn't. She nearly had a panic attack.

Mike Burke leaned against the doorframe. His arms were crossed over his chest. One eyebrow was raised, but his expression was unreadable. His dark blue *Cates Construction* T-shirt had a new tear in the shoulder. Threads held his jeans together at the knees. He'd taken off his work boots at the door and wore only his socks. He walked on cat's feet.

"You're home early," she managed.

"You're breaking our rules."

She'd never been more embarrassed. She blushed, and her entire body felt hot. "I'm sorry."

He shrugged, unaffected. "Don't be. You're welcome in my bedroom anytime."

He stepped in the room and pulled his shirt over his head. He continued to undress, unbuckling his belt, and then drawing down his zipper. He toed off his socks.

Carrie couldn't help herself, she stood and stared. His shoulders were wide, and his chest was thick. The man was cut. A smattering of hair trailed from his navel to the open waistband. The bulge in his boxers showed he was packing more than most men.

"Stay for the show or go," he said. "Either way, I need a shower."

Her legs barely got her across the room. She was a bundle of nerves and shaking limbs. Mike caught her arm as she passed him. He rubbed his thumb over the soft inner skin of her forearm. He leaned in, inhaled her scent. Said near her ear, "Next time you wander into my bedroom, you stay and play."

Play meant sex. It was implied in the darkness of his eyes and his deepened voice. Goose bumps rose. An image of the man lying on silk sheets made her stumble. She somehow found her way back to the living room. She sat on the couch and buried her head in her hands. A quick peek into his bedroom had resulted in a sexual warning. Damn her curiosity.

Never again.

Mike came to her after his shower. His hair was damp and spiky. He was bare chested. His athletic shorts rode low on his hips. "I'm not naked," he told her, just before she looked up.

He settled in a leather chair, close to where she sat. "How was your day?" he asked.

His normal, end-of-the-day conversation surprised her. He could be civil. She was grateful. She cleared her throat and said, "Shaye Cates and I formed Team Barefoot William. You have great players to coach."

"Ah, coaching." He drew out the words, as if he'd tried to forget his part in slow pitch. "Who's signed up?"

She ran down the list, including herself at the end.

"What position do you intend to play?" Sarcasm crept in now. Clearly, he didn't believe she had an athletic bone in her body.

"I'd like to pitch."

"Your second choice?"

"Shaye agreed with me."

"Let her coach the team then."

"You're not backing out of this." She stood firm. He could come at her all night, be rude and annoying, but she refused to let him off the hook. He had committed to the team.

One corner of his mouth curved, the snide side. "You could show me your stuff if we had a glove and softball," he said.

She had *stuff*. "I have both."

"You travel with softball equipment?"

"I'm prepared for the game."

He rose and came to stand over her so close she inhaled almond soap and man. "Go wind up at the end of the hallway, and I'll play catcher."

She glanced at the enormous television, the blown-glass vases, and the sliding-glass doors. All breakable items. She didn't want to take any chances. "I'm not throwing in the penthouse."

"I doubt you can throw at all."

She got to her feet. They faced off. "Let's take it outside," she suggested. Lawn maintenance had recently mowed. She liked the scent of freshly cut grass.

He laughed then, deep and annoying. "You're sure you want to do this?" He still didn't believe she could pitch.

"As long as no one sees us."

"Even if someone did, we have a legitimate excuse. We'd tell him that I dropped by to discuss the softball team. No one's going to mistake this for a friendly visit." That was a good cover. "Put on a pair of tennis shoes," she warned. He was barefoot. "The ground crew spread fertilizer earlier." She went to change clothes and to get her ball and glove.

Mike Burke stared after her. He couldn't believe Carrie was out to prove herself. He didn't give a rat's ass if she could pitch. He'd hoped to stick her in left field, where there'd be little action. A part of him worried about her screwing up and feeling bad. She was sensitive. He wanted to protect her feelings. The fact he cared set his teeth on edge. He scratched his belly. A shirt and his Nikes, and he'd be set to go.

Mike left the penthouse ahead of Carrie. They rode down in separate elevators. He waited for her in the lobby. She crossed to him wearing a red tank top and navy sweatpants. She had nice breasts. A white headband held her hair in place. She carried her ball and glove with casual grace. Her sneakers were new and squeaky on the polished entrance floor.

He nodded to the security guard as they left the building. The man was aware of Mike's comings and goings, but with the change in shifts, he didn't know Mike had spread his sheets in the penthouse apartment. Mike wanted to keep it that way.

"Where to?" he asked Carrie once they were out on the sidewalk.

She pointed toward the side lawn. The building cast shade onto the grass. "That's as good a place as any," she said.

He ran one hand down his face. "Are you sure about this?" He gave her an out.

"It's forty-three feet from the pitching rubber to home plate. Walk it off."

He did so, give or take a foot. She called him on it. "Five more feet."

She wanted accuracy. The lady was a perfectionist. He went on to watch her loosen up. Her body had decent flexibility. She could touch her toes and twist so far sideways, she nearly faced backward.

"I'm kind of rusty," she said. "I haven't pitched for a while."

Since never, he thought. She was like the Tin Man.

She rolled her shoulders, shook out her arms. Then picked up the softball and slipped on her glove. "Get in position behind home plate," she called to him.

He could be her catcher. He bent his knees but didn't hunker down.

"You should have a glove," Carrie said. She drew a deep breath, gripped the ball in her right hand. Focused on him.

"Not necessary." This wasn't a hundred-mile-an-hour fastball crossing the plate. It was slow pitch. There'd be no sting.

Mike had once watched his grandfather play at a retirement village in Key West. He knew the arc of the ball had to be at least six feet high and lower than twelve. Carrie's throw rose in-between but fell slightly short of home plate.

Holy shit, not bad for ball one, Mike thought. "Can you do that again?" he asked.

She nodded. "But hopefully better."

He scooped up the ball and tossed it back to her.

Her next pitch would have made any batter swing.

She had softball in her blood.

She practiced for an hour, honing her skill. He gave

her little direction. She'd played before. She made her own corrections.

"Not bad," he said. She was damn good. "Where'd you learn to pitch?"

Her smile was immediate. There was a lot of metal in her mouth. "I volunteered at a senior center in Philadelphia, close to where I grew up," she told him. "I'm fond of the elderly, and when the social director asked me to join their slow-pitch team, I jumped at the chance. My teammates were all seventy and older. Pitching came naturally to me."

He understood natural. He had been told by coaches that he'd been born with a pitching arm, which hadn't done him a lot of good in the grand scheme of his life.

He walked back toward her. "Any chance you can bat?" he asked.

"I can sacrifice bunt."

She was his ringer. "Are the Rogues aware of your pitching skills?" he wanted to know.

"Only Jillie Mac," she said. "She came to the senior center with me on occasion. She won't say anything."

"Where will Jill play?"

"The infield," said Carrie. "She's good at sports. I'm not."

"How about sex?"

She blushed, as he knew she would. "I've never considered it an athletic event."

"It can be," he teased her. "Hard, fast, deep, heavy breathing; both players win in the end. Climax ties the score."

No comeback from Carrie, although her color remained high. "Our team is set except for one alternate. Is there anyone you'd care to ask?"

He had an idea, but Aidan would kill him. "Agnes," he said.

"The receptionist?" Carrie was surprised.

"She's sixty-seven." Mike thought this through. "But she played women's softball in college, and is always reminiscing about her good old days."

"College wasn't yesterday for her."

"It was a long time ago," he agreed. "She's pretty fragile. But as an alternate, she'd be part of Team Barefoot William without actually getting on the field. She'd warm the bench and cheer us on. It would be the highlight of her year."

"There's an off chance if someone got hurt that she'd have to play." Carrie was practical.

Mike rubbed the back of his neck. "Let's hope that doesn't happen. This is a friendly community game, right?"

"You've yet to meet the Rogues. Retired or not, the guys are born sportsmen. They've never lost their edge. That's why Jillie Mac decided on slow pitch. It would even the playing field. A little," she added.

"Will you approach Agnes or should I?" he asked her. He couldn't wait to see the older woman's face. She'd be excited. She might even bake him his own batch of cookies.

"Let Jill do it," Carrie decided. "She's in charge of the event. I want her approval first."

"When's our first official practice?"

"Tomorrow night," she told him. "Shaye suggested we have three before game day."

They would probably need more than that, Mike thought, but three was better than none. They all had lives. Everyone worked. They'd be giving up their evenings to bat and learn the field.

"I'm glad you're coaching," Carrie said.

"That makes one of us."

She poked him in the chest then, to get her point

across. "Don't you dare take the fun out of this game,"
she said and meant it. "Keep your bad attitude and sarcasm away from the dugout."

Guess she'd told him, he mused.

She took off then, crossing the lawn ahead of him. He
appreciated her backside. Her curves brought sexy to
softball.

He walked more slowly. He could play nice.

It was only for one day.

Ten

Twelve Richmond Rogues arrived in Barefoot William. Ten retired players, and two active. They were flown in on James Lawless's private company plane. The men traveled alone. They would be in town for only eight hours. Their families remained in Richmond. Those who had small children would be home in time to tuck them into bed.

Their celebrity impacted the town. Jillian Mac had stood back and watched as the beachside town swelled to three times its size. Richmond rallied around their boys of summer. Loyal followers of the team traveled great distances.

Fans embraced the rookies, and had never forgotten the veterans. James Lawless, Richard "Risk" Kincaid, and Cody "Psycho" McMillan would always have their respect.

The men had greeted Jill and Carrie with fist bumps and hugs. Jill had a soft spot in her heart for each one of them. Especially Psycho. He'd pulled out his wallet and shown her recent pictures of his wife and daughter. He was one proud father.

The day rested heavily on Jill's shoulders. A great deal of time and planning had gone into this weekend. She and Carrie had begun preparations months in advance. Still, the enormity of the turnout overwhelmed her.

Shaye Saunders had hometown muscle. Her connections extended throughout the county. She'd been instrumental in helping tie up loose ends. Jill would always be grateful to her.

Tailgate celebrations had begun with breakfast; hundreds of trucks and campers had parked just outside the guard gate leading to the site. The partying would continue long after the slow-pitch softball game. Aidan had beefed up security. Just to be on the safe side.

History was made with the ground-breaking ceremony. James, Aidan, and Trace Saunders were drawn together for a photo op. Their first scoop of dirt drew enormous applause. Somehow Psycho managed to get in the picture. He had a way of popping up unexpectedly. He'd wanted his own Lucite shovel, but shared James's instead. Jill had promised to order him a commemorative spade, which had pleased him greatly.

Trace Saunders and Aidan Cates had been given special baseball jerseys. They'd become honorary Rogues. The men had all looked handsome in their suits, Jill mused, looking back on the morning. Aidan had stood out to her. He'd worn a navy suit with a white shirt and burgundy tie. He'd gotten a haircut since she'd last seen him. His gaze had warmed her when their eyes met. She grew so hot she'd fanned herself with the program of events. She hoped to see him again on a more regular basis following the weekend. She'd missed him.

He had apparently missed her, too. His get-well wish for her sunburned feet had arrived in a bouquet of hot pink, orange, and yellow gerbera daisies. A vase of white roses awaited her on the day she and Carrie moved into the Rogues store. She did love flowers. No man in her life had ever been so generous. She appreciated Aidan.

The morning had flown by; it was now one o'clock. Game time. She stood behind the low fence in the Team Rogue dugout. She gazed at the crowd. Additional collapsible bleachers had been delivered to the ball field at parks and recreation. The stands stretched the entire fence line. Those seated as far back as the outfield raised their voices for a home run. Fans in standing-room-only stomped their feet. Concession stands were set up on the grounds. Peanuts, popcorn, hot dogs, and cheese nachos scented the air. The sky was clear; the temperature was moderate. It was the perfect day to play ball.

Mila Carlyle from Dreams had approached Jill moments before. The owner of the store had thanked her profusely for the tickets. Jill had also included one for her associate, Sabrina. She'd felt a little fresh air and a box of Cracker Jacks might make Sabrina less of a tight ass.

Jill glanced between dugouts. The players on both teams had exchanged pleasantries. All but Mike Burke and Rylan Cates. They'd stared at one another, but neither acknowledged the other's presence. Surely they knew each other, Jill thought. However there was no sign of friendship.

The crackling of the microphone gave way to player introductions. The crowd went wild, not only for the professional ballplayers, but for their hometown competitors, too. Team captains Aidan Cates and Risk Kincaid had the crowd on their feet, cheering at the tops of their lungs.

Rylan Cates received a hero's welcome. Ry was tall and lean with sandy hair. He had very blue eyes and a slow smile. He seemed more surfer than baseball player to Jill.

Psycho and Trace did the coin toss. Psycho won and

chose to bat first. The head umpire took his position behind home plate. A second official stood between first and second base. The day was all about fun and fair play, although Psycho was clearly amped to win.

The Rogues selected their bats and took a few practice swings. The men were all in their late thirties; handsome and fit. They promoted an active lifestyle. There were no beer bellies or couch potato butts.

"The ball's so big and round, it's like batting a pumpkin," Psycho grunted, standing on deck. He watched Carrie warm up, obviously amazed by her pitching ability. He turned toward Jill and shouted, "Why isn't she on our team?"

Jill hadn't shared her best friend's skill. She'd let the Rogues find out for themselves. Carrie deserved to shine. This was her moment. Jill noticed Mike Burke couldn't take his eyes off her. He was checking out more than her talent. That made Jill very nervous.

Psycho dug in at home plate. The team had decided to wear the classic Rogues' uniform colors, and did so with red-and-white baseball jerseys and blue jeans. He wore his baseball cap backward.

His grin was cocky as he pointed down the first baseline at Agnes Spencer. The older woman had stubbornly insisted she be in the starting lineup. Aidan had been apprehensive, concerned about her age and her fragile bones. He'd been outnumbered, and eventually he'd given in. He had walked with her to first, a protective gesture. Jill crossed her fingers that the medical team would not be called for an emergency.

Agnes now bent her knees and punched the pocket on her glove. She had a determined look on her face. "I'm coming your way, Aggie babe," Psycho called to her.

She motioned for him to bring it on. Agnes was feisty. Her light blue Barefoot William T-shirt hung nearly to her knees. The tee covered her khaki shorts. She looked as if she was wearing a dress. She was happy with her look. No one asked her to tuck it in.

The game was underway, Psycho leading off. Fans were chanting "Psycho, Psycho, Psycho." He'd been bad-ass crazy during his career. *Try anything, do anything* had been his motto. He'd lived a wild lifestyle until he'd met his wife, Keely. She'd brought him up short. Now Jill respected him as a husband and father.

Jill exhaled when the game began. Carrie pitched to Psycho with the relaxed presence of a player who knew she could strike him out. He swung at a ball that dropped two feet before the plate. "Shi-shoot," he corrected. He shook himself off, got ready for her next underhanded toss.

He connected with the next pitch. The ball flew down the first baseline, straight toward Agnes. The crowd held its collective breath as the older woman scooped, then stepped on the base. Psycho was out by a fraction of a second.

He snarled, bent down, going nose to nose with her. The crowd erupted when he kissed her on the cheek. Agnes may have made the out, but Psycho won everyone's heart. Jill felt her throat tighten, for no reason at all.

A man's man, Risk Kincaid batted second. No one could match his reliability and calm. He landed a double.

Jill hit third: a solid single.

Team owner James Lawless came fourth. He struck out. He shook his head, then surprised everyone by applauding Carrie. She was on fire. The crowd clapped for him, too.

Two outs, and Carrie next faced Rylan Cates. Ry was confident. He gave her an exaggerated wink. She winked back. The fans whistled their approval. Their silly flirtation drew Mike Burke's scowl. Jill could easily see him from first base. He was within her line of vision. His mood had visibly shifted, turning dark and dangerous. His hands were now fisted at his sides. He rocked heel to toe, a boxer's stance, ready to throw a punch.

What in the world was going on? she wondered.

Aidan had taken notice, too. He was playing left field, but now moved toward third base. He could see into the dugout. His gaze shifted from the Barefoot William bench to home plate, then back again. He seemed concerned about Mike.

It was fortunate for the home team that Aidan played close in. Rylan powered the ball over one of his cousin's head at third and Aidan caught the pop fly.

Three outs and the Rogues took the field.

Shaye got the team lined up to bat. Jill had no idea what was going on in their dugout, but Aidan now sat by Mike at the end of the bench. Their heads were bent, and it appeared that Aidan was doing most of the talking.

Agnes Spencer soon walked to home plate. The crowd rose and applauded her. She positioned the bat, which had to weigh as much as she did. The woman was a lightweight.

Rylan was to pitch. He played centerfield during the regular season, but today he stood behind the pitching rubber. James Lawless chose to catch. Jill played second base. Psycho took right field. Risk Kincaid headed to center. The rest of the Rogues fanned out, covering the remaining positions.

Carrie had told Jill that her team had practiced together. Their practices had paid off. Mike made a good coach. He pushed a little, praised a lot. He said not a word to Carrie.

"Agnes, hit the ball to me," Psycho shouted. "I'm waiting, sweetheart."

Agnes had other intentions. Jill watched in amazement

as Granny Aggie smacked the ball over her head. And on the very first pitch. Agnes made it easily to first base. Jill was impressed. Risk jogged and collected the ball. He returned it to Rylan.

"Out of the park, boss," Agnes yelled to Aidan, who was next up. The lady had a strong set of lungs.

Jill held her breath. She'd love to see Aidan score the first home run of the afternoon. Yet winning or losing mattered little to her. Today was all about welcoming fans and leaving them wanting more. That *more* would come with spring training. Psycho didn't share her feelings. "Strike him out," he hollered to Rylan.

Ry faced off against his older brother. Rylan could pitch, but he wasn't nearly as good as Carrie. Four pitches and the ball never fully crossed the plate. Aidan took his base. Agnes was spry; she trotted to second.

Shaye Cates had a competitor's heart. It didn't matter that Rylan was her brother, too; she was out to score. He pitched, and she drove the ball straight back at him. The softball caught his thigh, near his balls.

Ry did the shit-fire shuffle. He danced around the softball that bounced off him and rolled to his right. Shaye was safe at first by the time Jake Packer, a team rookie playing shortstop, made the recovery.

"What the—?" Psycho growled from right field. "Bases are loaded and there are no outs."

"It's only the first inning," Jill reminded him. Aidan now stood beside her on second, and his body bumped hers lightly. She discreetly brushed him back. She shivered in the heat of the day.

"Let's go, ladies!" Psycho rallied his teammates.

Retired pro volleyball player Dune Cates took his turn batting. Risk caught his high fly ball, but that didn't stop Agnes from crossing home plate. The townies went crazy. Agnes was all smiles.

The next two Barefoot William players went down on strikes. "It's about damn time," said Psycho as he jogged to the dugout. "You pitch like a girl, Rylan."

"Too bad he doesn't throw like Carrie," Jill said as she ran past him.

"She's your friend—rub it in," said Psycho.

The afternoon progressed with laughter, a few taunts from Psycho, and a lot of teasing when players made mistakes. Carrie took Barefoot William to the top of the ninth inning. Her pitching had slowed somewhat, and Jill grew concerned for her friend. Carrie was visibly tired. She now rubbed her shoulder between throws.

Jill called a time-out and the umpire stopped the game. She crossed the field to Mike Burke. He was far from welcoming. "What do you want?" he asked. "You're holding up play. A game we're winning by the way." Barefoot William was ahead by two runs.

"Take Carrie out," she said.

He looked at her as if she were crazy. "What the hell for?"

"She's hurting."

"You know this how?"

"Watch her next pitch and you'll see her flinch."

His brow creased. He looked uneasy. "I hadn't noticed."

"That's because you're busy glaring at Rylan. Get a grip. Whatever's going down between you, deal with it after the game. But pull Carrie now."

"If I don't?" He was being his disagreeable self.

"You'll wish you were wearing a cup." She darted back to her dugout.

"You fly just fine without your broom," he grumbled after her. Still she heard him.

"Flying monkeys to you, too."

Carrie got in one additional pitch before Mike withdrew her from the game. Jill breathed a whole lot easier. Psycho came to stand beside her at the dugout fence. He nudged her with his elbow. "Is she okay?" he asked, concerned.

"She's done for the day," Jill told him. "Ice on her shoulder, and she should be fine."

He ran one hand down his face, and she knew there was more to come. "I saw you body-rub the contractor. Is there anything between you?" he asked.

Psycho missed nothing. Ever. "I was just trying to distract him," was the best she could do.

He looked dubious, but didn't press her further. "You were successful. Aidan looked dazed." He went back to the bench.

Mike Burke soon called a second time-out. The umpire allowed three minutes. The team formed a circle and seemed deep in discussion. Jill wondered what was going on. Five minutes passed, and Psycho shouted across the field, "Violation."

Aidan Cates walked from the dugout and motioned to Risk Kincaid. They met at home plate. As team captain, Aidan had to choose a new pitcher; he wasn't sure he'd picked the proper person. Right or wrong, the decision rested on his shoulders.

Risk stood with his hands on his hips; Psycho joined them, too. He refused to be left out of the conversation.

"Our pitcher is hurt," Aidan said, coming right to the point. "We need to make a switch."

Risk nodded. "You have two alternates."

"I'm not sure of the rules, but I'd like to appoint Mike Burke as our player/coach," said Aidan.

The umpire scratched his head. "This isn't the World Series. An exception to the rule won't hurt today. It's the top of the ninth, the game's almost over."

"Unless we tie it up and get a rally going," Psycho put in.

"I have no objection to the substitution," said Risk.

"Is he any good?" asked Psycho.

"He's the best we have," Aidan said.

"Let's get back to it." Risk nudged him toward the visitor's dugout.

Mike glared at Aidan on his return. "Three up, three down, that's all we need," Aidan said.

Mike shook his head. "My pitching days are over."

"We need you, dude," said Dune.

"You can keep the trophy if we win," Shaye offered. And everyone agreed.

"I don't need a trophy." Mike was being obstinate.

Carrie came to stand beside him. She pinched his arm. His skin turned white where she squeezed. "You may not need this, but I do," she said. "I've played hard. I gave my heart for eight innings. Get your ass out there and close this for me."

Mike narrowed his gaze on her; his hate face was in place. He wore it well. He pulled free of Carrie's hold, and flexed his hand. Aidan debated Mike's capabilities. The man could grip, but how well could he toss these days? They were about to find out.

"Son of a bitch," Mike mumbled when Carrie gave him her mitt, and he and his team took the field. The man wasn't happy.

Aidan had pushed Mike into a position Mike had never planned to play again. Softball wasn't fastball, yet the electric charge of the crowd had built to major-league proportions. There was clapping and stomping. Cheers and whistles. The air vibrated with a life of its own.

Mike stood on the rectangular-shaped rubber, his chest rising and falling as he warmed up. The catcher gave him a thumbs-up with each throw. Team encouragement ran high.

"Whenever you're ready," the umpire called to him.

The time was now. It was the top of the order for the Rogues. Psycho, Risk, and Jill were to bat.

"You can do this, Michael," Agnes called to him from first base. "Psycho's an easy out."

Psycho looked down the baseline at Agnes. "Get ready to eat your words, Aggie."

Agnes rolled her eyes. "Pshaw."

Mike locked his jaw. Do or die, he threw his first pitch. Psycho connected with the ball, a grounder that flew past the shortstop. One man was now on base. No outs.

"Told you so," Psycho bragged to Agnes.

"You're not home yet." The older woman gave back as good as she got.

Dune Cates caught Risk's high fly ball to center. His long legs covered a lot of the outfield in a very short time. One down.

Jill batted next, attempted a bunt. The ball tipped back and was caught by the catcher. Two away.

James Lawless stepped aside and offered Rylan his turn at bat. No one questioned his motive. Ry belonged to both the Rogues and Barefoot William. It was a hometown courtesy. If Ry should get a hit, James would then follow. If not, Rylan would still get the final round of applause.

Aidan noticed that his brother seemed reluctant to bat against Mike; up until the time Psycho shouted, "Bring me home, Ry."

Rylan passed on three balls before he found his pitch. Once he did, he smacked the shit out of the softball. He totally killed it. The bat broke and shattered. Splinters flew all the way to Mike.

Mike should've ducked, but he didn't. His eye was on the ball. Aidan watched as he dove for it. He managed to make the catch. He was back on his feet in a heartbeat, throwing the ball to Agnes at first.

Mike threw hard. Aidan was afraid Agnes wouldn't be able to handle the catch. She managed, using both hands. Rylan was running toward her. Psycho was four feet off the base, but he had yet to commit to second. He'd been watching the action. Mike had awed the crowd. He'd performed like a major league player.

The third out was yet to be made. Agnes had her choice: would it be Rylan or Psycho? Ry was the easy out. Instead she chose Psycho. She lunged, tagged him.

Psycho looked so stunned it was comical.

Agnes pumped her arm in victory.

Three down. Team Barefoot William had won.

Celebration erupted on the field. Dune Cates cheered with the same enthusiasm he'd once shown when winning a volleyball tournament. Aidan watched as his family and friends hopped up and down and acted like kids. There were high fives, fist bumps, and slaps on the back.

Risk Kincaid approached Aidan shortly thereafter. "Got a minute?" he asked, looking serious.

Aidan nodded. The two men walked toward right field.

"I want to discuss Mike Burke." Risk got right to the point.

Mike had been tense all day. Aidan hoped his superintendent hadn't offended Risk or any of the other Rogues. "What about him?" Aidan asked.

"You're aware of his history with Rylan," said Risk. And Aidan nodded. "Ry came to me several weeks ago after one of our assistant pitching coaches announced his retirement. The man's leaving after this season. Ry brought college film of Mike for me to watch. Skill, mechanics, and vision don't always come together for a pitcher. Mike had it all."

Risk paused, then continued with, "Mike saved Ry's life from what I understand. Rylan has always wanted to repay him."

"A simple thank-you would've sufficed," Aidan said. "But my younger brother never felt words were enough. Over the years he's thought about buying Mike a house, a boat, a car, but always changed his mind. He told me the right gift would come around in time."

"That gift could be now," Risk informed him. "I'd like to interview Mike for the coach's position; bring him into our organization next spring if we're a fit. I wanted to check with you first though. Mike's worked for Cates Construction a long time. I don't want to break anything up."

Aidan's stomach dropped. He couldn't swallow. Mike was his right arm. Losing him would be a sad day. Yet there was no way he would stand in the way of a future Mike had always wanted and truly deserved. Mike would never stand on the mound and be cheered by a stadium of fans, but he could still be part of major league baseball. He'd have a second lease on life. Mike's old wounds might finally heal.

Aidan sucked it up. "Talk to Mike," he agreed. "Rylan did a good thing by bringing Mike to your attention. Mike would serve the Rogues well. I'm sure of it."

"No hard feelings then?" asked Risk. "Mike wouldn't be joining us until the training facility is built."

"I appreciate your coming to me first," said Aidan. "I don't like to be blindsided."

"Neither do I," Risk said, "especially not when it comes to business. My wife, Jacy, is cute and quirky and knocks me off balance every single day. She brings me all the surprises I need in my life."

Aidan understood that feeling. Jillian Mac did much the same to him. She made his life interesting.

Risk offered his hand, and Aidan shook it. "We'll stay in touch. I'll fly down on occasion to see how things are progressing."

The two men walked back toward the infield.

Most of the Rogues now mixed with the Barefoot William players. Risk Kincaid singled out Mike Burke. The retired center fielder put his hand on Mike's shoulder. Their exchange was quiet and private. Reserved. People were curious over their conversation, but no one interfered. Not even Psycho McMillan.

Once Risk had made his offer, Mike looked to Rylan. The two men stared at each other for a significant time. Ry raised one of his eyebrows in question. Mike's expression gave nothing away. Coming to a decision, Mike nodded and smiled. Risk handed Mike his business card.

Aidan cut his gaze to the Rogues dugout. Psycho and Jill had retired to the bench. They sat close, looking chummy. Aidan's chest squeezed when Psycho hugged her and Jill rested her head on his shoulder. They stayed that way for a long time. Aidan grew more and more uneasy. Wasn't Psycho married? Jill had mentioned his wife and daughter. Then why did she kiss him on the cheek? Why did he take her hand?

Aidan returned to the home dugout. The heat of the day had beaten him down; he was in need of hydration. The iced cooler offered grape Gatorade or bottled water. He went with water. He'd finished off the bottle by the time Jillian Mac joined him.

The lady was full of surprises. She walked up to him, stood close. Grinned. "Congratulations on your win," she said. "This was an amazing day."

It had been, up until the moment he'd seen her with Psycho. "Decent," he agreed.

She seemed to sense something was wrong. "Talk to me, Aidan."

He had nothing to say. "Everything's fine."

She shook her head. "No, it's not. I'm psychic, remember?"

How could he forget? He stared at her now, at her mussed hair and dirt-streaked chin. Her eyes were bright; her nose was sunburned. Her Rogues jersey had a tear in the hem where she'd dove for a ground ball. Psycho had run in from right field to make sure she was okay. She'd gotten up quickly and dusted herself off. Then given him a thumbs-up. Her jeans were loose fitting. Her sneakers were tied with red and blue laces. He liked looking at her.

Aidan wasn't a man for public affection. However a quick kiss wouldn't draw a lot of attention. Or so he hoped. He reached for her then, cupped her face with his hands. His kiss was as soft as her breath. He deepened it slowly. A nip to her bottom lip, a flick of his tongue to her upper. She bit him back, hard enough to arouse and make him sweat.

Sensations escalated. He wanted to feel her. All of her. He drew her flush against him. She rubbed her belly against his zipper. He nearly lost his mind.

He needed more, but he got less. The sound of someone entering the dugout snapped them apart. "Dude, get your mouth off Jillie Mac." Psycho's voice was deep and firm. Threatening. He'd gone from friendly on the field to formidable in the dugout. A muscle jerked along his jaw line.

Jill wasn't intimidated. She remained close to Aidan. She went as far as to slip her arm about his waist. A bold move, Aidan thought, given Psycho's dark expression.

"We were celebrating," she informed the Rogue.

"With tongues?" he asked sharply.

"It was a friendly celebration," said Jill.

"A bit too friendly, if you ask me."

"No one's asking you," she huffed.

Psycho and Jill had a stare off. One Aidan didn't understand. Neither gave an inch. What the hell was going on? Something, obviously. It apparently involved him. He wasn't invisible. Enough was enough.

Clearing his throat, he said, "We're consenting adults." Which made them both blink. He eyed Psycho. "Do you have a problem with that?" he challenged. The man was a celebrity athlete, yet Aidan refused to give up his girl. He liked Jillian Mac.

"The feeling must be mutual since she kissed you back." Still, Psycho frowned. "What are your intentions toward my sister?"

Sister? Holy shit! Aidan was so taken aback, he had momentary brain freeze. "You're related?" sounded lame.

"Guess she forgot to tell you." Psycho laughed.

"You need to mind your own business," said Jill.

"I could, but you know I won't."

"Try." She glared at him.

Psycho gave it some thought. Eventually he shrugged. He then went on to deliver a message from the team's owner. "James wants to speak with you and Carrie before he leaves for the airport. He's waiting in his limo," he told her.

Business called, and Jill responded. "I'll be right there."

Psycho gave her one last look. "Your niece misses you, by the way. Cammie wants you to meet her new stuffed dragon. She calls him Fire. He likes toasted marshmallows. Take a weekend off and visit us. We all miss you."

Aidan felt Jill relax. She crossed to her brother and hugged him fiercely. "Love you, Cody."

"Right back at you." His gaze was on Aidan as he turned to leave. "Take care of her, contractor. I know where to find you." He was gone.

"Wait here for me," Jill requested of Aidan. "I can explain. I won't be gone long." And she hurried off to find James Lawless.

Jill was Psycho's sister. A fact she'd forgotten to mention. Aidan eased down on the wooden bench; sat in disbelief, feeling frustrated. He didn't want to get ahead of himself, but if their relationship progressed, Psycho could be his brother-in-law. His mind wouldn't wrap around it. Not yet anyway.

Dune wandered into the dugout. "The crowd has thinned, and I'm gone, too," he said. "My sweet wife tired herself on the sidelines, cheering for our team. Sophie yelled so hard she lost her voice." He rolled his shoulders. "It was a good day, don't you think?"

"I was proud of Mike."

"So was Carrie," said Dune. "She tried to reach him after the last out, but he was surrounded by players and fans. Then Rylan waylaid her."

"Is Ry interested in her?"

"Who knows?" answered Dune. "Rylan has James Lawless's permission to stay in town two extra days, so he can visit family. He'll catch a commercial flight to Richmond Tuesday morning. The Rogues season opener is a week away. They play the Colonels. Ry faces his old team."

"He'll be fine." Aidan had every confidence in his younger brother.

Dune grabbed two bottles of water for the road. "Ry's headed to Shaye's beach house. She's opened the door to anyone who wants to stop by. Catch up with you later?"

"Most likely." Or not. Much would depend on how long it took to straighten things out with Jillie Mac. Or Jillian McMillan, as he now knew her.

When speaking with Risk he'd been appreciative of the surprises Jill brought to his life. But this was one surprise too many. The woman confused the hell out of him. She'd once said her brother lived in Philadelphia and worked in sporting goods. That was definitely a stretch. He'd have preferred the truth.

The dust had settled on the field and the bleachers had been dismantled by the time Jill returned. The concession stands were now closed. The cleanup crew had emptied the last trash receptacle. The ballpark was deserted. The dinner hour drew the last fan home.

She knew where to find him. He was right where she'd left him. She hesitantly entered the dugout and sat down on the opposite end of the bench. She leaned forward, rested her elbows on her knees. "James was pleased with today's outcome," she said with a sigh, sounding relieved.

"You did a great job." He gave her that.

"The crowd was larger than we expected."

"No one got too rowdy or out of hand."

"No one but Psycho," she said. "I'm sorry he got in your face."

"He was worried about you." Aidan understood a brother's concern for his sister. He would protect Shaye with his life.

Jill rubbed her hands down her blue-jeaned thighs. "My white lies always catch up with me. I need to make amends. Where do we go from here?" she asked him. "Or do we call it quits?"

"I'm not a quitter," he said. "But you need to keep it real. Full disclosure from now on."

"I'll do my best."

"Come sit by me," he said.

He didn't have to ask her twice. She slid down the bench. She sat so close, their shoulders, hips, and thighs brushed. He liked the feel of her. He covered her hand with his own. He was confident they could work this out.

"Tell me about Jillian McMillan," he said.

She stared out across the ball field, and was slow to say, "My childhood memories aren't pretty. My father deserted my family when I was three; I have no memory of the man. My mother never spoke of him. She worked two jobs and was seldom home. Being the oldest, Psycho raised us kids. I have brothers and sisters, too."

She paused. "We were poor. Food was scarce. Have you ever made tomato soup with a ketchup packet and hot water? Split a candy bar five ways?"

He shook his head.

"I have, and I've known hunger." She bit down on her bottom lip. "I'm aware of Cody's faults. There isn't a rule he hasn't broken. He's fought for everything he has. He's fiercely loyal to those he loves. He's an amazing dad. He even built his daughter a playhouse. The man can throw a tea party. No guy looks better in a pillbox hat, a pink boa, and a strand of pearls."

She crossed her ankles, squared her shoulders. "He has always been my champion. I've worked dozens of jobs, but never had a career. Not until he told me about the community liaison position with the Rogues. My brother casts a big shadow. I applied as Jillian Mac, wanting to be hired on my own qualifications, not because I was his sister. He never interfered. Few people outside the Rogues Organization know we're related. I came on board and was able to interview an assistant. I chose Carrie."

Aidan understood. Nepotism caused jealousy. Jill hadn't wanted preferential treatment. She earned her own way. He liked that about her.

"On a personal note," she wrapped up, "I'm thirty-three years old. I like sports and being outdoors. I'm opinionated and pushy on occasion. I don't give my friendship freely. Should I like someone, I like him for life. I'm not an Indian giver. Permanence isn't easy for me. I always have an escape route."

She nudged him with her elbow. "It's your turn."

He gave her the short version. "My great-great-great-grandfather founded Barefoot William. I grew up here. I have an extended family that stretches the entire coastline. I seek balance in my life. I don't like chaos. From an early age, I wanted to build. Legos and wooden blocks were my favorite toys. I constructed a two-story tree fort when I was twelve. The fort had running water."

"I like a man who works with his hands," she complimented him.

"Your heart is in the right place most days."

"I like Sadie," she added.

"She likes you, too."

"Then there's Agnes."

"You are her new best friend after today," he said. "Opportunities for new challenges are far and few between as a person gets older. You gave her a chance to feel young again."

"She made the final out."

"There was a photographer taking pictures on the sidelines," he recalled. "Agnes may make the front page of the newspaper."

Jill went quiet on him then. He left her to her thoughts, for the moment anyway. Until she was able to say, "Guess I should call it a day."

"Spend the night with me."

She brushed dust off her forearm. "I'm in need of a shower and change of clothes."

Easy fix. "Follow me home in your car. You can clean up there. I have a T-shirt you can borrow."

Her lips twitched. "Only a shirt?"

"Unless you'd rather be naked."

She closed her eyes, sighed. "This could be a very good evening."

Aidan would make sure it was.

Barefoot William was bursting at the seams. Rogues fans and vacationers packed the streets, so he took to the back roads. He had built his house away from the beach, away from the tourist trade and in-town traffic. He liked his privacy. His retreat sat on twenty acres.

"It's not your typical Florida home," he said to Jill when she parked her car next to his in the brick courtyard. Dusk crept in, and automatic spotlights kicked on. A Japanese boxwood hedge bordered the walkway. White and purple bougainvillea and red firecracker plants provided color at the front entrance.

Jill climbed from her Triumph and came to stand beside him. Her eyes were wide; her mouth parted. "Another house that Aidan built," she softly said.

He took her by the hand and led her to the double-wide entry door. "The outside's finished, but the inside still needs work," he told her.

He watched her closely when they entered. He wanted to see her initial reaction. Her breath caught in her throat; her hand covered her heart. "Your place is incredible." Her approval meant a lot to him.

"Look around," he offered. He now saw his home through her eyes. The octagonal structure was made of cedar and glass. Each room faced a circular sunken living room. He could stand in the middle and take in the entire view. Sliding pocket doors allowed privacy when necessary.

He had minimal furniture, adding pieces as they caught his eye. His crescent-shaped couch faced a big-screen television. His computer sat on a rolltop desk. He kept an antique pharmacy apothecary cabinet for his personal papers. Brazilian cherry hardwood added richness to the floors.

"Sadie?" he called out, checking on his dog. She didn't always hear him come in.

Sleepy-eyed, with her tail wagging, the pointer came from the direction of the kitchen. She liked to sleep by her food bowls. They were always filled. She stretched out on her heated orthopedic bed, placed in front of the kibble bin.

"Sweet girl." Jill went down on one knee and greeted Sadie. "She seems glad to see me."

"We're not used to having company," he said.

"No visitors?" She seemed surprised. "You have lots of relatives." She eyed him with interest. "No dates?"

"I wanted to finish my house before I opened the doors to friends and family," he said. "This has become an ongoing project. I'm out of town ten months out of the year. I have a caretaker. The house will get finished, eventually." He shifted his stance, added, "No female has slept here." It was important that she knew that.

Her throat worked, and she buried her face in the soft fur at Sadie's neck. Her sigh of relief touched his heart.

She looked back at him in her own time. "Your home could use a woman's touch," she said lightly. "It's very masculine with its sharp angles and rough wood. A little softness might be nice, too."

"Your suggestions are welcome," he said.

"I'm not an interior decorator."

"Neither am I. I buy what I like."

"Basic fabrics are good with pops of color."

He could live with that.

"I love overstuffed rocking chairs."

"So do I." His grandmother had one.

"Comfy loveseats for two," she added.

"Good to know." He didn't mind cuddling.

"I'm crazy for those leather club chairs that seem to hug you when you sit down."

He kept a mental list.

"Hand-painted curtains," she continued. "I love dressers that become sideboard tables."

Those were all interesting ideas.

"Round, oversize ottomans where a dozen people can rest their feet and—" She laughed at herself. "Sorry, I got carried away."

He hadn't minded in the least. "Fun thoughts," he said.

"They came from catalogues," she admitted. "I didn't have a lot of toys growing up, so I'd cut out pictures and design my future home. That was as close to a dollhouse as I ever got."

The puzzle pieces that were Jillian Mac were slowly fitting together. Communication was important to him.

She gave Sadie a final pat, then got to her feet. Sadie came to him then; nudged him with her nose. She wanted his attention, too. Aidan rubbed her shoulders. Satisfied, Sadie ambled back to the kitchen.

"You can check out my appliances later. Let's shower now," he suggested. It was time to own up. "I've wanted you since that first day in Three Shirts."

"In the dressing room?" She was surprised.

"Small and tight."

"Your reputation preceded you. You'd already been there with another woman."

Aidan rubbed the back of his neck, clarified, "My date was trying on swimsuits. She'd stripped all the way down, instead of leaving on her underwear. Her piano-wire bracelets got caught on a shoulder strap as she was slipping off a one-piece. She called for help. I entered the changing room, and she was all over me."

"You couldn't fight her off?"

"She was a bodybuilder," he remembered. He'd met

Ava Anderson at Parks and Recreation, during the summer activities fair. Barefoot William liked to keep its kids off the streets. The facility had offered everything from craft projects to a variety of sports. Ava had been in town for a month, a guest lecturer on good health.

She'd come on to him, asking him out. He'd agreed to a casual afternoon on the boardwalk. In a shirt and slacks, she'd looked fit and feminine. Naked, she was as ripped as any man. Her muscles had muscles.

"The woman was strong," he told Jill. "I couldn't get her off me. We were noisy, and customers complained. Jenna walked in and my date flexed." It had been embarrassing on so many levels.

"Would you have had sex, had you not been caught?"

He shook his head. "I would never disrespect my cousin; I wasn't even into the woman. Finding you and me together a few weeks ago set Jen off again."

"I wasn't naked."

"My cousin wasn't aware of our circumstances."

One corner of her mouth tipped. "You did barge in."

"I would've taken the changing rooms apart to find you."

"You were on a mission."

"There was something about you," he confessed. "Something beyond your lies. Something I couldn't define."

"Can you define it now?" She wanted to know.

"Not completely," he replied honestly.

"When you wrap your head around it, let me know." She drew in a breath. "What do we do now?"

"I'm going to do you."

Eleven

Aidan took her by the hand and they crossed the room together. They entered the bath, and he slid the black lacquered pocket doors closed behind them. Inside, full-length mirrors caught them from every angle. He dimmed the lighting, which left them in a pale glow. Jill ran her hand over the brown marble vanity, then wiggled her fingers under the automatic water faucet. A gentle spray moistened her palm.

"Very modern," she appreciated. "I like the two sinks."

Aidan did, too. Couples shouldn't have to fight over space in the morning, especially when washing their faces or brushing their teeth. The double basins solved that problem. The large rectangular shower with benches, along with the sunken tub, could also accommodate two people.

He came up behind Jill and eased her back against him. Her desire met his arousal and the air crackled with sexual intent. They stared at each other in the mirror. She shivered ever so slightly. "Feel me," he whispered as her back molded to his front. "I want you."

Her shoulder blades pressed into his chest as tightly as her bottom snugged his groin. He surrounded her with his strength; his sex strained against the fly of his khaki shorts.

He brushed her hair off her neck with inordinate care. Then breathed near her ear. He felt her heartbeat quicken when he placed an openmouthed kiss just beneath, then lightly blew on the spot. A hot shudder flashed through her body. He liked turning her on.

Moving down her neck to her collarbone, he kissed and nuzzled, kissed and nipped; his seven o'clock shadow abraded her sensitive skin. Her chest rose and fell beneath the cotton of her Rogues jersey.

Pushing the neck of her shirt off her shoulder, he explored the curve with his lips and tongue. "More skin." His voice was deep and dark with wanting her.

He took his time, so what should've taken seconds rolled into minutes. They had all night. He slid his hands down her sides to the hem, then eased the shirt up and over her head. All along the way, he teased her belly, her ribs, her breasts, leaving her breathless.

He tossed her jersey aside. Then drew her sports bra off next. Her freed breasts rose, catching the dim light. The soft undersides were in shadow. Her reflection left him so hard, his entire body tightened.

She dropped her head back against his chest and closed her eyes. His hands fanned the fullness of her breasts. Her nipples puckered. He traced down her ribs to the smooth, taut hollow of her stomach.

Slow hands. Slow burn. He made her hot for him.

Timelessness. His foreplay had no end.

She inhaled long and deeply when he fingered the silver snap on her jeans. Her breathing sharpened as he unsnapped them, scraped down the zipper. The sound was loud in the stillness of the room.

When he slid his hand beneath the elastic of her panties, stretching his fingers toward her sex, Jill went weak in the knees. The full weight of her body rested against him now. Sweet curves and warm woman.

Anticipation played where their bodies touched.

Expectancy spread like a fever.

She was naked to the waist, her skin flushed. Her lips were moist and parted. Her jeans had shifted lower on her hips. The zipper was pulled all the way down, the material on either side spread wide. She was available to him.

Aidan's hand was visible beneath the sheer nylon of her panties. The stretch and stroke of his fingers had her pressing into his palm as he penetrated her with his forefinger. In and out. She was wet for him.

Lifting her gaze, she found him watching her in the glass. Watching her reaction to each graze and slide of his finger. Her features bore signs of strain and naked longing.

Filling her with two fingers, he kept her on edge. He increased the pressure, sharp and enveloping. As her climax built, her back arched and her knees buckled. She clutched his arm.

He was there to catch her when she came. He trapped her close until her breathing eased. Slipping his hand from her panties, he turned her within the circle of his arms. He stroked her hair out of her face, kissed her lightly on the forehead. Then removed the rest of her clothes.

Goose bumps scattered on the soft flesh of her inner thighs as he eased down her jeans and panties. The callused pads of his thumbs skimmed the sensitive backs of her knees, then trailed down her calves. Her legs were smooth and lightly tanned. Her tennies and socks came next. Once her jeans and bikini briefs reached her ankles, she stepped out of them.

His mouth descended, and he teased and tasted her. She sighed as he parted her lips and deepened the kiss.

She shivered when his tongue rubbed hotly over hers. He felt her pleasure.

She responded with passion and a desire to please him, too. Her hands found their way down his back and beneath his Barefoot William T-shirt. It came off with one smooth tug. His khaki shorts dropped next. Then his boxer briefs. She untied his tennis shoes. He toed the heels.

He stood naked before her now. Heat twisted inside him, heavy and urgent. The tip of his sex strained upward; his testicles pulled painfully tight.

Time was lost to sensation as Jillian Mac's world went into soft focus. She pressed him with her body. Her breasts brushed the hard contours of his chest; her abdomen sought his sculpted stomach. She stroked every muscle, every bone.

He was breathing heavily when he walked her backward and into the shower. Frosted glass surrounded them. He proceeded to push a panel of buttons. In seconds, warm, inviting water cascaded from dual showerheads. The spray filmed her skin. There was nothing sexier than being touched beneath the sensual spray. Awareness magnified.

A selection of sponges hung from a shower caddy. She squeezed Burberry shower gel onto a natural sea sponge. Grapefruit and cedar scented the air. She bathed him, slowly, thoroughly. The scrape of her nails followed the scrub of the sponge, over the rounded muscles of his shoulders, the masculine cut of his chest, and his flat belly. When she caressed his erection, he jolted. When she squeezed him lightly, his eyes dilated. He groaned low in his throat.

Melting heat and thick, swelling pleasure deepened the moment when Aidan captured his own sponge, added lots of shower gel. Inch by soapy inch, he massaged her neck, her breasts, the curves of her hips. Her lips parted when he eased the sponge between the V of her thighs; the teasing force had her rocking against him.

Their intimacy threatened her sanity. Lust and longing and white-hot sensation filled her. Hunger and burning.

He released her for what seemed like a lifetime, but was only seconds. He took a condom from his water-proof shaving kit on a shelf above one of the benches. He ripped open the foil packet with his teeth and sheathed himself. He was ready for her now.

He backed her against the slick, tiled wall, cupping her bottom. His muscles flexed as he lifted her against him. She wrapped her arms about his neck, her legs about his hips. He slid into her.

Once she'd received him, she rolled her hips, taking him deeper, as deep as she could. He filled her fully. Their joining soon quickened, becoming fierce. Her pulse beat to his racing heart.

She bit his neck, scratched his shoulders, and scored his back.

He clutched her hips and bottom so tightly, he was certain to leave bruises.

Ultimate pleasure brought them to orgasm at the same moment.

She gasped, trembled, convulsed.

His whole body shuddered as he sank into her.

Sated, he supported her with one arm as he turned off the water. A further selection of buttons, and the shower became a steam room. Thick whirls rose all around them, clouding the glass.

He moved to one of the benches and sat. She straddled his thighs. They both exhaled at the same time.

He rested his chin on the top of her head.

She pressed her cheek to his shoulder.

They held each other so tight, not even the steam could squeeze between them. A feeling of contentment embraced her. The fleeting sense of stability petrified her. Relationships had not been good to her over the years.

She tried not to dwell on permanence. Instead she embraced the night with Aidan. The man was considerate. He loaned her an extra-large gray T-shirt after they tossed their dirty clothes in the washer.

She liked the airy feeling of not wearing panties.

Aidan liked her accessible, too. Twice more they had sex, on his living room couch and again in the garage on his workshop bench when she asked to see his tools. She'd gotten one tiny splinter; Aidan had removed it from her thigh. They had yet to reach his bedroom.

Two a.m. came and went. Her stomach growled.

"Care for a late-night snack?" Aidan asked while nuzzling her neck. She presently straddled his thighs as they sat on a metal antique glider on his wide-screened verandah. The sex they'd just had on it had been amazing. The back and forth slide combined with the roll of their hips provided her strongest orgasm of the night. Aidan proved insatiable. He'd worn her out.

She was definitely hungry. Food sounded good. Her T-shirt hung off her shoulders, exposing her breasts. She pulled it down, and then pushed to her feet. Aidan rose as well, tugging up his athletic shorts. They'd come outside to appreciate the cool night air, to stargaze, to talk. Her light touch on his thigh had turned their conversation into frantic glider sex. One of her best memories ever.

Aidan's kitchen was large and modern. A six-seater restaurant booth sat in one corner. Here was the casual setting that offset his formal dining room. She liked the open area and long counter space.

Then hem on her shirt covered her bottom as she slid

across the black leather seat. She rested her elbows on the Formica tabletop.

"Your choice," Aidan said, "healthy or junk food."

"Mix it up?"

He nodded. "That I can do."

Sadie cracked one eye and sniffed the air when he scrambled eggs and fried bacon. Aidan gave his pointer a small bite of egg. It didn't take much to satisfy her. She went right back to sleep.

He melted a Snickers bar in the microwave, then drizzled the chocolate, caramel, and nuts over toaster waffles and sliced bananas. Jill liked his cooking style.

"Coffee, orange juice, or both?" he asked her.

"Juice is fine." Caffeine would keep her up. She needed to sleep eventually, if Aidan would let her.

He served her picnic-style, with paper plates, cups, and plastic silverware. He sat down across from her. Stretching out his legs beneath the table, he trapped her knees. The brief pressure made her shiver. They relaxed and ate.

She moaned with the first bite of her warm chocolaty waffle. "I recognize that sound," Aidan teased her. "Sexy."

She wasn't the least embarrassed. She'd let herself go when they'd made love. Their bodies had spoken.

The flick of his tongue to her nipples had drawn her sigh. Her breath had been ragged when he'd entered her.

She'd heard him groan when she'd kissed his sex. Then listened to his chest hitch when she'd taken him in her mouth.

She cleaned her plate, and then ate off Aidan's. He didn't mind. One corner of his mouth tipped as she polished off the last strip of bacon. Two bites of banana, and she licked chocolate off her fingers.

"You are a turn-on, Jillian McMillan," he said.

"You do it for me, too."

He pushed their empty plates aside and took her hand. His gently kissed her palm. "Talk or sleep?" He left the choice to her.

"We can chat a while."

"We can ask questions, get answers."

"Do you think confessions make a relationship stronger?" she asked.

"Honesty strengthens a couple. We'll take it slow. There's no need to tell me everything tonight. You can save something for tomorrow."

She smiled at him then. "I'll go first." She wanted to keep things light, so she went with, "What was your first impression of me?"

"That you were the hottest psychic I'd ever seen."

Good answer. "I'd heard your name mentioned at James River Stadium. Then again by Lila at Steamers. I wasn't ready for you, Aidan Cates," she admitted. "You have a big presence. You fill a room, including the corners."

Her next question was asked tongue in cheek. "Do you have a favorite memory of us?" They'd known each other only three weeks. "It can't be sex."

"You coming to the construction site and meeting my girls meant a lot to me."

"That was a good day for me, too," she agreed.

"Are you a romantic or a realist?" from Aidan.

"I love Valentine's Day," she confessed. "What does that tell you?" Sadly, she'd never had a boyfriend in February. That hadn't stopped her from buying her own personal gifts. Last year she'd enjoyed a small box of chocolates while wearing red lounging pajamas. Extravagances, yet they'd made her feel special. "Do you have a favorite holiday?" she asked next.

"Thanksgiving," he said. "No matter where my family

might be living, we come together for a long weekend. Someday I'd like to host a big dinner party here. Holidays are best shared."

"You have plenty of room." She could picture the gathering. The dining room festively decorated. Fall centerpieces and seasonal wreaths. Lots of food and laughter. Kicking back and watching football. Or feeling full and taking a nap. Then savoring a second piece of pie.

"I have more space than I know what to do with most days," he said. "I built a big house in anticipation of a big family."

"How many kids?" She was curious.

"My parents had five. We'd take sides, two and two, and one would break the tie."

"Same at my house," she said. "Although Cody always had the last word; he was the oldest."

"Both Trace and Shaye and Dune and Sophie are wanting to start families. I'm waiting for baby announcements any day now."

"They'll make good parents."

"Ever been in love, Jill?"

This seemed important to him. She had strong feelings for Aidan. They hadn't known each other long; she had no idea if her feelings would last. So she shook her head. "Can't say that I have. How about you?"

He grinned. "Ninth grade, her name was Bethany Michaels. She was the only female to take shop. My kind of girl."

"She broke boundaries."

"And my heart," he said. "She wouldn't give me the time of day outside class. My life lost all meaning."

"You recovered?"

"Lily Louise brought new meaning to my sophomore year of high school. She liked to French kiss."

"What defines you, Aidan?" She was curious.

"Honesty, hard work, my family, Sadie," he answered. "You?"

"My intuition," she told him. "I'm also loyal and protective of my friends."

"Good qualities."

"There's always room for improvement." She reflected on her white lies. She was working toward telling the truth.

They grew quiet, sitting together in a compatible silence where words were no longer necessary. A smile, a wink, a touch meant so much more. His dark gaze was warm and inviting. She realized in that moment she could stare at him forever. She would never tire of this man.

"I like you, Jillie Mac." He became serious.

I like you more, died in her throat. "It's nice to be liked," she said lightly.

"It's even nicer when it's reciprocated."

She'd disappointed him. She could see it in his eyes. Her life seemed suddenly complicated. Indecision weighed her down. She hated second-guessing herself. What if she felt more for him than he felt for her? What if she was reading more into their night together than was actually there? She'd been fooled too many times.

Her previous relationships had ended poorly. Once emotion slid between the sheets, she always got hurt. She couldn't afford that with Aidan. She was already in too deep.

She yawned then. The pressure of the day had caught up with her. She could hardly keep her eyes open. Aidan sensed her need for sleep. He rose and cleared the table. Scooping her up in his arms, he carried her to his bed. The king-size headboard was designed as a bookcase and shelved with books. Mysteries, biographies, and science fiction. The man liked to read.

He lowered her on soft blue cotton sheets and then lay down beside her. He drew her to him, and she settled close. He covered her with a navy satin comforter. Gently kissed her on the forehead. She was snug, secure, and scared to death. Nothing lasted forever.

His body soon relaxed, and she knew he slept.

She closed her eyes for two hours.

Then quietly crawled out of bed, dressed, and greeted dawn on her drive home.

Monday morning, and Aidan Cates was determined to locate Jillian Mac, even if it took him all day. She'd left his home between four and six a.m. on Sunday, without saying good-bye. She was now avoiding him. His instincts had told him not to chase her. He'd stayed away an entire day. Today he would find her.

I like you. He had meant what he'd said. He'd wanted to gage her reaction. He'd hoped for a smile; instead her face had fallen. She'd given him sad eyes and a frown. Definitely not what he'd expected.

He knew she had feelings for him. Their connection was strong. She'd made love with her heart. He wanted to know her better, if she would give him half a chance. Sneaking out hadn't set well with him. They needed to talk things over.

Jill had stayed one step ahead of him all morning. He'd stopped by her houseboat at first light, only to discover she'd left earlier than usual for work. He knew her routine. The Cateses were a grapevine for news. Secrets were shared. The family stood tight. Jill was now part of their community. He had only to listen to learn her whereabouts.

He'd gone by Brews Brothers, where she often bought a cup of coffee and a bagel with strawberry cream cheese. She would then sit on an outside bench, watch the beachcombers, and enjoy her breakfast. She'd feed her favorite seagull, named Gilligan. There'd been no sign of her at the coffee shop. The barista indicated she had long come and gone.

He now scanned the boardwalk to see if she was window shopping, one of her favorite pastimes. She seldom went inside a store to make a purchase. The lady was thrifty.

His third stop was the Rogues Shop. There were no customers. He found Carrie at her desk in the back room, buried beneath a stack of files.

"Good morning, Aidan." She peered around the mound of paperwork. "How can I help you?"

"Where can I find your boss?" he asked.

Carrie checked her desk calendar. "One of three places," she told him. "Today she's handing out Rogues souvenirs: sun visors and hats at Parks and Recreation, beach blankets and balls by the pier, and key chains and cup holders at the opening of Save-a-Buck, the new dollar store on Hibiscus Boulevard."

"Her first stop?" He hoped Carrie could be more specific and narrow down his search.

"Jillie 'floats' most days." Carrie used air quotes. "She has an agenda, but she'll take care of business in her own way and on her own time. She's not a clock watcher. She moves with her biorhythms. They serve her well."

Aidan ran his hand down his face, considered his options. He would find her, at some point during the day. He had people he could call at each location, including the pier. Someone would spot her.

The community center was closest to the construction site. He'd start there. He needed to stop by the trailer and check in with Mike and his girls, just to make certain there weren't any problems. While Mike could deal with most matters, Aidan remained a hands-on owner. He'd experienced theft and vandalism over the years. He kept his finger on the pulse of his company.

Next week he planned to take a few days and fly to Tampa to see how the cardiac unit was progressing. He wondered if he could talk Jill into traveling with him. He could make the trip both business and pleasure.

"Anything else, Aidan?" Carrie asked. Her smile was tentative.

"Have you heard from Rylan?" He was curious. He'd hoped to see his brother before Ry returned to Richmond.

"I haven't seen him since the softball after-party at the beach house," she told him. "You missed the celebration."

He'd had his own good time. Nothing could match his night with Jillian Mac. He wouldn't trade it for the world.

He had one last question for Carrie before he split. A personal one. "You and Rylan seem close," he hinted.

"We're friends, nothing more," she said easily. "Rylan's a good guy. We have a lot in common, but he's not my type." She grew thoughtful. "Ballplayers are a breed unto themselves. They're intense and competitive; winning is everything. Not every woman is cut out to date an athlete. I'm one of them."

Good to know, Aidan thought. "I'm off," he said, only to stop a moment later before a display of baseball caps. "Do you mind if I grab one on my way out?" He'd left his on the kitchen counter, in his hurry to leave the house. The sun was blinding. "Put it on my account."

"Take two," she called after him.

He did, one for him and one for Mike, although Mike would probably stick with his *Screw Driver* cap. Returning to the boardwalk, he stood within the shadow of an overhead awning and made a few phone calls. His contact at the pier hadn't seen Jill, but the receptionist at the community center said she was out by the pool at that very moment.

Aidan jogged to the parking lot, climbed into his SUV, and drove to the public park. He let up on the gas pedal two separate times when he realized he was speeding.

He felt disjointed. A part of him seemed to be missing. That part was Jillian Mac. She made him restless. He'd begun pacing on Sunday, and he hadn't stopped. He'd taken Sadie for so many walks, she finally went into hiding when he pulled out her leash. There hadn't been a movie or sport on television that held his attention. He'd clicked the remote through all seventy channels. Over and over again.

Jill was his primary focus.

He followed a long line of traffic toward the main recreational facility. Schools were closed for teacher planning and professional development. Students headed for the park.

The center supported both Barefoot William and Saunders Shores. Trace Saunders had donated the land and building as a wedding gift to his wife. The man was generous.

There was no immediate place to park. Aidan drove around the lot eight times, waiting for someone to leave. He located a corner space just as a woman with a carload of kids pulled up. The lady looked harried. He gave her the spot and found another. He ended up parking on the grass by the picnic area; from there he walked to the main entrance, where he went in through automatic doors.

Once inside, he took a moment to look around. The complex was a combination of sage walls, wide windows, and open spaces. There were signs posted throughout, directing people to the basketball, handball, and tennis courts, as well as the baseball diamonds and skate park.

Two indoor rooms were designated for arts and crafts. He peered into one and found a female counselor instructing five young girls on how to make individual and chain paper dolls. Construction paper, buttons, yarn, fabric, and glitter were strewn over a long table. The girls smiled, giggled, and squealed as they cut out and decorated their projects.

A room down the hallway provided training courses for babysitters, CPR, and youth fitness. He noted a list of upcoming events: summer theater tryouts, martial arts, dance, and music, along with several scheduled field trips.

The recreational center had something for everyone, he thought as he passed through the men's changing room and stepped out on the pool deck. Here were swimmers and sunbathers who preferred the pool to the beach. Swimming lessons were offered and organized games were conducted in the shallow end.

"No splashing allowed in the baby pool." Aidan recognized Jill's voice a second before he spotted her. She clapped her hands, then pointed to a young boy with spiky hair and a mischievous smile. "That means you, Kenny Novak. You're six, and the other children are two and three. Scoot."

Several of the mothers sitting on the cement edge with their kids nodded their appreciation when Kenny obeyed and hopped out. But not before he swung his arm and sprayed a tiny blonde in the face, making her cry. The girl's mom dried her daughter's eyes, and then cuddled her close.

"Drop by the snack room for a juice box, Janie," Jill offered the girl. "There's apple and fruit punch."

Aidan crossed his arms over his chest and leaned back against the chain-link fence that surrounded the three swimming pools, built for different age groups. Six lifeguards were on duty, yet Jillian Mac appeared in charge.

She was a chameleon. She had the ability to fit in easily and without question, while he stood out amid the bikinis and board shorts. He was overdressed. He rolled up the sleeves of his blue shirt to his elbows. His work jeans were worn white at the seams. His steel-toed Timberlands stood out among all the bare feet. He'd have to be careful not to step on anyone's toes.

He stared at Jill, appreciating her as a woman. Her hair was damp, as if she'd taken a dip in the pool. A red Rogues visor shaded her eyes from the sun. Her navy nylon swimsuit clasped her body and showed off her curves. A white whistle was clipped to a coiled elastic cord at her wrist. A large canvas beach bag filled with Rogues souvenirs hung over her shoulder. It was apparently heavy. She leaned left as she walked around the base of the low diving board, heading toward the concession stand.

She greeted everyone as if they were family. She'd made it a point to learn people's names. Her smile was contagious. She accepted hugs from the small children and shook hands with their parents. She passed out ball club memorabilia. She made sure every person received something.

She was good at her job, Aidan thought. She built anticipation. Barefoot William would be in frenzy by the time spring training rolled around next year. He was a baseball fan, and was as excited as the next guy.

"No running, Chris," Jill called to a boy of eight or nine. "Jacob, you're dripping ice cream on the pool deck. There's no food allowed beyond the red line." Jacob backed up and finished off his cone in the proper area. Jill rewarded him with a sun visor.

"Hey, Jill," a male lifeguard shouted to her from across the pool. He pointed to the large gray clock shaped like a dolphin near the refreshment stand. It was eleven. "It's beach ball hour."

Jill gave him a thumbs-up.

Aidan watched as the guard crossed toward an enormous bin of Rogues beach balls. He unhooked the fish netting that kept them contained, and dozens of balls in an assortment of sizes bounced onto the cement deck. Eagerly, the kids chose their favorites.

A skirmish broke out when two boys simultaneously reached for the largest one. They pulled, tugged, and exchanged fighting words. Jill stepped in. She blew her whistle, raised her voice. "Damian and Rocky, share the ball or I'll give it to someone else." The boys backed off, and took turns. "Much better," she praised them.

A leggy young girl shyly approached Jill. The girl's bathing suit was faded and had seen better seasons. "I'm Cassie Lane," Aidan overheard the girl say.

"I'm Jillian Mac," she replied.

The girl pointed to the solid silver bracelet on Jill's right wrist. "I like your jewelry."

Jill held up the bracelet so Cassie could have a better look. "It has the Rogues inscription on the inside," she said. "We sell them at our store on the boardwalk. We also have charms."

"I'm a fan," said Cassie. "I'll start saving my allowance so I can buy a bracelet." She scrunched her nose. "I watched the Rogues televised games last year. They lost a lot."

"They'll have a better season this year," Jill predicted. "We now have Rylan Cates. He's a superstar."

Aidan agreed with Jill. Ry would add dimension to the team. He was a born leader.

"I play softball," the girl went on to say. "Right field."

"I'm sure you're an awesome player," said Jill.

The girl looked down, wistfully said, "I'm growing into my legs."

Jill smiled. "Psycho McMillan used to play right for the Rogues. You need long legs to cover the outfield."

Cassie sighed. "I better go. There's no school, but my mom still has to work. She cleans houses. I need to ride my bike home and babysit."

"You have brothers and sisters?"

Cassie nodded. "Two younger brothers, who don't always listen to me."

"I have something for you to take to them," said Jill. She set down the canvas bag and dug deeply through the souvenirs until she found the perfect item. She straightened. "Here's a pack of baseball cards." She passed them to Cassie. "Those will keep them occupied for a while."

The girl giggled. "I'll have their full attention."

"I also have something for you," Aidan heard Jill say.

Cassie's eyes went wide. "You do?" She was surprised.

Jill slipped off her silver bracelet and handed it to the girl. "Here's a special souvenir, just for you. It goes with everything—jeans, shorts, even a dress."

Cassie beamed. "My swimsuit and pajamas, too." Her hand shook as she slid the bracelet on her wrist. She breathed deeply. "I'm never going to take it off."

"You're now a walking advertisement for the Rogues," Jill teased her.

"I like you, Jill," Cassie said.

"Back at you, sweetie."

Jill had yet to see him, Aidan realized. She'd been too busy. He now made his move. He pushed off the fence and met her at the shallow end of the adult pool near the handrail. Her back was to him. The water glistened, blindingly bright. He tugged down the bill on his baseball cap to protect his eyes.

"I like you, too," he said over her shoulder.

She turned toward him. Cocoa butter and chlorine

scented her skin. Her lips flirted with a pale pink lip balm. She drew in a breath, and he forced his eyes off her chest. Firm breasts beneath thin nylon made a man's fingers itch. His hands were already prickly.

"I like your baseball cap."

No hint of commitment, but at least there was something about him she liked. "I'm promoting the Rogues."

"You look good doing it." She shook the canvas bag, went on to ask, "Can I interest you in a key chain? How about a cup holder for your SUV?"

He lowered his voice. "I want you."

Had she blushed? Or were her cheeks slightly sunburned? "You've had me," she whispered back.

"You're more than a one-night stand."

Her sigh was weighted. "We were good while we lasted."

Lasted? They hadn't gotten started. "Are you breaking up with me?" He was afraid of her answer.

"We were never really a couple."

The lady confused the hell out of him. He was feeling frustrated. "We need to talk," he stated.

"I'm working."

"You're floating."

"You've seen Carrie."

"She gave me your agenda."

"My best friend ratted me out."

They stood so close they could've touched, yet Aidan kept his distance. He'd never felt more insecure around a woman. After a heartfelt second her gaze softened. She was into him, he was sure of it. That was all he needed. He refused to give up on her.

He shifted his stance; slipped his hands in his pockets. He stared down on Jill. She looked up at him.

"You're here to stay, aren't you?" she asked.

"I've got all day."

She gave in. "There are picnic tables around the side of the building. It's too early for lunch. We'll have privacy."

"After you." He had no problem following her. He didn't want her slipping away from him.

She squared her shoulders, eased around him. She left the canvas bag at the refreshment stand for safekeeping. He appreciated her backside as she walked stiffly before him. Her slender shoulders were squared. Her spine was symmetrical. She had a small, bite-able ass. Her legs were toned. Her navy toenail polish had a metallic sheen. The lady was hot. He wanted her in his life. Convincing her was another matter entirely.

They rounded the corner of the building. There was no one in sight. Alone was good. He took advantage. Catching her by the arm, he gently pressed her against the cement wall. He covered her with his body, and stole a kiss.

Her lips parted in surprise, and he slipped her his tongue. Her body remained stiff, but she didn't fight him. He worked his leg between her thighs. Skin against denim. His hands cupped her bottom; he tucked her close. He wanted her aware of how much she affected him.

He was hard.

Her body slowly softened against his.

For a heartbeat of seconds they were one.

He lifted his head then, his breathing heavy. "I don't know what's going on in that pretty head of yours," he said. "I thought we'd connected on Saturday, but apparently I was wrong."

"Not completely wrong," her voice cracked.

"I want to see you again," he was honest. "Should you feel the same way, you know where to find me."

Her silence spoke for her.

He'd said what he needed to say. That was that. He wanted more than a one-sided relationship. He'd made his move; it was up to her now. He desperately hoped she would come to him. Only time would tell.

He released her as quickly as he'd kissed her.

He took his leave.

Twelve

Carrie Waters wondered when Rylan Cates would be leaving the penthouse. She was one nervous woman. She feared Mike Burke would arrive home and find her with the other man. He wouldn't be happy. She'd broken one of their house policies. She'd allowed a visitor into their private space. She'd set the rules, and Mike would definitely call her on it.

It wasn't her fault, not totally anyway. Rylan had asked Aidan where she lived so he could stop by before he left town tomorrow. He'd shown up unannounced. Carrie had answered the door, expecting to see Mike, who still knocked on occasion. A precaution in case Jillie Mac came over. Instead of Mike, there stood Ry in a T-shirt, board shorts, and flip-flops. His hair was shaggy and he hadn't shaved. He looked like a beach bum.

She'd last visited with Rylan at Shaye's beach house. She'd noted that the hostility between him and Mike had eased somewhat. Still, they'd kept their distance and hadn't actually spoken. Apparently silence worked for them.

Mike had given her the evil eye whenever she'd talked to Rylan. She had no idea what prompted his dislike, though she had every intention of finding out, sooner rather than later.

It was nine p.m., and Rylan sat comfortably on her

sofa, his feet propped on the ottoman. He looked cool and collected, and far too comfortable. He was in no hurry to leave.

Carrie perched on the edge of a leather chair. She sighed heavily. She'd spent a long day at the Rogues Shop, moving boxes and baseball memorabilia. She'd aggravated her shoulder further. She hadn't fully recovered from Saturday's softball game. All she wanted was to sink into her Jacuzzi. Warm swirling water and almond bubble bath would soothe her soreness. She anticipated a good long soak. Once Rylan left.

She had yet to offer him a sandwich or something to drink. She should be polite. Ry was her friend. "I have cold cuts and soda, if you'd like a snack," she said.

He stretched his arms along the back of the couch. Sank deeper into the cushions. "Thanks, but no," he said. "I need to take off shortly."

Now would be good, she thought, but didn't push him. She nearly fell off her chair when he speculated, "Tell me about your relationship with Mike Burke."

Her breath caught, and she covered with, "I don't know what you mean. I barely know him."

He narrowed his gaze on her. "There's more, and we both know it."

Her heart skipped. "Why would you say that?"

"I watched the two of you at Shaye's," he told her. "You tried hard to avoid each other, which made it obvious to me."

"Mike has more attitude than I can handle, so I keep my distance." She didn't want to give too much away.

"He's damn stubborn," Ry agreed.

"And sarcastic." She knew this to be true.

"He's only sarcastic with people he truly cares about," Rylan told her.

He must be crazy about her, Carrie thought, which

was hard to believe. The man had been on her case from the moment she'd mentioned liking devil's food cupcakes. He was sharp and short. Often rude. He still called her Vanilla.

"Staying out of someone's way usually means there's more going on than meets the eye." Ry wouldn't let it go.

"What you see is what you get with us," she stated. "We're worlds apart. Besides," she added, "you also avoided Mike at Shaye's."

Ry shifted on the sofa, sitting straighter now. His jaw worked, and he seemed to want to tell her something, but was hesitant to do so. Minutes passed before he said, "Mike and I have a history."

They did? That took her by surprise. She hadn't known. The slamming of the front door further shocked her. It shook on its hinges. Mike Burke now stood in the entryway, mad as hell. He fisted his hands. He appeared ready to punch something or someone.

"You have no business discussing me with Carrie, not now, not ever." Mike's gaze was shuttered, his expression dark, as he walked toward them. "What the hell are you doing here?" he growled at Rylan.

"I could ask the same of you," said Ry.

"I stopped by to check on Carrie," Mike said. "To see how she was recovering."

Ry wasn't fooled. "You entered without knocking," he said. "Do you have a key?"

"The door was ajar."

Carrie was certain she'd locked it, but she wasn't going to argue with him, not in front of Rylan. Ry was too suspicious of their relationship as it was.

She swallowed hard. When had Mike arrived? She and Ry had been so engrossed in conversation, he'd snuck in unnoticed. Now he was a force to be reckoned with.

Rylan pushed off the couch and approached Mike. They were of comparable height, although Mike was thicker across the chest. Mike's badass attitude made him appear even larger. Both could hold their own in a confrontation. Mike with muscle, Rylan with logic.

Carrie wasn't certain what to do or what to say. She instinctively moved to stand between them, which made them both blink.

Mike's lip curled. "What are you doing?" he asked her.

"There'll be no arguing or fighting in my penthouse," she said firmly.

"Another new rule?" Again from Mike.

"To be added to the old list."

"I wasn't aware of your rules," said Rylan.

"You wouldn't be," Mike said harshly. "You don't live—"

Live here. Carrie silently finished his sentence.

Mike ran one hand down his face, angry with himself for giving their living arrangements away.

One corner of Ry's mouth curved; he appeared amused. He had the balls to wink at Carrie. "Definitely nothing between you," he said. He looked at Mike over the top of her head. "Sorry for bringing up our past."

Mike didn't accept his apology. "You've also discussed me with Risk Kincaid."

"You're the perfect candidate."

"That's yet to be seen."

Carrie was confused. She looked from one man to the other, but neither offered an explanation. Frustrating men.

Mike nodded toward the door. "You were just leaving?" he asked Rylan.

Ry took the hint. "I've overstayed."

"You damn sure have."

Mike stiffened when Rylan gave Carrie a hug. The embrace went beyond casual, leaning toward intimate.

Mike cleared his throat, a threatening sound.

Ry let her go. "Later, babe," he said to her.

He and Mike exchanged a look that was far from pleasant. However there was less heat in their eyes than when Mike had first arrived. Ry left and Carrie sighed. She hadn't realized she'd been holding her breath. Their confrontation had exhausted her.

She poked Mike in the chest with her finger. "Way to blow our cover," she accused him.

"Rylan won't tell anyone."

"How can you be sure?"

"He owes me," he said, but didn't elaborate.

Carrie let it go, for now. She'd pry later. She crossed to the kitchen, removed the house rules she'd posted on the front of the refrigerator. She located an ink pen, then said, "I'm adding *no eavesdropping* to our list."

"I wasn't eavesdropping," he defended. "I happened to walk in on your conversation."

"You didn't immediately make yourself known."

"Nothing important was said until Rylan mentioned my name," he pointed out. "You broke our agreement. What happened to *no visitors*?"

"Aidan gave Ry my address."

"There's a peephole," he reminded her. "You didn't have to answer the door."

"Rylan's my friend," she said.

"Buddies don't hug as long as he hung on to you."

Carrie liked the fact he'd noticed.

"Since you broke a rule, I can break one, too."

"I didn't do it on purpose."

"Doesn't matter," he stated. "I want Jacuzzi time."

She frowned. "I was headed to the tub when Rylan arrived. I planned to be in and out by the time you got home."

"Your shoulder still hurts?" He looked concerned.

"Feels tight," she admitted.

"I could loosen you up, if we got in together."

Loosen you up sounded sexual. Her heart quickened.

"There's no need to feel uncomfortable."

Easy for him to say. He was secure in his skin; she was not. She hesitated. "I'm not certain."

"I'm sure for both of us."

He took her by the hand and led her down the hallway. Her bedroom door was cracked and he pushed it open with his work boot. Her breathing was uneven by the time they reached her bath. She was nearly hyperventilating.

He rested his hands on her shoulders, looked at her closely. "You sound like you're already having sex," he said. "Easy does it, Vanilla. You're way ahead of me."

She dipped her head, felt her cheeks heat.

He tipped up her chin with two fingers and said, "Don't be embarrassed. I like you excited."

"It's panic," she corrected him. "I don't want you to see me naked."

"You're scaring me a little. What are you hiding?" he asked. "Three breasts, a penis?"

A smile tipped the corners of her mouth. "Nothing like that," she assured him. She had weight issues. Pounds packed on faster than she could lose them. She had a stomach. Her thighs were thick. She wore a full support bra and control-top panties.

"You can always keep on your underwear," he said.

She appreciated his suggestion. "Will you?" she asked. She'd feel a whole lot better if he did.

His smile was wicked. "What do you think?"

He released her hand and entered the bath. There, he adjusted the dials on the platinum acrylic Jacuzzi tub. It quickly filled with hot, steamy water.

Carrie squeezed a significant amount of almond bath

gel beneath the dual faucets. Bubbles rose on the surface. She chose a soft bath mitt from the silver-wood cabinetry. She only had one mitt. They would have to share.

The two-seater tub was soon full. Mike turned off the water. He then began to undress. Carrie couldn't move a muscle. Off came his shirt, then his boots and thick, white socks. He stood before her. A man so cut he could have been sculpted. Broad chest, buff abs. He was pure female catnip.

"Need help getting out of your clothes?" he asked.

Her throat worked, but she couldn't manage a word. He took the initiative. Goose bumps scattered over her skin before he even touched her. She shivered when he rested his hands on her hips.

"Are you afraid of me?" he wanted to know.

She swallowed hard. "Not . . . exactly."

"Then what exactly?" he pressed. "You're pale, stiff, and nervous. I'll leave if you really want to bathe alone. I thought we could relax, talk, share our day," he said simply. "I'm not going to make a move on you. I won't push you into something you'd regret."

"Promise," she said so softly she wasn't sure she'd even spoken.

"We'll be seated across from each other. You'll stay on your side and I'll stay on mine. Agreed?"

Very little room separated them in Carrie's eyes. They'd be sitting incredibly close. She was attracted to Mike. Her sigh gave him the go-ahead.

His expression was unreadable as he unbuttoned her white blouse and slipped it off her shoulders. He then eased down her elastic waist slacks. She wore a lot of black, in hopes of looking thinner.

She held her breath, certain he would make a snide remark. Surprisingly, he did not. His eyes darkened. "You have a great body," he told her.

"I'm overweight."

"Don't put yourself down. Stick women don't have the same appeal as a woman with curves," he said. "A man likes to feel a woman beneath him, and not be afraid he'll break her bones."

She was relieved. Holding on to the handrail, she took the wide marble steps up to the Jacuzzi. It was a short stretch over the edge. Mike assisted her. She managed to settle on one of the benches without making a giant splash. She slid down into the water. The bubbles covered her breasts.

He unsnapped his jeans, drew down the zipper. The slight rustle of denim, followed by the smooth slide of his silk boxers, made her stomach flutter.

"I'm coming in," he warned her, in case she wanted to avert her gaze.

She chose not to. He climbed over the side, and she took him in, all of him. Raw, ripped, and masculine came to mind. She wanted to touch him. She fisted her hands under the water instead.

He landed on the bench with barely a ripple. His gaze was hooded by his ink-dark lashes as he stretched his arms along the edge of the tub and smiled lazily at her. Here they sat, enjoying the same warmth and comfort. As long as he didn't move, she had no problem sharing the Jacuzzi.

Steam licked her lips and the bubbles embraced her. She released a soft sigh. All tension and strain slowly left her body. This was the ideal way to end her day. She closed her eyes and relaxed to the fullest, up until the moment Mike turned on the jets. All twenty-one of them. She experienced an invigorating hydrotherapeutic jolt.

Her eyes widened when one of the high-powered

nozzles shot her left buttock. "Goosed," she said, scooting over.

Mike grinned. "Goosed now, gratified later."

She shook her head. "Not a chance."

"It's fun on occasion to let yourself go."

"I'm sure you've experienced lots of good times."

"Definitely my fair share," he admitted. "How about you?"

Not that many, actually. She'd never made love in a Jacuzzi tub. "A few," she hedged.

He stretched out his legs. The ball of his foot grazed the inside of her calf, working its way up toward her knee. He distracted her. She was glad she'd shaved her legs that morning.

"How's your shoulder feeling?" he asked.

"Better." But not great.

"The pulsating jets won't penetrate your deep tissue." He flexed his fingers. "I can give you a massage."

She wasn't sure that was such a good idea. She might melt if he touched her.

"Give me one minute," he said.

What could happen in sixty seconds?

She was about to find out. "Make it quick."

"There's nothing quick about me, babe."

He gently cuffed her wrist, helped her to turn around. The bottom of the tub was slippery. She soon reclined against his body. Her shoulders rested on his chest; her bottom was cradled on his groin. She couldn't help but notice that he was hard. He poked her.

He brushed his stubbled jaw against her cheek, said, "Lean forward."

He went to work on her shoulder. The man had magic thumbs. He kneaded deeply. The knot soon loosened. Her pain eased. His increasing pressure made her moan.

He rubbed her arms. Her eyes closed. Her body floated, drifted. She felt as light as the bubbles.

How long had he massaged her? She'd lost track of time. She blinked back to reality. She found her breasts were now bare. He'd made her bra disappear. He palmed the delicate undersides while his thumbs grazed her nipples. He stroked them to points. Her chest tingled. She forgot to breathe.

"My shoulder's fine now," she somehow managed.

"Let me relax you fully."

Tempting, but not sensible. Touching would change their whole dynamic. She bit down on her bottom lip; debated too long for his liking. He decided for her. He ran his hands down her sides to her waist. He made good use of his thumbs once again. Hooking them into the elastic on her panties, he eased them off. She was buoyant, her knees were bent, and the control tops soon cleared her feet.

He clasped her hip bones, shifted their positions. He lifted her off his lap, and set her by his side. Reaching around her, he tilted her hips forward. She gasped when a spiraling jet of water sprayed between her thighs. Her arms flayed.

He drew her arms against her sides when she sought to escape. He calmed her. He nuzzled her neck. His teeth grazed her shoulder. He bit the smooth flat of her back. He reset the panel that controlled the jets. "Go with the flow." His voice was deep and sinful.

The water pulsed, streamed, surged. Sensation and pleasure. The warm whirl of the water seduced her belly. Her hips twisted. Mike's hand settled on her pubic bone; he touched her intimately. Sweat and steam filmed her brow. Her breathing rasped. Her orgasm soon shook her. She collapsed against him.

For a timeless moment, she was carried outside of herself, loose and languid. Mike had reset the jets to a low pulse. The sound of the bubbles and the gentle slosh of water against the sides of the tub lulled her.

She rested her head against his shoulder, sighed. "Don't let me drown."

"I'll be your water wings."

They sat for what could've been five minutes or as long as an hour. Mike Burke didn't care. He eased her back onto his lap and crossed his arms beneath her breasts. He was comfortable, and in no hurry to leave the tub.

Flushed and feminine, Carrie glanced at him over her shoulder. She reached back and burst the bubbles on his chin, then several more at the base of his throat. He brushed them off her eyebrows, traced her cheek with his fingertip.

He unplugged the tub. They both stood. As the water sank away, he reached for the shower massager and began washing the almond suds off her body. The water fanned as he swept her neck and breasts and belly. He rinsed her legs and inner thighs. Her lips parted and her eyes glazed when he switched the spray to pulse and the water began to thrust in forceful bursts. He aroused her once again, took her to the edge, but didn't take her over.

Moving the spray away from her, he rinsed himself off, too. Wrapping her in a heated bath towel from a nearby rack, he drew her from the Jacuzzi tub and dried them both off. He liked touching her. He took his time, lingering over her breasts and at the juncture of her thighs.

He rested his forehead against hers. Cautious of her braces, he dropped a soft kiss on her lips and savored her taste: moist and sweet with a hint of almond. He nipped the fullness of her bottom lip; she flicked her tongue against his upper. He wanted to deepen their kiss but chose to do so in bed. Where they could stretch out and enjoy each other.

"Pratesi?" he asked.

"Your room or mine?" There was no hesitation on her part.

He was relieved. "I want you in my bed."

He shifted then, stepped on his discarded T-shirt, and smiled. "We've both broken another house rule," he said. "We're leaving the bathroom a mess. There are clothes and towels everywhere."

"We don't always have to be neat. We'll clean up in the morning."

He could live with that. Naked, his body pulsing, he swept her off her feet and carried her to his room. She protested that she was too heavy, but he disagreed with her. He wanted her and, in his mind, she weighed less than air.

"Another rule bites the dust," he told her. "We're walking around naked."

"I'm throwing away the list tomorrow."

"Best idea I've heard all day," he agreed.

Easing her onto the black silk sheets, he then sank down beside her. She was on her back, he was on his side. His bedroom curtains were drawn back, and his room was cast in moonlight. Slivers of silver played across his chest and hip and also tipped her nipples.

He stared down on her. "You're good with us?" he asked. He wanted her to be perfectly sure.

She turned onto her side and faced him fully. "I'm here, aren't I?"

"That you are, Carrie." His release of breath was rough. Telling. He had expected her to change her mind. She seemed pleased he'd called her by her real name.

He leaned closer and their bodies touched.

They were now breast to chest.

Thigh to thigh.

Sex to sex.

He could've entered her with a slight shift of his hips. But he didn't. She wasn't ready for him. He hadn't been with a woman since he'd arrived in Barefoot William. He preferred experienced women; those who knew the score.

He realized in that moment he'd been waiting all his life for sweet, sensitive Carrie. He'd wanted her since their first meeting at the Saunders's barbeque. His feelings toward her had been immediate.

She'd scared the hell out of him. His sarcasm had been a defense mechanism. He didn't date nice girls. He'd tried to push her away, yet she had stuck by him. He planned to stick by her now, for as long as she'd have him.

A deep need drew him back to her mouth. He ran his tongue over her braces, teasing and testing. He kissed her gently, yet deeply. She responded with care.

Dipping lower, he kissed her throat, the point of both shoulders. Raw pleasure pushed him down her body. His dark hair whispered across her pale naked breasts like the touch of a shadow. His cheek rested just below, as he placed openmouthed kisses across her belly, her hips, slowly reaching the center of her heat and all sensation.

Her hips came off the bed, and he cupped her ass. Tonight was all about Carrie. He teased and caressed her with a slow intimacy that threatened his sanity. Feeling the tightness in her body, the throbbing between her legs, he knew it was time to protect them both. He rose, went for a condom. He found the box in the medicine cabinet in his bathroom. He grabbed several packets and returned to their bed.

"Let me put one on you," Carrie said.

He consented. She took her sweet time. She liked

touching him. And he liked being touched. She skimmed her fingers over his abs and thighs before reaching his sex. Her hands shook slightly as she opened the foil packet and fitted it over his erection.

Her touch alone had Mike fighting for control. The moment had arrived when the air between them was saturated with longing and a need for release. He wanted to take her swift and fierce. That would come later.

Lying back down, they faced each other again. Tongue to tongue, hip to hip, their bodies came together. The blend of cool silk sheets and hot-bodied woman nearly undid him. She curved her leg over his hip, and he strained as he took her slowly. She was tight. Incredibly tight. He didn't want to hurt her. He gave her a moment to receive him. Once she had, time had no meaning and reality was lost as skin moved over skin.

She took what he was feeling and made it her own. They became one motion, all flow and thrust, driven by sharp breaths, arching backs and undulating hips.

They breathed in frantic rhythm, the pounding of her heart resounding in his soul. The rise of intense pleasure pushed them to release.

They both stiffened. Both moaned. Both shuddered.

Both took a long time to recover.

Afterward, he tucked her so tightly against his body, she became an imprint on his skin. He held her while she returned to reality. Her hair was wild and she was slow to focus. When she was finally able to look him in the eye, he saw her satisfaction and contentment.

He removed his condom, tossed it in the small trash can by his bed. "Stay the night with me?" he asked.

"I'm not going anywhere." She snuggled so near, he felt her under his skin. In his heart. His dick was definitely fond of her, too.

He cared about her enough to share his past. It seemed

only fair, since he planned to keep her in his life indefinitely. That was, if she chose to stay.

He rested his forehead against her own, breathed in her almond-scented hair. He stroked her shoulder, her back, then went on to say, "Rylan Cates was my best friend in college. We attended on baseball scholarships." He hadn't opened up to anyone about his past, and the words felt rusty.

She didn't pry as he gathered his thoughts. Minutes passed before he was able to continue. He told her everything; he held nothing back. He spoke of the poker game and the bar fight. His injury. He recalled his pain and disappointment. His depression. How Aidan had offered him a job that changed his life.

His boss was as close as a brother. Aidan withstood Mike's sarcasm. He'd never questioned Mike's isolation, or the fact he lived at the construction trailer, where he suffered in silence.

"I felt whiplash," he slowly confessed. "I thought I was going to do something, to be someone, only to lose my identity."

"You saved Rylan's life."

"I would do it again in a heartbeat," he realized. With those words, all his frustration and anger left him. A sense of relief settled about his heart. His chest warmed. Through it all, Carrie squeezed him tightly, as if she were trying to infuse her strength into him. She was sympathetic. Her eyes misted in understanding. "Nothing happens by accident," she whispered against his neck. "Life is a journey, our destinations aren't guaranteed. It's how we adjust, adapt, and accept change that makes us resilient. You were able to bounce back."

Her support overwhelmed him. He no longer felt defeated. No longer felt alone. "There's one more thing," he added. He then mentioned his conversation with Risk

Kincaid. "I'm headed to Richmond on Friday for my first interview."

She eased back, met his gaze. She placed her palm on the center of his chest. She waited a moment before saying, "Your heart's not racing. Aren't you excited?"

"I've had my heart-pounding moments," he admitted. "I've thought of nothing but the Rogues since Saturday. Then—"

"Thoughts of Aidan crept in." She read him well. "You realized how much he's done for you. You're loyal and are having second thoughts."

"Aidan has been supportive of the move," he said. "He had his girls schedule my flight. He paid for my first class ticket. The ladies located a hotel near the stadium. They booked a suite. Risk will send a car for me."

"What if you're offered the assistant pitching-coach position?" she asked.

"I face a major decision." One that would change his life once again. He didn't want to think about anything but Carrie tonight. She was his priority. He eased her onto her back and covered her with his body. They made love a second time. His box of condoms got a workout.

The end of the week came far too soon. Carrie Waters faced the weekend alone. She didn't mind. Up until Mike, her evenings had been spent before the TV with chips and dip or a bowl of peppermint ice cream. Tonight, she ate romaine salad. She would begin her exercise routine in the morning. The apartment complex had a gym, but she wasn't ready to sweat in front of a lot of people. She planned to take a walk. The weather was beautiful.

Mike had inspired her transformation. The man was fit. She liked his muscles. He'd told her several times he found her beautiful. But this was personal. She'd feel better about herself if she dropped a few pounds.

The light rap on her front door surprised her. Mike was in Richmond; he'd left that morning. He'd promised to text her, and had been true to his word. He'd kept her updated on his flight, noting the delay in Atlanta. Once he'd landed, he'd sent her pictures of his hotel room. It was luxurious. She felt as if she were right there with him.

She set aside her dinner, and answered the door. Jillie Mac stood in the hallway. "Can I come in?" she asked, her voice sounding small. She wore a tie-dye *Under the Boardwalk* tank top, blue jeans, and beaded sandals. There were dark circles under her eyes and hollowness to her cheeks.

Carrie hadn't seen her for several days. Jill had called the office each morning, and given Carrie her general whereabouts for the day. She'd wanted to introduce herself to the community. She'd walked the halls of the local government building, then gone store to store, passing out information on upcoming ticket prices.

Carrie took her by the arm and led her inside. Something was wrong with her friend. She hoped Jill would open up to her. "Join me for dinner?" she offered.

"I'm not very hungry."

"There's always room for lettuce."

"Creamy French dressing?"

That was Mike's favorite, too. "Recently purchased, in hopes you'd stop by." She motioned Jill toward the living room. "Make yourself comfortable. I'll fix you a plate."

It didn't take long for Carrie to put together the salad. She made it with lettuce, cherry tomatoes, chopped mushrooms, and a sprinkle of croutons. Jill liked a lot of salad dressing, and that's what she got.

Carrie found her friend curled up at one end of the couch. This wasn't the Jill that Carrie knew. She'd lost her spirit. She appeared tired and very sad.

Carrie set the salad on the coffee table. She went back to the kitchen for a glass of plum iced tea, a napkin, and silverware. She returned, and noticed Jill hadn't moved; hadn't started eating.

Things were going well at the Rogues Shop, so she figured Jill was having man problems. Aidan Cates came to mind. Carrie was aware they had dated. Jill hadn't spoken of him all week. That wasn't a good sign.

She started the conversation by asking, "Did you deliver our appreciation gifts to the softball players?"

Jill had wanted to extend a special thank-you to those who had participated. She'd purchased crystal softballs and had them inscribed with Barefoot Rogue and the inaugural date. Carrie had placed her ball on the designer shelving in the penthouse.

"I still need to hand out gifts to Mike, Agnes, and Aidan," Jill said. "I thought you might do that for me on Monday."

"No construction trailer for you?" Carrie guessed.

Jill shook her head. "I'd rather not."

"Why not?" from Carrie.

Jill reached for her salad. She took several bites, but that didn't distract Carrie. "Is it because of Aidan?" she asked.

Jill swallowed hard. "He likes me."

"That's a definite reason to avoid the man."

"No need to be sarcastic."

"No need to be stupid."

Jill blinked. "You've never called me stupid."

"You haven't been until now." Carrie eased up a little. "What's the problem, Jillie Mac? I know you've got feelings for him."

"I've never done well in relationships."

"There's always a first time." She thought of Mike Burke, and how different he was now from when she'd first met him.

"I'm not good with commitment."

"It gets easier with the right person."

"I just don't know," she said with a sigh.

"Aidan's a strong, honorable man," Carrie said. "He's kind and dependable. You should give him a chance."

"I'm afraid."

"Afraid of Aidan or afraid of you?"

"Me," Jill admitted. "Aidan is special. I don't want to screw things up with him."

"Apparently you already have. You look miserable."

"I am miserable."

"Fix it," Carrie gently advised. "You've had men come and go in your life. Make room for Aidan to stay."

Jill went back to eating her salad. Her thoughts were her own. Carrie reached for the television remote and turned on the set. *SportsCenter* announced the evening baseball game. The Richmond Rogues were playing the St. Louis Colonels, at home.

"What a great start to the season," said Carrie as the players were introduced and the National Anthem was sung by a local recording artist. "We need popcorn."

She returned her own salad plate to the kitchen and searched the cupboards for a box of Orville Redenbacher Kettle Corn. Finding it, she opened a bag and put it in the microwave. There was something soothing about the popping of the kernels. She made two bags, emptied them both into a big plastic bowl.

Jill had moved to the center cushion for a direct view of the TV. She'd angled the coffee table left, so she could pull up the ottoman. Her gaze was now on Carrie, and not on the game. Her expression was curious, puzzled, and slightly amused.

She held up a single white sock along with one Nike tennis shoe. "I found these under the table. Not your size," she said. "You wear a seven, these are twelve."

She dangled a pair of men's Armani boxers by the waistband. Her lips pursed. "Who do I know who likes silk?" she asked.

Oh, crap! Carrie was so startled by the question, she tripped over her own feet. She spilled the popcorn. She dropped down on her hands and knees and quickly cleaned up her mess. "Where did you find those?" Her voice squeaked.

"The boxers were wedged between the couch cushions." She set the underwear aside.

Mike's clothes. She hadn't bothered to pick up after him. The evidence was damning. Could she avoid the question? she wondered. "Back to the microwave," she tried.

"Not so fast." Jill stopped her. "How long have you been seeing Mike Burke?" she wanted to know.

"How do you know it's Mike?"

She pointed to an empty can of Guinness on a side table, then produced a folded sheet of paper. "Mike's favorite beer," she noted. "I also found his travel itinerary."

"Snooping, were you?" She couldn't take offense. Jill was her best friend.

"Everything was out in the open," Jill told her. "You weren't expecting me to stop by. Otherwise you would've cleaned up. The place would've been spotless. There'd be no signs of your man."

That was true. Carrie had yet to recycle the can of beer. She could still picture Mike sitting and enjoying the Guinness after a long day at the construction site. She'd sat beside him; his arm had been around her. It had been a very cozy, comfortable night.

"How long have you been together?" asked Jill. "How serious are you?"

"We like each other," Carrie said as she headed to the kitchen to pop another batch of popcorn. More careful this time, she returned to the sofa. She positioned the bowl between them, then took a few bites before adding, "I have no idea where our relationship is headed, but I like what we have now. We enjoy each other's company, especially in the Jacuzzi." She felt her cheeks heat. "Those jets can blast."

"I'm sure they do." Jill started to laugh, and couldn't stop. She nearly fell off the sofa. It was a release for her, Carrie realized. She laughed until the moment she buried her face in her hands and cried.

Carrie had never seen her friend so sad. Jill had always been the strong one. Yet at that moment, she shattered. Jill was visibly vulnerable. Broken. Carrie set the bowl of popcorn on the ottoman and hugged her.

Hugged her until her tears dried, and she sighed heavily. "I need Kleenex," Jill said.

Carrie stood, hurried down the hallway to her bedroom, and brought back a box. It was half full. She patted Jill on the back as she would a child. Then brushed her hair behind her ears.

Jill blew her nose loudly. "I'm sorry," she said. "It's been a long week. I've worked a lot of hours, gotten little sleep. And"—her breath caught—"I miss Aidan."

"I'm sure he's missed you, too."

Jill wiped her eyes. "I always screw up serious relationships."

"Because you weren't with the right man," offered Carrie. "Telling someone you like them shouldn't send them running."

Jill reached for another Kleenex. "I'm the one running now."

"Slow down, Jillie Mac. Aidan's a decent guy."

"I should probably talk to him."

Carrie nodded. "Probably should."

"What's happened to us?" Jill asked. "We came to Barefoot William to promote spring training—"

"And were fortunate to find two men who care about us," Carrie finished for her.

Jill lifted an eyebrow. "You're sure about Mike?"

"Positive." She grinned then. "He no longer calls me Vanilla."

"A very good sign," Jill agreed.

Carrie then shared Mike's history with Rylan, and how Ry had recommended Mike for the assistant pitching coach position. That was the reason Mike wasn't at the penthouse. He was in Richmond for the weekend, being wined and dined and interviewed.

"He's got a big decision ahead of him," Carrie stated. "Will he stay in construction or head to the major leagues?"

"Whatever he decides, I wish him well."

Carrie touched Jill's shoulder. "Are you going to be okay?" she asked.

"I'm better now," Jill told her.

"Let's watch the game then," said Carrie. She turned up the volume. "It's the Rogues' season opener. I hope they kick St. Louis's ass."

The game was action-packed. No team led for more than an inning. Bottom of the ninth, and the score was tied. Richmond faced two outs. No one was on base. The game could go into overtime.

Rylan Cates was on deck. The stadium rocked. Fans were on their feet, cheering, stomping, pointing foam fingers toward the sky. They wanted a home run.

"Major pressure," said Jill. "Rylan needs to prove himself."

Carrie watched as he went full count, three balls and two strikes. She could barely breathe.

"Now!" both she and Jill shouted as a fastball crossed the plate.

Rylan didn't hesitate. He hammered the ball over the center field fence. Long and gone. He ran the bases, came home. The final score was Rogues 9; Colonels 8.

Excitement broke on the field and in the stands. The Rogues were superstitious. Winning the home opener was a good omen. The season was theirs.

The women watched the interviews that followed. The press caught Rylan on his way back to the locker room. He was hot and sweaty but stopped for reporters and answered their questions. He gave credit to team effort and downplayed his final home run.

"He's good looking and gracious," said Jill. "The Rogues have a new hero."

Carrie grinned. "Surfer dude can definitely play ball."

Jill pushed off the sofa, said, "I'm calling it a night. Thanks for everything, Carrie."

"What are friends for?"

"We've been through a lot, haven't we?" asked Jill.

"Our best days are ahead of us, I'm sure of it," Carrie said as she walked Jill to the door.

They exchanged a sisterly hug before Jill left. Carrie held her breath. The next person to walk through the door would be Mike Burke. She couldn't wait to see him.

Mike appeared Monday evening, just in time for dinner. He'd texted Carrie when his plane landed. He wanted to meet with Aidan before he came home. She was on pins and needles, but she understood his need to square things with his boss. He'd take care of business, and then she'd give him pleasure.

Two hours later, he didn't knock, merely walked in.

She met him in the hallway. He picked her up, swung her around. Set her down gently. "I'm home," he said simply.

She flashed her braces. "I'm so glad."

"I have a lot to share with you."

"Dinner or discussion first?"

"Let's talk."

She went to the kitchen and turned down the oven on her hamburger casserole. She'd discovered Mike liked simple but hardy food. She could cook the basics.

She joined him on the couch, sitting close. He curved his arm about her shoulders. He then kissed her with the passion of a man who'd missed his woman. Carrie liked being missed.

It took him a while to say, "Traveling to Richmond was the second best experience of my life. You were my first best," he wanted her to know. She was pleased by that fact.

"The front office treated me like a first-round draft pick. It was a busy weekend with the season opener. I met and talked to everyone involved with the team. I watched the game from the owner's box. I was impressed."

"Where do things stand?" Carrie asked, suddenly anxious.

"I had expected to fly back for further talks, but Risk Kincaid indicated on Sunday that the job was mine if I wanted it."

Carrie's throat swelled with emotion. "Congratulations." Tears filled her eyes. Mike was about to enter major league baseball. She was happy for him.

He rolled his hip, reached into the pocket of his navy dress slacks, and removed two business cards. He held up the first for her to see. She read the script on the cream-colored velum: *Risk Kincaid, Richmond Rogues Organiza-*

tion, Managing General Partner/Co-chairman. Mike went on to rip the card in half.

Carrie's jaw dropped. She felt a moment of panic. "What are you doing and why?"

"Easy, babe," he said, calming her. He fingered the second card, kept it just out of her reach. He built the suspense. "This is where I'm meant to be." He passed the white business card to her.

She held his decision in her hands. Carrie's eyes blurred once again when she read the bold block letters: CATES AND BURKE GENERAL CONTRACTORS. "You're sure?" Her voice was watery.

"I believe in us as much as I believe in my future in construction," he said with conviction. "Aidan had planned to make me partner after the softball game. Risk offered me a position with the Rogues before Aidan could pitch our partnership. Aidan didn't stand in my way. He pushed me to go to Richmond; to be a part of the team."

Mike grew thoughtful. "Rylan and I are square now. He took me out to dinner Friday night. We talked. I can't relive my past, but I can move forward."

He couldn't help but smile at her. "I offered to pay Aidan rent for staying here. He declined. He's giving us the penthouse for a wedding present."

Carrie had a hard time taking it all in. "You want to marry me?" she asked.

"The sooner the better," he said. "I wasted much of my life wishing for something I could never have. Now what I want most is you. Celebrate forever with me, Carrie Waters."

His words touched her heart. "I want to spend my life with you," she said. "You, me, and the jets in the Jacuzzi."

Mike threw back his head and laughed deeply. He rose

then, tugged her to her feet. "Dinner's going to have to wait. It's been three days. I want you."

She wanted him, too.

They had sex in the Jacuzzi tub, and then ate her blackened casserole. It was overcooked, but neither of them cared. There was nothing wrong with crunchy noodles.

Midnight drew them to Mike's bedroom.

Pratesi tucked them in.

They slept tight.

Thirteen

Jillian Mac was wrapped so tight she couldn't breathe. She'd driven to the construction site to deliver the crystal softballs to Agnes, Mike, and Aidan. She'd sat in her Triumph for an inordinately long time. Three o'clock crept up on four.

She leaned back against the headrest, curved her spine into the leather seat. Slunk low. She hadn't seen Aidan for two weeks now, which was far too long. It was her fault. Yesterday she'd gotten in her car and headed to the site, only to turn around at the gate. The administrative trailer loomed large and intimidating, and she'd chickened out.

Today she'd gathered her courage and given her name to the security guard. He'd let her pass. She'd parked next to Aidan's SUV. The Armada cast shade onto her car. She let her vehicle idle. It would be so easy to back up and leave.

What was wrong with her? She'd always been gutsy. She hated feeling vulnerable. She wondered if Aidan had changed his mind about her. She hoped not. She was just coming to grips with their relationship. All she needed was a little more time.

A low-rumbling Porsche pulled in beside her. Mike Burke cut the engine. High-maintenance vehicle; high-octane man, Jill thought. He climbed out and strode around to her side of the car. He tapped on her window; tapped until she acknowledged him. Irritating man.

She rolled down her window, glared at him. His hair was mussed; his jaw unshaven. He wore a black T-shirt scripted with *Armed and Dangerous with a Nail Gun*. His jeans were torn at the knees. His work boots were worn.

He eyed her critically and said, "You look like shit."

She glanced in the rearview mirror. Her eyes were red and puffy. She had little color in her cheeks. Her hair was dull. "You've interrupted my meditation," she informed him.

He grunted. "You haven't found peace, given the tone of your voice. Maybe you need a new mantra."

"Maybe you need to mind your own business."

He leaned his hip against her car door. "Looking for Aidan? He's in his office."

Mike could be her ambassador of goodwill. She reached across the console, gathered the box of crystal softballs, and tried to hand them to him. "Would you take these inside for me? Appreciation gifts for those who played."

He shook his head. "Deliver them yourself."

"You could be more helpful."

"You're not helpless."

She scowled at him.

He squinted at the gift box. "I should have a bigger ball than everyone else. I was both coach and pitcher."

She came back with, "You have brass balls, Mike. Two brass are worth one crystal."

He grinned. "Suppose so."

Congratulations were in order for this man who irritated the hell out of her. She'd heard from Carrie that Mike had proposed. He'd also become Aidan's business partner overnight. She forced herself to get along with him. "I wish you and Carrie well," she managed. "Take care of her always. Otherwise I'll come after you with both knees raised."

"Same goes for you and Aidan," he said, looking serious. "You're killing him. When he's not happy, I'm not happy. You don't want me miserable."

Could Aidan possibly be feeling as bad as she? According to Mike, it was a distinct possibility. She needed to see for herself. She turned off the engine, palmed the key. He moved and she climbed out, carrying the box.

He followed her to the trailer. "Watch your step," he said when she'd taken her first. "You don't want to break any balls."

Once she was through the door, Agnes greeted Jill warmly. "How do you like my makeover?" the receptionist asked. She patted her hair. "Playing softball, being in the sun, inspired my highlights."

"You look gorgeous," Jill said, admiring the older woman. Her transformation was stunning. Pale streaks of blond made her look ten years younger. The pink blush on her cheekbones gave her a glow. She was styling with her new cat's-eye glasses.

Jill set the gift box on Agnes's desk. She then presented Agnes with a sparkling softball. Agnes was so excited she cleared away all paperwork, sweeping a stack of files into her desk drawer, so the ball would have a place of honor by her nameplate.

"Mike?" Jill held the next softball out to him.

He took it, tossed it in the air. The crystal ball caught the overhead lights and cast rainbow prisms on the ceiling. "It goes home with me," he said. "Carrie and I will have a matched pair."

Jill liked that idea. A sneeze so loud it blew from Aidan's office into reception preceded Sadie's entrance. The pointer shook herself, then ambled toward Jill. The dog's nose was runny, and Jill reached for the small box of Kleenex on Agnes's desk. She gently wiped Sadie's nose, then tossed the tissue in the trash can. Sadie looked at her with cloudy, watery eyes. Jill felt awful for her. "What's wrong with Sadie?" Jill asked, concerned.

"She has spring allergies." Aidan had appeared in the hallway. "She sneezes, same as a person. She's on medication."

Jill's heart quickened. She stared at Aidan, tried to define the moment. He stood tall and handsome; his tone was cordial. His expression was closed. He had his own dark circles under his eyes. There was leanness in his cheeks that sharpened his features. He wore a yellow-and-white striped button-down and khakis. A brown sport coat was slung over his shoulder. He carried a large manila envelope in one hand and a leather athletic bag in the other. He looked ready to travel.

"Going someplace?" she asked, wondering if he would be gone long. Hoping not.

"I'm headed to Tampa," he told her. "I want to check on the cardiac unit we're building."

"He's driving, and will be gone a week," Mike added. He stood by Agnes's desk; his hand was in the bear cookie jar. "Oatmeal raisin. You are good to me."

"Who's watching Sadie while you're away?" Jill asked.

"Olive wanted to babysit Sad," Aidan said. "She's good at it. The parrot squawks at Shaye when Sadie stands at the door needing to go out. Olive knows when it's mealtime." He rubbed the back of his neck. "Unfortunately Sadie's allergies are at their worst. I don't want her sneezing on Olive."

"There'd be ruffled feathers," said Mike. He then offered, "I'm happy to take her."

"You'd let her nose run," Aidan said.

"I wouldn't," Jill said softly. "I'd love the company." A second heartbeat at the houseboat would be welcome.

Aidan met her gaze, considered her offer. "If you're sure. But should it not work out, call my sister. She'll come get Sadie."

"We'll be fine." Jill was her own boss; she could set her own hours. She looked forward to spending time with the pointer. "Can she ride in my Triumph?"

"There's not a lot of room on your passenger seat. I'd rather she wasn't cramped," said Aidan. "I can drive Sadie to the Horizon. Leave her with you."

"That will work," Jill agreed. She reached into the box and gave Aidan the last crystal softball. "A memento of the day."

Instead of taking it to his office, he surprised her by slipping it in the pocket of his sports jacket. Aidan walked to the door; gave one last instruction to his girls. "Should anyone be looking for me, refer them to Mike," he said. "It's time to break in my new partner."

The ladies clapped their approval.

"Walton Masonry will have the perimeter sidewalks poured by the time of your return," Mike promised, aware of the work schedule. "We'll have electricity in the stadium grounds by then, too."

"I want the sidewalks smooth." Aidan was emphatic. "One solid sheet, no lines or cracks."

Jill listened, had a flicker of an idea. "Tell me more about the walkways," she requested.

Mike responded with, "They lead in from the parking lot and surround the ballpark."

Jill's mind worked overtime. Aidan would be out of town, but she wanted to discuss her thought with Carrie before they approached Mike. He was a partner now, after all, and might be more receptive than Aidan.

Mike stepped up and lifted Sadie against his chest. "You look too pretty to get fur all over you," he said to Aidan. Sadie took that moment to sneeze. Mike made a face. "My arm's wet; I need a Kleenex."

Agnes hurried from behind her desk, two tissues in hand. She quickly cleaned him up. "Much better now," she said.

Aidan held the door for Mike, Sadie, and Jill. They trooped out. Aidan came down the steps right behind her. Jill could feel his breath on her neck; the warmth of his body. She'd missed their closeness.

Mike loaded Sadie in the back of Aidan's SUV. The men bumped fists. "Have a good trip," Mike said over his shoulder as he headed back to the trailer.

Jill and Aidan left the construction site amid outgoing cement trucks. She lost sight of him behind the concrete mixers. She drove slowly, avoiding the potholes. Her Triumph swayed with each truck that passed her. They were moving at a good clip. She clutched the steering wheel tightly, until she reached the turnoff to the main highway. She breathed easier then.

Aidan pulled up beside her. He rolled down his window, and she did the same. "It got crowded back there," he said. "Are you okay?"

She responded with, "Next time I visit your site, I'm driving a tank."

"Much safer than your sports car," he agreed. "I'll contact Mike. We need to post speed limits."

They reached Land's End within minutes. They parked, and Aidan helped Sadie out of his vehicle and onto the houseboat. He then unloaded two brown grocery sacks of food and treats, several toys, and Sadie's therapeutic bed.

He handed Jill the pointer's allergy medication, saying,

"She's had her pill for today. Dr. Schober's office and emergency numbers are on the label. He's been the Barefoot William veterinarian for forty years. He makes house calls."

"Hopefully I won't need to reach him."

Sadie nudged Jill's hand with her nose. The dog wasn't sure what was going on. She needed reassurance. Jill scratched her ear. "A girls' week," she said. "I'll take good care of you." Sadie wagged her tail.

"I'm off," Aidan said when there was nothing more to say. He gave Sadie a hug, but remained distant with Jill. "See you both when I get back."

He walked to the door, and Sadie trailed after him. "Stay, girl," he told her. Sadie whined.

"I have treats." Jill offered. That got Sadie's attention. Her ears perked up. She returned to Jill. Jill reached into the paper bag and gave her a soft Milk Bone chew. Sadie lay down and ate it. It took her a while to finish—she didn't have many teeth.

Aidan was halfway out the door when he turned back to her. She froze that moment in her mind. "My feelings haven't changed, Jillian McMillan," he said. "I still like you." And he was gone.

Her heart went with him. The man cared for her still, and he wasn't afraid to say so. She needed to open up to him, too; perhaps when he returned from Tampa. She didn't want to miss another opportunity.

Jill relaxed with Sadie the rest of the day. They ate dinner together, though Sadie ate much slower than Jill. Jill had finished her grilled cheese long before Sadie worked through her bowl of kibble. A walk followed. Jill climbed down the ladder, then lifted Sadie from the front deck. The dog cooperated. No wiggling. They sauntered down the dock, and Sadie seemed fascinated by the pelicans.

She would sniff the air, then point. She held the three-legged position for several seconds. She was still a hunter at heart.

It took them over an hour to reach the end of the dock and return. The houseboat residents called to Sadie, a few came off their vessels to pet her. Jill met several more of Aidan's relatives. They all loved baseball.

By the time they made it back to the Horizon, Sadie was moving slower than when they'd started. She'd also begun to wheeze. Deep, long-heaving wheezes. Jill rubbed her chest, but that didn't seem to help. Sadie couldn't catch her breath.

Jill grabbed the dog's medicine bottle from the grocery bag. Read the label. Cell phone in hand, she dialed the veterinarian. She was amazed that he picked up and not an answering service. Afraid for Sadie's health, she heard her voice shaking as she explained the situation. Dr. Schober agreed to make a house call. Jill gave him her address.

Jill stared at the wall clock, counting down the minutes. The vet couldn't arrive fast enough, as far as she was concerned. She sat on the floor, holding Sadie, praying she would be all right. Twenty minutes later, a fit man in his sixties arrived on a ten-speed bike. Jill was very glad to see him.

Dale Schober climbed the boarding ladder carrying a backpack. He didn't knock, but entered with purpose. He introduced himself as he knelt down beside Sadie. He unzipped his pack, brought out his stethoscope, and gave the dog a thorough examination.

"She started wheezing when we came back from our walk," Jill told him. "She scared me, not being able to breathe."

"I understand your concern," he said. "Aidan recently had her at my office for her yearly exam. She's healthy for a senior. She could be allergic to ragweed, spring tree pollen, whatever's blooming. She may have inhaled something on your walk."

Jill felt awful. "I had no idea our walk would cause her distress."

"It could've happened to you or to Aidan had he been home," the doctor reassured her. "She's calmed down now and is already breathing easier."

Jill sighed in relief. "I feel very protective of her."

"Seniors are special," Dr. Schober agreed as he gently rubbed Sadie's shoulders. "Steam will help relieve her congestion. Next time you take a shower, bring her in the bathroom with you. Let her sit outside the shower door. Steam from the hot water will clear her sinuses and help her breathe easier. It's similar to a nebulizer treatment."

He stood then, his backpack in hand. "Call anytime," he said. "Babysitting a geriatric dog can be as daunting as taking care of an aging grandparent." He gave Sadie one last pat, then departed.

Jill was sitting cross-legged on the floor beside the pointer. Sadie rested her head on her knee. Her breathing was still a little raspy. "I could use a shower and you could use some steam," she told the dog. She helped Sadie up. They headed for the bath.

Over the next few days, Jill ran a lot of showers. Sadie's breathing gradually improved. Jill refused to leave the pointer while she worked, so she switched vehicles with Carrie, and now drove the Cube. Sadie could stretch out in the back to her heart's content. Jill could keep a constant eye on her.

The sacrifices people made for their pets, Jill mused, as she pulled up at the gate to the construction site four days later. Every one was worth it.

Her heart quickened with anticipation. Her promotional plan was in place. Today would prove as exciting as the ground-breaking ceremony. She'd sent out a press release. Reporters were on-site.

The masonry workers would soon pour the long, winding sidewalk around the perimeter of the stadium. Fans would then be allowed to leave their footprints for future generations.

A fan walkway was innovative. It had never been done at any spring-training facility. This would be a first.

James Lawless had approved her request without hesitation. He'd given her kudos. Mike Burke had raised both eyebrows and sucked air when he'd learned of the promotional event. The man was in charge. Decisions had to be made quickly. He'd come around.

There would be an honorary plaza for the Rogues' footprints next spring. They deserved their own special ceremony.

Mike approached her the second she stepped from the SUV. "The crowd's getting antsy," he said. "The first cement truck is in place and the concrete finishers are eager to get started. Once the 'crete is poured, they will smooth the top layer. It's quick-drying, so we need to move fast. Fifty fans will line up at a time to leave their footprints."

"You're very organized," Jill complimented.

"It's all Carrie." He gave the credit where credit was due. "She's handing out pencils so everyone can add their name, too. Carrie will write *Rogues Number-One Fans* at the start of the sidewalk."

Jill nodded her approval. "I want to leave a space for Aidan's footprints," she told Mike. "A square of cement can be poured at a later date."

"The man wanted smooth and we're giving him heels and toes and signatures."

"I'll take any and all blame."

"I'll be the first to point my finger at you."

Jill couldn't help but grin. "I'm sure you will."

"Let's get to it," Mike said.

"I'd like Sadie's paw prints for posterity," Jill decided on the spot.

Mike rolled his eyes. "I'll hold her, and you can press down on her paws. Two men are standing by with hoses to wash excess concrete from shoes. We'll clean Sadie's feet, too."

"Then I'll put her in the trailer. It's too hot for her to be outside."

"You're such a mom."

The expansion of the cardiac care unit in Tampa was moving forward without a hitch. Aidan Cates was pleased to see the progress. He signed off on his inspection. The superintendent was competent and would bring the project in early. Guy Clarion would earn a bonus.

"Hey, boss, come into my office. You've got to see this," Guy called out when Aidan stopped by the administrative trailer. He'd wrapped things up earlier than planned. He was ready to head home; ready to see Jillian Mac. He also missed his dog.

"What's up?" Aidan asked from the doorway.

Guy had turned on the television and was flipping through the channels. "I just caught the end of a news segment, and hoped to hear the story on another channel," he told Aidan. "You're getting some major press." He paused on ABC. "A newscaster was reporting from the spring-training facility."

The reporter was animated. "Richmond Rogues and Cates and Burke General Contractors have come together to please their ticket holders," he said. "A pathway of fan footprints circling the stadium has created quite a buzz. This is an amazing tribute to those who support the team. Contractor Mike Burke and community liaison Jillian Mac spearheaded the event. It's a day to remember." The announcer chuckled. "Even Aidan Cates's dog got in on the action." Footage from earlier in the day was shown. Aidan stared as Sadie set her paw prints. He swore his dog smiled. So much for his smooth sidewalk, he thought. Once again, Jill had thrown a curveball into his life.

He stuck his hand in the pocket of his sport coat, where he carried the crystal softball. He squeezed it hard, then unclenched his fingers. His jaw worked and he released his breath. His stress slowly evaporated.

Did he care? he asked himself. Not nearly as much as he thought he might. The lady was creative. He had to give her that.

The reporter returned to the moment at hand. The cameraman now panned the long length of sidewalk. Cement trucks were still lined up. People continued to press their footprints in the concrete. Those gathered were sunburned and laughing. Their excitement was tangible.

"Great move, Aidan," Guy complimented from behind his desk. "That's a feel-good broadcast. Fan appreciation is key. You've got your own Grauman's Chinese Theatre. Affiliates all across the country will pick up the piece. Cates and Burke is about to become a household name. You've shown goodwill."

Aidan thought about Jill on his drive back to Barefoot William. He had two hours to get her straight in his mind. There'd be no further ultimatums. She'd come to him in her own time. All he could do was wait for her to realize that she liked him back. He believed he would hear her words. He believed they had something special. Jill was close to realizing that, too.

It was after eight when he hit the outskirts of Barefoot

William. The construction site was slightly out of his way, but he wanted to see the sidewalk before he saw Jill. Mike Burke's Porsche was parked at the trailer. Aidan went and got his partner. He wanted Mike to know he was proud of his decision.

Mike was at his desk, working at the computer. Aidan cleared his throat and Mike cut him a look. "You here to chew me out?" Mike asked, shutting down the screen.

"You've already had your nuts twisted." He couldn't help but smile. "Carrie and Jill can be persuasive when they set their minds to it. I had a text from James Lawless. A cost addendum will be added to the contract for overtime."

"The cement truck operators and concrete masons chalked it up. There'll be no additional charges. Many of the workers are from Barefoot William. Jill promised them spring-training tickets. Everyone was happy."

"I want to see the sidewalk," said Aidan.

"Walk or ride?" asked Mike.

The stadium was a mile away. Aidan chose to walk. He needed the exercise and fresh air. The electrical poles were up and spotlights illuminated the grounds. He and Mike had time to talk.

"How's it going?" he asked.

"It's going," Mike answered. "Today was disruptive, but we're on schedule. I'd like to stay ahead of the game, in case Jill and Carrie come up with further promotions."

Mike ran one hand down his face. "You should've seen Shaye and Trace doing their footprints. Pretty damn funny. They faced each other, so their prints were set in opposite directions. Dune took dozens of pictures. You're looking at tiny and gigantic when you see his feet beside his wife, Sophie's."

"Then there was Sadie," said Aidan.

"Don't sweat any bullets, we were careful with her,"

270   *Kate Angell*

Mike stated. "Jill was her protector. We got all traces of cement off her paws. Swear."

Mike picked up a rock, tossed it across the lot. "Carrie and I did our footprints, too."

"What about Jill?"

"She waited for you to return. There's a square of cement yet to be poured."

Aidan's chest warmed, expanded. He liked that she'd held back. The sidewalk stretched just ahead. Approaching, he understood the commotion. The community had come together. Baseball was the all-American pastime. Enthusiasm for the sport was evident in each set of fan footprints. He was responsible for building the stadium. But Jill would fill the seats. They were a team.

He and Mike walked the length of the sidewalk. Aidan recognized nearly every name, so many were relatives and extended family. Even his Grandfather Frank had come out for the occasion. A widower, Frank seldom left his house. Yet he was fond of baseball.

"Let's head back," Aidan said when they came to the end of the sidewalk, which could be extended at any time.

Mike walked beside him. "Life is good," he said. "I still can't believe I met my future wife at a barbecue."

"You were a total ass that night."

"Carrie makes me want to be a better person."

"You were always a good guy," Aidan said, "if first impressions could be overlooked."

His cell phone rang, and he removed it from his pants pocket. He glanced at the screen. "Incoming psycho," he muttered. Mike looked at him questioningly. "Psycho McMillan," he iterated. To answer or not to answer? That was the question. "Aidan Cates," he finally said.

"I can't reach my sister." The man didn't believe in hello. "She's not answering her phone."

"Maybe she turned it off."

"Or maybe something's happened to her."

That thought bothered Aidan. He kept his concern to himself. "Your sister is living on a houseboat with an alarm system that would waken the dead. Her weapon of choice is a baseball bat."

"Go by the houseboat and check on her."

"I can and I will. She's been babysitting my dog. I need to pick Sadie up."

"Get a move on, contractor." Psycho hung up.

Aidan stared at the phone for several seconds before putting it back in his pocket. "He's going to be a meddling brother-in-law."

Mike didn't seem surprised by his comment. He grinned. "Carrie told me that Jill and Psycho were related. He will always look out for his sister."

"To be expected." Aidan picked up his pace. "Psycho could be an alarmist or a matchmaker. Either way, I'm headed to the Horizon."

"I need to lock up the trailer, and I'm gone, too."

Both men left within a few minutes of each other.

Parking places were limited at Land's End. Aidan parked a block away. He jogged to the houseboat. The blinds were pulled, but the lights were on inside. He climbed the boarding ladder and banged on the door. No answer. He turned the knob—it was unlocked. He entered.

The Horizon seemed unusually warm. The sound of water running came from the bath. He wandered down the hall. He listened and heard, "*Breathe*, Sadie. Deep breaths, girl. Don't give up. You can do it."

Aidan's heart nearly stopped. It appeared his dog wasn't breathing. Was Sadie giving up the ghost? He knew canine CPR. He'd taken a course when he'd adopted the pointer. He rushed into the bathroom. Right into a sauna. The heat and steam stopped him cold. The shower ran full blast, and the curtain was partially pulled back. A towel had been spread where the water splashed and puddled on the floor.

Jill sat on her knees, her back to the wall. Her hair was wet and stuck to her forehead and the sides of her face. Her white tank top stuck to her breasts. Her blue boyshorts hugged her hips. She braced Sadie, who stood on wobbly legs. His pointer drooled and her fur was damp. She now breathed without difficulty. Both of them looked bedraggled.

He took it all in, relieved the situation wasn't dire. "What's going on?" he asked.

Jill rose slowly. And Sadie sat down. His dog sneezed. Jill wiped her nose with a paper towel. "We're nebulizing," she told him. "Dr. Schober's orders. I had to call him the first night you left town. I'd taken Sadie for a walk, and she got very congested. Your vet suggested steam to clear her sinuses. It works well. I give her treatments three times a day. They last an hour."

He now knew why she hadn't answered her phone. She'd been busy taking care of his dog. "Psycho tried to reach you," he told her. He slipped her his cell phone. "Call him."

She did. "I'm fine, love you, too," was short and sweet before she disconnected. She handed back his phone. "You're sweating," she said to him. "Give us five more minutes, and we'll be done."

"I'd rather stay here with you."

She patted her clothes hamper. "Have a seat."

He eased down on the wicker top, hoping it would support his weight. "You're amazing, Jillian Mac," he said, and meant it. "Thank you for taking good care of Sadie."

"She's had her moments, but pulled through. She'll be glad to go home with you tonight."

"It's good to be back in town."

"Was your trip to Tampa successful?"

"The cardiac center is coming along nicely." He paused, pursed his lips. "But not as well as the sidewalk at the stadium."

"You've heard?"

"And seen," he said. "I stopped by the site on my way here."

Perspiration ran down her forehead, and she wiped her brow with the back of her hand. "The idea came to me the day you left town," she explained. "I had to act fast. The sidewalk was scheduled to be poured. Carrie and I worked our butts off to meet the deadline. Community cooperation was phenomenal."

"So I saw on the news."

"Not the best way to find out, was it?"

"A text might have been nice."

"You left Mike in charge."

Aidan was thoughtful. "He handled the situation much as I would have."

"Honestly?" Her eyes were wide.

"I'm not the one who stretches the truth."

She bit down on her bottom lip. "What do you think of the fans' footprints?"

"I like it enough to add a wall for handprints to a children's cancer clinic we'll be building next year in Orlando. A celebration of connecting hands for the cure."

"That would be beautiful."

"I have you to thank for the idea."

Sadie started getting restless. She wiggled away from Jill and came to him. He hugged her, damp fur and all. She sighed with contentment.

Jill rose, turned off the shower. Then wiped up the remaining water on the floor. Aidan opened the door and the hot air ran out behind them as they left the bath. Jill turned on the ceiling fans and the air stirred, cooling the living room.

"I should get going," he said. She hadn't asked him to stay, and he didn't want to prolong his departure. His hands itched to touch her. He wanted to pull her close, kiss her until she melted against him. They'd yet to make love under the sea.

"I'll pack up Sadie's food." Jill filled a paper bag with the leftovers. "I bought her a new tennis ball and tug toy that squeaks."

No other woman had bought his dog toys.

She looked from Sadie to the brown paper sack and therapeutic bed. "Where are you parked?"

"We'll be fine," he told her. "I'm within a block."

Jill held the bag until he'd climbed down the ladder and Sadie was safely on the ground. She then passed it to him, along with the bed.

"Have a good rest of the evening," he said.

"You, too."

It would be better if she were with him. "Maybe I'll see you this weekend."

"Maybe you will."

Or maybe he wouldn't. He knew the flip side of the coin too well. He watched as Sadie started down the sidewalk ahead of him. She sneezed once, but the sound was no longer heavy and congested.

"I like you, Jill."

"I know you do."

At least she was aware of how he felt. Now if she'd only respond in kind, he'd marry the woman.

Saturday came and went, overcast with light rain. There was no sunshine when Jillian Mac was gone, Aidan thought. Sunday didn't prove much better. He made himself a big breakfast, but ate only half. He sat at the kitchen booth and imagined Jill sitting across from him. He liked sharing a meal with her.

He mowed his backyard, pushing an electric mower. It was his way to expend energy. Hot and sweaty, he took a shower. He didn't have the motivation to shave. He caught the Rogues baseball game. They played a three-game series in Yankee Stadium. Game one, and they burned the Yankees with a bunt that brought in a home run. Their pitcher didn't allow a hit in the bottom of the ninth. Richmond led the National League East. It was early in the season.

A series of commercials followed, and Aidan decided to take Sadie for a short walk. Her sneezes were sporadic. He'd kept up with her medication and shower nebulizer treatments. She was holding her own.

They headed out the front door together. Halfway down the sidewalk, Sadie pricked her ears and picked up her pace. What the hell? Aidan went after her.

He rounded the hedge and immediately spotted a car in his driveway. A vintage Triumph with the windows rolled down. Jillian Mac sat in the driver seat, her head thrown back, her eyes closed. Sadie's enthusiastic bark startled her. She jerked forward and looked around, spotting him immediately.

He walked over to her car, leaned in the passenger-side window. The scent of a hamburger and fries clung to a discarded foil wrapper. A ketchup packet was torn open. Napkins littered the seat. Condensation covered a soda can.

"Out for a drive?" he asked.

"I knew my destination when I started."

"You found your way here." He stared at her closely. Perspiration had collected on her upper lip and her clothes were wrinkled. "How long have you been sitting in your car?"

"Two, maybe three hours." She pointed to a silver lunch box on the floorboard. "I brought dinner, too, in case I didn't have the courage to ring your doorbell."

"Why haven't you come in?"

"I wasn't ready."

"How about now?" he asked.

She swallowed hard. "Soon, Aidan, soon."

He rounded the hood of the sports car. Came to stand beside her. His hand was on the door handle, but he didn't draw her out. He wanted her to make the first move.

Sadie had come to sit beside him. She didn't understand Jill's apprehension. She barked louder a second time. An encouraging *woof*.

Aidan was at a loss. He was afraid to say something that would have Jill shifting her car in reverse. He didn't want her leaving. "I like you," seemed only natural. He said it quietly, hoping it wouldn't scare her away. "Like you a lot," he added with conviction.

There were tears in her eyes when she next looked at him. Her lower lip trembled slightly when she said, "I love you."

He was so stunned, it took him seconds to respond. He nearly ripped the car door off its hinges to get to her. He lifted her off the seat and high against his chest. "Took you long enough," he breathed against her mouth, right before he kissed her. A deep, drugging kiss that had her gasping for breath. "I love you, too."

"You're certain?" She was expectant, insecure.

"Damn sure."

"You're not going to walk away tomorrow?"

"Not ever. I have proof I want you in my life."

He went on to show her the stability he could offer. Sadie led the way back to the house. The dog's step was light, almost prancing. Not bad for an old girl.

"Nothing is set in stone," he told her when he kicked open the door. "I ordered the furniture, but when it was delivered, I wasn't sure how I wanted it arranged. It needs a woman's touch."

He released her slowly, let her slide down his body in the entryway. "There are mostly basic fabrics, as you suggested. Decorative pillows add color."

Her eyes were huge as she looked around the sunken living room. "Loveseats and leather club chairs," she murmured. "An overstuffed rocker. The ottoman is as big as a bed."

"I'll leave the curtains to you," he said, coming up behind her and wrapping his arms about her waist. He held her close. Late-afternoon sunshine shot through the picture window, warming the cherrywood floors. "My house is your house, Jillian McMillan. I want you to permanently unpack your suitcase."

"That I can do."

Sadie barked her approval before heading to her dog bed.

Aidan's life had returned to normal, or as normal as it was going to get with this woman. She would bring chaos and crazy into their future. He would remain calm and constant. They would find the perfect balance.

"We made it," he said, kissing her cheek.

"I knew we would." She sounded positive.

"How did you know?" He hadn't been sure until moments ago.

She tilted her head so their lips brushed. "I'm psychic, remember?"

"What's your prediction for our future?" he asked.

"You're about to make love to me."

He liked that thought. He reached for her left hand, brought it to his lips, and kissed her wrist. "I'd like to complete the heart tattoo on your ring finger," he said.

"You're a man with marriage on his mind?"

"Whenever you're ready." He would not rush her.

She turned to face him. "Soon," she promised.

He kissed her then with love and passion.

She kissed him back with joy and certainty.

Jillie Mac was home to stay.